JENNY T. COLGAN

Spandex
AND THE
CITY

ORBIT

First published in Great Britain in 2017 by Orbit

3 5 7 9 10 8 6 4 2

A CIP catalogue record for this book
is available from the British Library.

ISBN 978-0-356-50544-2

Typeset in Caslon by M Rules
Printed and bound in Great Britain by
Clay Ltd, St Ives plc

Papers used by Orbit are from well-managed forests
and other responsible sources.

MIX
Paper from
responsible sources
FSC® C104740

Orbit
An imprint of
Little, Brown Book Group
Carmelite House
50 Victoria Embankment
London EC4Y 0DZ

An Hachette UK Company
www.hachette.co.uk

www.orbitbooks.net

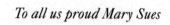
To all us proud Mary Sues

Chapter One

When my brother was about eight or so, and I was fourteen, I took him (heavily bribed by our mother, who was raising us on her own, and had remarked several weeks in a row that if she didn't have an afternoon off to get her roots done and drink several margaritas, she was going to crash the car on purpose) to a superhero movie, and he didn't enjoy it one tiny bit.

He was an unusually literal child, and he came out scowling.

'What's up?' I said, finishing up the horrible blue candy he'd insisted that I buy him and then didn't eat. I was still calling it 'sweets'; hadn't learned to call it candy.

'The baddies,' he said.

'Yes,' I said.

'There were goodies and baddies,' he said.

Then he looked at me, blue eyes frowning in the freckled face which was so similar to mine. The freckles looked cute on him. I looked like Peppermint Patty. My sole goal in life at fourteen was to get enough of a suntan to join them all up. This is what dermatologists call the 'kamikaze' method.

'Yep' I said, not really listening. There hadn't been nearly as many cute guys in the cinema as I'd hoped.

Vincent shook his head.

'The baddie kept doing an evil laugh, Holly,' he said. 'Like, he knew he was evil and he really enjoyed being evil.'

'Yes, he did,' I said. 'In case the horns and the fangs didn't give away that he was quite evil enough. And the poisoned tail. And all that killing and destruction that he did.'

He shook his head again, even more crossly.

'I don't think real baddies look like baddies.' he said. 'I don't think they even *know* they're baddies.'

And he wandered off to the subway ahead of me – leaving me licking blue sherbet off my fingers – and I never knew why that stuck in my head.

'No. Definitely not, absolutely not, totally no and also no way.'

'What do you mean, "no"?'

The bar was dark and pretty noisy, but anyone could hear my no, and I really wasn't enjoying Gertie asking me about absolutely every man in there over and over again, like some kind of single-ton torture interrogation.

Twelve years on from taking Vincent to that movie, my freckles were under quite a lot of make-up, my sandy hair was ironed into submission, but I was still eating – or in this case, drinking – blue stuff.

Gertie was in one of her 'PIN HOLLY TO THE GROUND ON TOP OF ANY AVAILABLE MALE' moods, and all I could do was let her talk and drink her curaçao cocktail, mostly exactly at the same time.

I sighed and glanced again at her latest suggestion. He looked like a tree trunk had wandered into a bar by mistake.

'Oh, for goodness' sake. Look at the muscles! They're one, gross, and two, I don't think a gym bunny is going to be very interested in girls, do you? Come on, he's like all sculpted and stuff. Can you imagine? He probably eats nine raw eggs a day. And looks at himself in the mirror all the time. Oh, and you know – sleeps with men.'

'I can't believe you have a problem with handsome.'

'I don't have a problem with handsome. Handsome has a problem with me.'

'That's not true at all.'

'You never fancied the handsome one in the boy band, did you?'

'No.'

'You used to like Louis not Zayn, right?'

'Where are you going with this?'

I squinted once more at the man at the other end of the bar. He appeared to be all jawline. He looked uncomfortable, like he didn't know what he was meant to be doing there, and also faintly familiar. He caught my eye and smiled in basically a pretty cheesy way.

'Argh,' I said. 'Okay, oh God. Right, he just stared straight at me. And smiled! Weirdo!'

'The problem with you is—'

'Oh, how I love a game of "the problem with me is",' I said. Gertie was my friend, but she was also all loved-up and was buying a place with DuTroy in the suburbs, so she totally had the answer to everything all the time, telling everyone she knew that all they had to do was fall in love and behave exactly as she had. You can tell what good friends we are in that we can still bear to go out for a drink together.

'You have talked yourself into not deserving the handsome

boys. Because of, you know, thinking about stuff too much. And complaining about your freckles. Which are cute, by the way. So you go for the less handsome guy, thinking they'll be an easier get for you, but they're not, because you know why?'

'Tell me.'

'Because you think they don't know they're not the handsomest guy. But they know what you're doing. Trading down. And that makes them furious and resentful. So they won't be very nice to you because they know they're second-best. And then it gets worse.'

'How does it get worse?'

'Because when we turn thirty, everything flips, and suddenly the geeky, weird-looking guys start making tons of money and growing into their looks while the big lunks all get fat and bald. So then the weird ones really are the hot ones, and all the women want them. And now they really *are* furious and out for revenge for all the times they got treated second-best when they were younger.'

'So what are you saying?'

'I'm saying that handsome guys are probably going to be nicer to you just because they're more basically confident underneath. Plus, added bonus: they're handsome.'

DuTroy was extremely handsome and he treated Gertie really well. I wondered if she had a point. After two years with a furiously nerdy cartoonist who always looked faintly disappointed in me – not of my job, or the way I looked, or what I was saying, but just gently overall – and a variety of interesting, moody, often horrible poets and beardies, I did wonder.

I snuck another glance at Mr Muscle. He smiled again, showing very white teeth.

'I think he's a serial killer,' I said. 'There is absolutely no other explanation.'

4

'You are wearing the red dress,' said Gertie. The red dress, it was true, was a definite hard-worker. I didn't have the lucky pants on – this was a night out with my best friend – but the dress was a definite sign of some kind. Gertie didn't get out much since she'd met DuTroy, which was why she was sucking down blue cocktails like she secretly just wanted a hosepipe plugged into the bar, and urging me on to the kind of bad behaviour she didn't get to do any more.

'Hmm,' I said.

'Well, go get more drinks,' she said. 'Stand close to him. See what happens.'

'ARGH,' I said. 'Is this what people used to do before Tinder?'

'Physically stand in places?'

'Physically stand in places,' I said. 'Yuk. Bleargh. Plus I love being single.'

'What, even the Sunday mornings?'

'Yes! No. Not the Sunday mornings.'

If I could get it together, I'd launch a breakfast club just for those Sunday mornings when you wake up alone and try to convince yourself you're enjoying it. And you go out to get coffee and sit and read the papers with all those other people also trying to pretend they're living in a commercial and love sitting by themselves on a Sunday morning being cool and drinking coffee. At the Breakfast Club, we'll all get coffee and read the papers, but in a kind of all-together companionable silence. Maybe. The problem is, if someone else ran a Sunday morning breakfast club, I would absolutely totally one hundred per cent not go.

I stood at the overcrowded bar. It was hot and incredibly noisy. He was just a foot or so away, nursing a fizzy water, I think, and looking around.

It occurred to me suddenly that he didn't look like a guy

hanging around a bar – there were a few, and they were all pretending to talk to their friends, intensely involved with their
telephones, eyes casting around the room in a slightly suspicious
manner. He was quite still. Observant, as if he was looking for
something very specific. I swallowed, moving towards the bar.
As I got closer, I realised he was gigantic, easily six foot five and
built – not heavily muscled, but sinewy, strong. Nice. If I had a
beard, I told myself sternly. And a penis. And testes.

He scanned the room, saw me again, smiled distantly.

The drinks were pulsing through me. And I *was* wearing the
red dress. I made an uncharacteristic decision. I smiled right back.
Although his hair was very black, his eyes were blue.

'Hey,' he said, and even though I was sure this was all an absolutely pointless exercise, and I had no real idea as to what I was
doing, I said 'hey' back.

The next second, he grabbed me and threw me across the bar.

Chapter Two

I landed heavily, in among the shocked-looking bar staff, banging my elbow hard against the beer fridge; it hurt like hell.

'What the . . . ?' I started to swear, but in the very next instant, I heard an enormous crash and all the bar staff ducked down beside me.

I glanced at the girl next to me, who had a full sleeve tattoo and half of her head shaved. She was shaking. I gave her what I hoped was an encouraging glance, then sneaked a quick peek above the bar. Someone had unplugged the music system and turned on the overhead lights. What was a sophisticated, buzzing nightspot was suddenly just a big bare room, devoid of magic or excitement; rather seedy in fact.

The trembling girl showed me her phone: she'd called emergency services and simply left it off the hook. I nodded.

'Everybody down!' came a calm voice. It was unhurried, almost relaxed. Weirdly, this made me feel even more frightened.

I blinked and risked a peep over the bar top again. A large man with bad skin and a mask was standing in the doorway, with several murky-featured guys behind him.

'Phones, wallets, valuables, blah blah,' he was saying. His voice was surprisingly soft, but everyone was listening to him nonetheless. 'Thanks. That's so kind of you. It's all right really ... '

He turned to the nearest woman, an ageing blonde with overworked-out lines on her face. She recoiled.

'It's all right,' he repeated, almost soothingly. 'I'm just stealing from you.'

'You ... you ... ' she spat, but was unable to say any more.

He gently reached over and carefully unhooked a silver necklace from her neck. The blonde jumped as he examined it.

'Oh dear dear dear,' he said. 'This isn't real. Did you know that? Or was it a present?'

The woman stared at it angrily as the man handed it back.

'Phone,' he said.

Meanwhile, his men were lurching round the room with empty sacks, and people were emptying their handbags and wallets into them immediately, without question. My ears were ringing from how noisy it had been before.

'Very good,' said the man. 'Thanks. Thanks, everyone. This will help fund us nicely.'

There was a commotion in one corner. I looked around and my heart stopped. It was Gertie, punch-drunk from all the cocktails.

'NO!' she was screaming. 'NO! You can't have it.'

I knew immediately what she meant.

DuTroy had given her an eternity ring for her birthday, and it's her most treasured possession. I know she thinks it means that he's going to give her a wedding ring one day, and I think she's right about that too. I cursed myself for being far away.

'*Gertie!*' I whispered loudly. '*Gerts! Just give it to them.*'

The masked man was walking towards her in a really menacing way. I looked around for someone to do something – anything – to

8

help, but everyone was terrified, staring at the floor, feeling feverishly in their pockets for the space their phones were moments before.

I swore mightily to myself. I am not in the least bit brave and will not pee in a room that a spider is in or has been in or might once have been in but –

'ARGH,' I said. I looked around for the big man with the blue eyes but he was nowhere to be seen. It struck me suddenly that he might have been with the robbers, scoping the place out, and my blood ran cold. I swallowed, and before I could think about it, I had jumped back over the bar.

Chapter Three

'LEAVE HER ALONE!' I shouted loudly, my voice shaking 'Leave her ring! Here. Take my watch. And my wallet. And my phone. Take anything you like, just ... leave that ring.'

'Holly!' said Gertie, her face looking utterly drained of all colour. The henchman – he was massive, dressed all in black – turned around slowly to face me. My teeth were chattering in my head.

'Here,' I said, pushing forward my bag, in which, I knew, was enough cash for two cocktails and a credit card which was basically maxed out completely, but he wasn't to know that. 'Take it, take it all, but leave the ring.'

You could hear a pin drop in the room. My heart was beating so loudly in my chest I could feel it. Where were the police? They'd been called for. Where were they?

Nobody spoke. Then the main guy, the one who had spoken, stepped aside from the blonde woman and started to move towards me, very slowly. Oh God, oh God, oh God.

This wasn't like me at all. The one time I went to give blood I pretty much threw up in the van. And I didn't even want to come out to a bar because I hate them. Also, it struck me, if I was going to be killed, I wish I *had* worn the nice knickers.

He loomed over me; he was very tall. He was wearing a large hat which cast shadows on his face, and of course a mask; I could tell his skin was bad. And something else: just where the hat finished, he had the oddest thing which my attention snagged on – a large, pale kiss-curl. The rest of his hair was smoothed down, but this curl stuck out.

I was trembling all over.

'That's the problem with bravery,' he said. His voice was light and airy, and he sounded rather sad. Somehow that made it worse, and I felt a big block of ice in my stomach. I couldn't seem to move.

'The problem with bravery is that it's incredibly time-consuming and, you know, potentially really dangerous.'

He leaned closer to me, searching my face. I turned my eyes to the ground like a cringing dog, utterly terrified. Next to me, his cronie was fiddling with his gun. I could hear metal clicking against metal and fingernails.

The oddest thing I noticed – all my senses were heightened – was that he smelled of lime and cedar. Something incredibly expensive, anyway. Who puts aftershave on to commit a massive heist? I found myself thinking. And where the hell were the police?

Without violence, he simply lifted the bag out of my hand and grabbed Gertie's wrist. Then he looked at me and sighed.

'Don't make me,' he said.

'Don't make you what?' I stuttered.

'Machete!' he said sorrowfully, and one of his goons jumped forward.

'No!' I said again in total disbelief. Then I looked at Gertie, who was pale and sweating, eyes wide.

'Give it to him!' I said. 'Give him the ring! And quickly!'

His shadowed eyes moved back to my face, and I flinched instinctively.

'Oh, thank goodness,' he said, then again moving like a darting snake, he grabbed the top of my arm.

'Well done.'

He was holding me. Not tightly, but I couldn't squirm. Gertie had somehow fumbled off her ring and handed it to him with shaking fingers, watching me the entire time. He took it without looking at her, but he wouldn't let go my arm.

'I like a fast learner,' he said, smiling. His voice was still so soft and calm. I wanted to spit in his face, but all my courage was gone, withered.

'Thank you, everyone,' he called out to the room politely. 'Your little trinkets will help fund our ... well, nothing you need to know about.'

He smiled again.

'Do enjoy the rest of your evenings.'

As he said that, his henchmen shot every single bottle of booze behind the bar. Glass shards rained down and I hoped the bar staff was all right. Yet still he did not let me go, and the horrifying thought dawned on me slowly: the robbery was over.

But he was taking me with him.

Chapter Four

People stared at me as I was dragged past them, and they cast their eyes down. Thank God, I found myself thinking, thank God they don't have their phones. I made a mewling sound. Gertie was being kept back by one of his goons, but I could see the horror in her eyes.

'Let me go,' I begged, but he was still pulling me along – not brutally, but there was no element of doubt – and didn't even show whether he'd heard. And everyone in that tacky, run-down, evil-smelling nightclub turned their faces away, saying without words, 'Don't pick on me, don't pick on me, ' and I will say, I did not blame them.

Finally, at last, I heard a siren somewhere and my neck jerked up. The man laughed as the siren grew briefly louder, then faded away.

'Think they're having a busy evening,' he grunted.

We were at the door. Outside, I saw under the streetlights a large van with blacked-out windows. I knew for a fact this was where he was taking me and I started to kick and struggle, but he held on to me – not strongly enough to hurt me, but enough.

'Don't struggle,' he said. 'It's tedious. Can't you just come along until I'm safely out of here? Honestly, it's standard procedure. But I really don't want to hurt you.'

'NO!'

I risked a yell. He pulled me close to him – I smelled that scent again – and leaned into my ear: it was a curiously intimate hold.

'Oh, for heaven's sake,' he whispered in my ear. 'On the other hand, you scream, and I'll cut a rainbow in your face, line by line.'

And I saw the solitary streetlight in the back alley glint off the blade of a knife he had in his palm.

My throat shuttered closed. I couldn't have screamed if I wanted to.

The street was dark and silent. My eyes closed; my shoulders sank: I was resigned to my fate, while in a simultaneous state of utter disbelief that this was happening to me. I work in PR, for goodness' sake. I share a flat where I can touch all the walls at the same time. I eat too much brown food, and I like my legs and dislike my freckly nose. My name is Holly Phillips, I am twenty-six, ten and a half stone, sandy hair, brown eyes: completely and utterly ordinary. And I was being kidnapped. I closed my eyes and let my head sag.

The next thing I heard was a kind of a swoosh. My head jerked up in confusion; the hand tightened on my arm. Something was blocking out the streetlight, leaving us in darkness. It was the figure of a man.

I started to struggle in my panic. Oh God no, I thought; it's one of those idiot vigilantes. You know, the ones that are always being paraded in the newspapers – portly, sweaty and uncomfortable in their Lycra robes sewn by their mothers or long-suffering girlfriends, stalking around town telling off teenage drug dealers and getting sworn at for their trouble.

Then I made a sharp intake of breath.

It wasn't one of the silly copycats. It's ... it couldn't be. Oh, for goodness' sake.

My relief to see his identity was balanced out by how absurd this entire thing was.

'Okay, what have we got here?' the figure said in disappointed tones.

'Oh, seriously? I've got a hostage and stuff. Can't you just get out of my way?' said the man holding me.

'What on earth ... ? There's twenty-two robberies taking place at nightclubs right across this city.'

'Twenty-five.'

'And they're all down to you? What are you? New?'

'Frederick Cecil. Nice to meet you.'

'Frederick Cecil?' said the man, still in shadow.

Really, I thought, even in my fear. That *is* a terrible name.

'That's a terrible name for a baddie,' continued the man. 'You sound like a butler.'

The grip on my arm tightened.

'I happen to like it,' said Frederick Cecil.

'What about Ferocious Freddie the Fearless?' suggested the man in the shadows.

'Yes, I don't really have time for this now,' said Frederick Cecil, dragging me along further.

It was so quick I couldn't see how he'd moved, not at all. It was like a flash, or a jump cut: suddenly, the man from the shadows was standing right in front of us. Seeing the light again was blinding.

'Oww,' I said.

15

It doesn't help that the man who had suddenly appeared in front of us was revealed, out of the darkness, to be wearing his full suit. I'd seen him in the papers, of course – he was everywhere. But I hadn't realised in real life it was quite so ... quite so ... purple.

'Put the girl down.'

'Yeah, I'd love to, but you know ... getting away and all that?'

'PUT HER DOWN.'

I felt my throat loosen up just a little.

'Um, hi, yeah, *could* you actually put me down?'

They both ignored me, but there was a quick intake of breath from Ultimate Man – seriously, that's what he calls himself. Ultimate Man. Our genuine city vigilante. I'd never seen him before, but DuTroy thinks he's totally awesome.

I always thought he was a bit of a ninny myself, probably with daddy issues – I mean, he wears a cape and everything. I will tell you: the cape has not caught on.

I thought that right up until two seconds later when two of Frederick Cecil's goons were creeping up on him.

With me barely seeing it, *bang*, Ultimate Man had knocked out two henchmen really quickly. It doesn't make a big crunch like punches being thrown on television. It was just a crack and a kind of strangled *groo* noise, and two huge men were lying on the ground and the back of the van was left swinging open.

Frederick Cecil looked like he didn't care in the slightest.

'Can we move it along?' he said, showing me the knife again, glinting.

Faster than I could see, Ultimate Man kicked it out of his hand, and it soared over the van and landed in the brickwork of the building across the street.

16

All three of us turned to look at it. Suddenly I heard the sirens start up again, encouragingly close this time.

Frederick Cecil turned his head quickly in their direction, and Ultimate Man took his chance. He booted the man's elbow, which reflexively curled up and set me free as Frederick Cecil buckled in pain and let out a small sigh.

I didn't need telling twice: I tore off down the alleyway. Panting, I couldn't tell if I was being chased, but when I finally hit the street corner, I slowed down, completely out of breath – Gertie's right: Pilates is rubbish for cardio – my hands on my knees, breath tearing from the shock. I couldn't hear footsteps.

I risked a look behind me. The van was starting to move in the opposite direction to me, and Frederick Cecil was running towards it, just as Ultimate Man bored into him.

I found I didn't want to watch; I didn't want to know what the stupid, stupid men were doing. I was suddenly overwhelmed, bursting into tears, fully realising the horror.

I just wanted to find Gertie and go home and curl up and cry.

As if on cue, something came flying through the air towards me. I stepped aside, but I needn't have done: it landed perfectly where my feet were. I glanced down. It was Gertie's eternity ring.

Chapter Five

'No, no, no, no; absolutely no way; definitely not.'

Gertie and I were sitting on the window ledge, with the local news on.

DuTroy was standing by the door with a rolling pin. He'd been standing there for thirty-five minutes and I think he was feeling pretty stupid about it now, but he couldn't seem to stop himself. 'Seriously, dudes, no.'

They were trying to get me to go to hospital, both of them, but I kept telling them I was fine; I wasn't hurt, just shaken up. Gertie assumed this meant I absolutely definitely had concussion, which is an impossible argument to win if you think about it.

Anyway, I knew I hadn't hit my head, and was telling them so vociferously. I didn't even show them my arm. There was nothing to see there anyway; it was only the memory of his fingertips.

My teeth were chattering as if I'd been submerged in cold water, but I was gradually coming back to myself. We didn't have any booze in the flat – or so I thought until Gertie unearthed a hideous little bottle of some thick liquorice liqueur she brought back from holiday that time, and she made me drink it, which was just about the worst thing that happened to me that evening. We stared at the incredibly repetitive television news.

Clubs and bars all over the city had been targeted in raids, diverting police resources and adding massive confusion. On the screen, a girl with long bits of hair hanging off her – extensions which had dropped out in the panic – was sobbing into the camera, great trails of mascara running down her face.

'Shouldn't you be more like that?' said Gertie. 'I'm just saying. You could have got on TV.'

'What, you think I've failed at being scared in a socially acceptable way?' I said. 'Great. I hope a dingo never steals my baby.'

'This city is getting worse and worse,' said DuTroy, and of course he totally had a point about that. He had so much of a point about that, in fact, that when my mother rang up to check I hadn't been anywhere near one of those 'awful bars', I lied my head off and told her of course I hadn't, look at me, talking from home, nothing to worry about. I took another slug of the filthy liqueur.

Gertie looked at me reproachfully, stroking her ring. She'd tried to apologise, but I waved it away. She'd panicked. So had I. It wasn't her fault any more than getting thrown over the bar was mine. None of us knows how we'll respond when something really awful happens. I know that now. I only just about got away with not wetting my knickers.

But I don't want to dwell on it. I don't want to dwell on the absolute worst thing. That when that man – when that thing, really; he doesn't deserve the term 'man' – told me to get into the van, I didn't fight. I didn't scream or complain. I let him take me. I'd obediently allowed him to tell me what to do. If Ultimate Man hadn't shown up, I know I'd just have gone. Like cattle. Straightaway.

So now I know that about myself. It doesn't really seem worth being scared any more. If they come for us, I shall march with my head down, into the van. That's the kind of person I am. Come the zombie apocalypse, I'll go down first wave.

I sighed heavily.

'You all right?' said Gertie for the billionth time. 'Aren't you going to give a statement to the police?'

'Four hundred other people saw him,' I said. 'What can I add? Anyway, they probably already know who he is.'

'So,' said DuTroy. He'd obviously been dying to bring this up, but waiting till a suitable moment.

'So, uh . . . You met Ultimate Man, huh?'

'Not really,' I said. 'He didn't even look at me or anything. We weren't formally introduced.'

'But he saved you, right?'

I shrugged. 'I suppose so.'

'Man, that's cool.'

'It's not cool!' said Gertie. 'He's a vigilante! He's a crazy show-off who jumps around the place making an idiot out of himself and encouraging steroid abuse!'

Up until tonight, this had also very much been my feelings on the Ultimate Man issue.

Other cities don't have a vigilante hero. Well, maybe here in America they do, but not where I grew up, in Britain.

It felt like it defined us. While also, by the way, constantly reiterating the message that our town was totally full of scum and crime and our police was rubbish. This is not the way to attract investment and tourists. We did get tourists, obviously. But they were, for the most part, incredibly creepy, always loitering around the really dodgy parts of town hoping they might get mugged and then Ultimate Man might come and rescue them.

I will tell you: first, it made more work for Ultimate Man and it made basically worse stuff happen, which is immoral in my opinion; and also, he is (apparently) only the one guy, which means there's loads of tourists who got mugged and *didn't* get saved, leading one of them to sue the city. And because those odds aren't bad if you're a mugger, then it becomes a self-fulfilling cycle. The more people are muggers, the less statistically likely it is that Ultimate Man will happen to be strolling by and be able to save you.

I know you think having a guy with superpowers in your city would be cool, but I can tell you from experience, it really wouldn't. He's a blooming liability and a bit embarrassing, with the purple suit and everything.

But undeniably, he had saved me.

'He was fine,' I said shortly. I wasn't thinking about him. I was still thinking about Fredrick Cecil and his van.

'Thank God he was there. I don't know what would have happened.'

Well, none of us wanted to think about that for very long.

'So did he, like ... did he feel really ... I mean, are those real muscles or was it just the suit ...?' DuTroy went on.

'Actually,' I said, 'I was really sorry about it. I kind of always thought *you* might be Ultimate Man.'

'Shut up!'

'Sorry.'

'I totally could be Ultimate Man.'

'Yeah, in tiny world,' said Gertie, snorting.

He's gorgeous, DuTroy, but not the tallest. He looked really hurt.

'Aww, you can be my Ultimate Man, baby,' said Gertie immediately, and I made gagging sounds.

'I don't think I want to leave you alone in the city any more,' said Gertie. 'Maybe we shouldn't move out.'

'I won't be *alone*,' I said. 'Not having a boyfriend doesn't mean you're alone! I've got friends! I've got work! I've got Vincent!'

Vincent now lived in an annoying luxurious apartment based on the annoyingly lucrative job he got when he escaped his boring technical degree and started making a ton of money turning his annoyingly literal brain towards logistics.

I am totally fine with the fact that my baby brother, who is only twenty years old, rents an apartment on his own that is six times the size of mine. And didn't ask me to move in.

'Hmm,' said Gertie, unconvinced. 'I just . . . I mean, what if he targets you now? That bad guy?'

'He doesn't know who I am,' I said, remembering again with a shiver the gentle pressure of that hand against my arm. 'He didn't even look at me. He was just grabbing anything to make his getaway. He'd have put a gun to a dog's head if there'd been one handy.'

'Are you sure about that? You've seen him now.'

'No, I haven't. He had a mask on. Look.'

I nod towards the television. There was a huge stupid photofit of a guy with stubble, bad skin and a mask over his eyes. You could barely tell what ethnicity he was.

'Four hundred people saw him as much as I did.'

But only one smelled him, I think to myself. Only one nearly stepped in the van.

Chapter Six

I considered taking a day off, but on balance decided I would keep some trauma leave in reserve for, frankly, a slightly sunnier day.

I work for the mayor, which sounds grand except I've never met her, and it's a tiny satellite department where I rewrite press releases about cheerful-sounding initiatives and try and get them in the paper, whereupon the few tired old hacks who are left working there generally just say yes, and sigh and talk about journalism not being what it was. I smile politely because obviously I know that, and clearly I'd much rather be a working journalist like them rather than churning out press releases on garbage pick-ups, particularly since the press release about garbage pick-ups has to rather skate over the issue that there's about to be dramatically less of them.

Anyway, naturally Gertie wanted me to take the day off, but there was the added bonus that I would be able to mention to the office that had I had been right in the middle of it and thus would be the focus of lots of gossip and I promise you, if you had a work day as boring as mine, you'd be grateful for that too.

I dressed in black to look demure and somehow a brave victim.

Maybe I would stare stoically out of the window and if anyone asked me what was wrong, I would say, 'No, nothing,' and perhaps bite my lip a bit. I wanted to milk the heroic, Ultimate Man bit. The more I focused on that, the less I had to think about the other bit.

The subway was mobbed as usual, and I looked around at people's tablets over their shoulders to read the news. I wasn't mentioned – as 'brave girl who got away' – annoyingly enough. Although I'm not sure they'd have got the most flattering photograph of me skulking up the road like a fleeing dog.

I swiped my security card at the office and walked up to the coffee room where my colleagues, Liz and Bettina, were chatting away.

'OMG,' said Bettina as I walked in. 'Have you heard what happened?'

I composed my features into a slightly saintly visage and looked enquiring.

'FINALLY!' said Liz. 'Finally, there's a man in the building.'

'What?' I said, wrong-footed.

'It's true,' said Bettina, nodding wildly. 'A *man*.'

There are lots of women in PR, my line of work. Lots. Even in the mayor's office, all the men are over in civil engineering, sharpening pencils and drawing manly . . . Actually, I have no idea what they do in civil engineering. I think it has something to do with slotting huge pipes into tight holes. I think possibly also I fantasise too much at work because I don't like my job. And also, there aren't enough men.

'Oh,' I said, interested but not ready to relinquish my starring role that easily. 'Anyway, so I was at this bar last night . . .'

'A tall man,' said Bettina.

'With hair!' said Liz.

'Are you sure you aren't objectifying?' I said crossly. 'And also, didn't you hear me? I was at a bar! The bar that got targeted by that bad guy!'

They looked at me.

'Oh that,' said Bettina. 'So was my mum. And all my other mates.'

'Yeah, everyone was,' said Liz. 'You're like the fortieth person this morning to say that. Actually you can't all have been there.'

She eyed me suspiciously but I'm pretty used to that. Liz is about a fifteenth of a salary grade above me though does the same kind of thing as I do, but she's been here longer and is a lot older than me and seems to think I am a major super-ambitious player out to snatch her 'incredibly senior' job, which shows she isn't really a very good judge of human nature.

'Well, I was,' I said, holding up a cream tote from Forbidden Planet. 'Look, no handbag – see?'

'Are we still talking about this?' said Bettina. She moves over to the glass wall of our little office. You can see across the main hall.

'There he is,' she said reverently. 'He's getting his security pass.'

'He can security pass me,' said Liz, which doesn't even make sense, but I follow where they're heading and glance down.

'A *man*,' said Bettina with some satisfaction. 'In *our* department. Ooh.'

Our previous incumbent, Shawna, had moved to Cyprus to get married, a fact which had been discussed at almost unbelievable length both with us and on speakerphone over the previous eighteen months, with everyone being well aware of the cost of paper napkins, the best font for save the date cards, the difficulties of sourcing French lace and how many alterations one required when dropping three dress sizes in three months before the big

25

day, whether nine groomsmen was enough, how you order personalised sugared almonds and what was best – an éclair cake or a chocolate one.

Then she didn't invite any of us. Liz kind of implied she was invited and had said no, but she wasn't really.

I looked down.

Sure enough, there was a large, slightly scruffy man trying to look tidy for his security pass photo. He was tall and wearing glasses and a suit which looked like his mother had bought it for him to grow into.

'He has hair,' marvelled Bettina. 'And he's tall! That already puts him, like, nine points ahead of my ex-husband.'

'Also, he doesn't eat squirrel,' Liz pointed out, squinting downwards.

Bettina rolled her eyes. 'At least I've got an ex-husband.'

The man moved over to the lifts and we scuttled back to our desks like children when the teacher comes back in. Bettina hastily put on some new lipstick and even Liz smoothed down her hair expectantly. I tried my best to pretend I was above all this kind of nonsense.

The lift pinged on our floor and slid open. We all desperately pretended not to be looking ... until Liz, unable to contain herself, leapt out of her seat. We never saw our actual boss: she was always in meetings or on courses; she normally just emailed work over. So Liz decided to do what she normally did and pretend she was in charge.

The man who emerged, blinking into the light of our office, was tall, right enough, but apart from that he wasn't a very impressive specimen. He seemed a little too big for his shirt; his shoulders were slumped over, presumably from being too tall for things all the time; he looked a little rumpled, like a dressed-up bear. He wore glasses, but unlike the slick trendy frames some people wore for fashion, they clearly had thick prescription lenses in them, which gave his eyes a slightly startled appearance, heightened now due to Liz turning her gimlet eyes on him.

'Hi,' she said. 'Hi there. Welcome to my team.'

Whose team? Bettina and I shared a glance.

'Now you are ... ?'

'Nelson. Nelson Barmveyer.'

He was carrying a large briefcase and wasn't quite sure where to put it down, so moved slightly awkwardly. Meanwhile, for a horrifying split-second I thought Liz was moving in to kiss him on the cheek. In the end, they managed to slightly dart past each other, and kind of grasp hands a little bit.

Oh well. I couldn't deny it: even though I had been trying not to get my hopes up, it was hard not to get a little bit excited about a new man in the office. Plus he might have hot friends.

Liz clearly wasn't in the slightest bit put off.

'Now, come meet everyone,' she said. 'This is Bettina.'

Nelson looked apologetic, then glanced round when he realised he'd forgotten to pick his briefcase up again.

'And this is Holly.'

'Hi,' I said. His hand was sweaty. He must be so nervous; I felt sorry for him. Especially when he found out he had to sit next to Liz.

'Welcome,' I said. He grinned awkwardly.

'Uh, yeah, thanks, right,' he said.

'You're over here, next to me!' said Liz cheerfully. 'Now, let me take you through it ... '

My phone rang. It was Gertie.

'Are you all right?'

'I'm fine. There's a new man in the office.'

27

'Oooh! Hair?'

'Yes.'

'Beating pulse?'

'Yes.'

'Go for it.'

'Gertie, you've just described a raccoon.'

There was a pause.

'So how about it?'

'Gertie, I'm in shock, according to you.'

'Heightened emotions, adrenalin rushing, pupils dilated ... This could work for you.'

'Gert! I have to go!'

'Well, get your stake claimed before Liz takes him home to chop him up for cat food.'

'Gert!'

'... Or whatever she does.'

Sure enough, Liz did have her head bent close to his and appeared to be giggling every time somebody said the word 'spreadsheet'.

I sidled off to my favourite place at lunchtime, which was behind a side street and was incredibly quiet so usually a good place to hide in a corner and eat food while reading, which wasn't a look I'd like to impose on the general public. I'd like to say Corelli's was a real hidden gem, but basically you could get a seat because it was pretty awful. It wasn't hip and trendy with exposed brick walls and good-looking staff yelling at you. It had horrid floral plastic tablecloths and old men who sat there all day with one cup of coffee and a fat guy who ran it and never looked pleased to see you however many times you went there a week, and a slight sticky residue on everything. But it had one massive advantage:

I was one hundred per cent guaranteed never to run into anyone from the mayor's office there. The mayor didn't even eat lunch; she thought it was for losers and said so in her supposedly inspirational memos she sent round every now and again, presumably composed in what would otherwise have been her lunch break.

I rifled through the stack of greasy-fingerprinted newspapers, hauled one out and made myself comfortable.

The newspaper report didn't mess around.

HANDBAGGER STRIKES

Handbagger? I thought. That wasn't the snappiest of nicknames. Next was the absurd photofit.

The criminal mastermind known only as the Handbagger –

That made him sound like some cross middle-aged lady having a tantrum after choir practice.

– struck at as many as twenty-five locations last night, including many popular night spots, relieving patrons of their wallets in a mass mugging many have compared to a terrorist attack.

Well, it was scary, but it wasn't a *terrorist attack*. Honestly. From a PR perspective, adding 'terrorist attack' to muggings, real vigilantes, fake vigilantes and a baddie was incredibly unhelpful.

Ultimate Man was believed to have made an appearance at seven of the twenty-five affected outlets, curtailing the criminal activities several times over.

Somebody cleared their throat. Ugh, I disliked having to share my tiny round table. That was the whole point of coming to the not-very-good café. With bad grace, I made to shuffle over.

Large brown eyes were blinking at me behind those beer bottle glasses.

'Uh, excuse me ... sorry ... is anyone sitting there?'

I blinked.

'Nelson, isn't it?'

'Uh, yeah,' he said, as if he weren't entirely sure.

I shuffled over. He was carrying a very dodgy-looking egg salad on a tray.

'Are you sure about that?'

He regarded the wilted lettuce rather sadly.

'I ... I don't really know the area.'

'I thought Liz was taking you out for lunch.'

He blinked.

'Uhm ... yeah. Then we kind of ...'

He tailed off.

'It's quite full on, starting a new job,' I offered, so he didn't have to make up some excuse. He sat down heavily – there was a lot of him; he looked like a friendly sack of laundry – and looked at my paper.

'So ... it's quite a trip this city, huh?' he said.

'You've just moved here?'

'No, but ... it is quite new being here in the city. Or ... I don't know. Maybe you always feel new. Or maybe it's just me.'

He turned a little pink, but I knew what he meant. Sometimes I felt that everyone was so busy trying to show each other that they belonged in Centerton, and having a brilliant time, that I felt like an imposter all the time. Hence my ability to let Gertie talk me into going to stupid night spots which get targeted by stupid idiots.

30

'No, it's not just you,' I said. 'Mind you, most people generally have a better grip on their salad.'

He looked startled by this, and half a boiled egg slid off his fork and onto the floor.

'Oh! Sorry!' I said, but he was already ducking down under the table, which – being far too big for it – he almost pushed into my lap, sloshing what Corelli's called a latte and I called boiled dishwater onto my lap.

'Argh!' I said. Fortunately, Corelli's didn't believe in serving its coffee at any temperature above lukewarm, so I wasn't scalded. Nelson's face, however, when he got up again, was the boiled red of a lobster.

'I am *so* sorry,' he said. 'So, so sorry.'

'That's okay,' I said, trying to brush off the worst of the damage with a tiny napkin that wasn't even vaguely fit for purpose.

'Oh my . . . I mean, I don't even know why I was going down to get the egg. I mean . . . '

We both looked at the floor. Then we both started to laugh.

'Seriously,' I said. 'What were you doing? Saving a dead egg?'

'I honestly don't know,' he said. 'Because if anything, the egg would have made the floor slightly cleaner than it was before.'

I giggled, and he put his head in his hands.

'Oh goodness,' he said. 'First day at work and I have already told one person in the office I didn't want to go to the Revolving Restaurant for lunch, and coffee-assaulted another.'

'It's an old skirt anyway,' I said, which was true.

'Can I pay for the dry-cleaning?' he asked.

'I don't know – can you?'

'Hmm,' he said. 'Well, if I go without lunch again tomorrow maybe.'

31

We looked at the remains of his very unpalatable-looking salad.

'Maybe,' I said.

We walked back to the office together, I slightly craning to see up to him. A bit of mayonnaise had got on his shirt, but I didn't want to tell him in case he got really embarrassed again.

Liz gave me the full on stink-eye as soon as we walked in together and glanced ostentatiously at the clock.

'You're late back,' she said. I wanted very badly to stick out my tongue and say 'you're not my boss!' but I didn't.

'Sorry,' I said. 'I had an accident.'

'It was all my fault,' said Nelson gallantly. Liz gave him the stink-eye too. Her penchant obviously hadn't lasted very long.

'Actually, Mr Barmveyer, we don't really encourage long lunch breaks here in the PR department. You never know when there might be an urgent breaking story we have to respond to.'

'Unless they're up the Revolving Restaurant,' I whispered, but Nelson looked thoroughly chastened.

'I'm sorry, ma'am,' he said. Liz did not like being called ma'am, I could tell. That's what happened when you pretended you were the boss.

'It won't happen again,' he added.

Liz sniffed. 'And you,' she said, pointing at me. 'The phone's been ringing off the hook for you! Didn't you have your smart-phone on?'

'Yes,' I said, which wasn't strictly a lie. The fact that Corelli's was in a signal black spot was one of the other reasons I liked it so much.

'Well, everyone wants to talk to you.'

Sure enough, as I took my phone out of my bag it started pinging and blinking red over and over again.

Chapter Seven

I walked over my computer – and that's where I saw it. Someone must have pulled it off the CCTV in the bar. So much for wanting notoriety for my experience. Suddenly I didn't want it at all.

In the evening editions of the newspapers, on Instagram and BuzzFeed – it appeared to be hitting all the outlets at the same time, there was a picture of me, like some kind of idiotic damsel in distress, ungallantly thrown over Ultimate Man's shoulder prior to being hurled over the bar. The picture was headlined 'The Girl Who Got Away'.

'Is that you?' said Bettina.

'Um, might be,' I said cautiously.

'My nights out never end like that,' she said.

'I did *tell* you I was there,' I said.

Liz came over and sniffed.

'You can see your knickers.'

'Thanks, Liz'

'Is that cellulite? Make the picture bigger.'

'Let's just forget all about it.'

'There is a big discussion about whether or not it's cellulite on

Instagram,' called Bettina from the other side of the office. 'Ooh. That's not very nice.'

'Stop it!' I said, suddenly appalled. 'Stop it.'

'Oh, they're putting their own caption on the pictures too.'

'This is a nightmare,' I said, collapsing in front of my computer. It really *wasn't* a flattering photograph. Also it had my bum, my knickers and my totally recognisable face in it all at the same time. My inbox started pinging like a maniac.

Liz smiled grimly.

'Well, we'd better get a statement out.'

'Why?' I said panicking. 'What? You don't need a statement! People get saved by Ultimate Man all the time. It's boring, like astronauts. Nobody even cares any more. I don't even know why they're running this.'

Liz tapped the monitor.

'Don't be daft. They're running some kind of story about you saving your friend.'

'The internet thinks you did it to throw yourself at Ultimate Man,' chipped in Bettina unhelpfully. Nelson, I noticed out of the corner of my eye, was awkwardly staring at the floor.

'No, this is good,' said Liz. '"Panties Girl Heroine of Mayor's Office".'

'Seriously,' I said.

'Sounds like an epitaph,' said Bettina.

'I don't want this to happen,' I said hurriedly.

'Bit late, Panties Girl.'

I don't think I'd seen Liz so happy since Gwyneth Paltrow and Chris Martin broke up.

Chapter Eight

So it was slightly like making one of those terrible pacts with the devil, where you want to be famous and the devil says all right then, and then does it in the worst way possible.

If it had just been the bum (or if they'd airbrushed the cellulite) that would have been okay, but no, they'd added the official photo of me, in case I wasn't visible enough from the side, so there I was, in my cheesy PR department official photo, totally recognisable, needing my roots done, looking slightly dazed and fundamentally stupid, seeing as the pic was taken on the first day I'd arrived and Liz had just given me the health and safety briefing, told me that she was pretty much the boss of the whole outfit, given me a shit desk in the corner – which I could tell from the hand cream in the drawer had been hers till about five minutes before I walked in – and asked if I had any single male friends.

So if I could once have got away with it for just the bum, I absolutely couldn't now they'd stuck my mug all over the place and Facebook was going berserk. And people were being rude about me and calling me BumBum and Panties Girl on Twitter (my surname is Barker, which sounds, I'm sure you'll agree, absolutely nothing like BumBum).

It took about four minutes for me to discover that being famous patently sucked ass. I glanced at my most recent telephone call. Oh lord – my mother. As if on cue, it rang again.

'Holly? Holly, are those the panties I bought you? Because you know they're obviously past their best. I mean, I was completely embarrassed down at bridge club – everyone saw it, and that awful Patty deFrancesco, well, of course, she picked up on it straightaway, said what size were you now because a lot of people got thinner when they moved to the city . . . '

'Can I phone you back, Ma? Only it's a bit crazy round here.'

'I just don't want Vinnie seeing it, that's all.'

I realise Mum worries about my baby brother, but really.

'Mum, I don't think he reads the paper, and if he did he wouldn't care.'

'Can you just call him in any case?'

'He won't pick up!'

She sighed. 'Oh, all right, Kim Kardashian. Don't let all of this go to your head.'

'Mum, my arse was put on a newspaper without my knowledge. How could having my arse in the paper go to my head?'

Liz hustled up and I quickly said my goodbyes and hung up.

'Of course, we'll turn it into a good promotional opportunity for the mayor's office.'

'What do you mean?' I said, watching my Twitter follower count zoom like a crazy thing. Then I noticed people starting to retweet things into my line from an account called '@bigUltimate Manass'.

They were not nice things.

'How?' I said, my heart starting to beat dangerously fast.

'We'll fix up a photo shoot,' said Liz. 'You and Ultimate Man. And the mayor. Ultimate Man and the mayor's office. Teaming up to beat the bad guys.'

'I don't think so,' I said, backing away.

'A lovely heroic press conference. It will be great. I think it might be your only chance not to be Pantie BumBum for the rest of your life.'

'How will you even get hold of him?' said Bettina. 'He hates all that kind of stuff.'

'He doesn't hate it so much that he stops wearing the suit,' I pointed out. 'If he really hated it, he could just join the police force like a normal person would. Plus didn't he do a calendar shoot?'

'Well, he's not a normal person anyway.'

'Seriously, there's no point in him saying he isn't interested in publicity, then swooping about in dramatic bank raids wearing a fricking mask and some spandex.'

'We'll get him,' said Liz ominously.

'How? You can't light that city in peril big light thing: they outlawed that.'

They had outlawed it after every kid with a torch had rigged up their own on top of the nearest highest building and called Ultimate Man out so often it nearly killed him.

'The mayor has ways,' sniffed Liz.

'I really am not sure about this,' I said. 'And of course he won't want to do it.'

'He might,' came a surprising voice. Nelson had been sitting in the corner, ears burning as five thousand reproduced copies of my bum popped up on every newsfeed and every local news channel.

'Why?' I said.

'Because this is awful for him too,' he pointed out. 'He looks like he's pulled the skirt up over your bum. On purpose. He looks like Ultimate Man's favourite thing to do is to turn ladies upside down and look at their panties.'

There was a silence.

'He's right,' said Bettina. 'I never thought of that.'

'Maybe that is his favourite thing to do,' I grumbled. 'Maybe that's exactly what he was doing. Maybe I should sue him or something.'

Liz narrowed her eyes.

'You will not.'

She marched out. 'I'm going to talk to the mayor.'

Which was how, the next evening – dressed in assuredly the best of my underpants just in case we got a really windy day or something – I found myself on the steps of City Hall.

'It'll be great,' Gertie had said, pleased. 'I'd love to meet him. And DuTroy would faint. Can we come?'

'No,' I said. 'Anyway, you've seen him in press conferences banging on about justice and rooting out corruption. He's going to be really boring and serious and it'll be rubbish.'

I sighed, looking at myself in the mirror. If I'd known I was going to become a small-scale local scandal, I'd have stuck to the 5:2 diet a bit more than half-heartedly .5:0.5.

'Maybe I'll wear some bum-lifting pants,' I'd said. 'That's where they're going to focus.'

I'd come off my social media altogether: it was getting worse and worse. There seemed to be an awful lot of people who either disliked my bum and felt it should not have been given visibility in a robbery situation, or liked it a lot and requested permission to get much closer to it. I wasn't fond of either viewpoint.

I looked through our window out at some million windows in

the city. It felt so strange that behind most of them, sure, were people just doing their best, like Gertie and DuTroy and me, but there were different types out there too.

People who planned to rob nightclubs, and did so. People who wrote filthy disgusting messages to strangers on the internet. People who put on skin-tight costumes and did vigilante martial arts. The world was a strange, strange place.

'Sometimes,' I said to Gertie. 'Sometimes I think we're the only normals left in this city.'

'That's why I'm getting the hell out of here as soon as I possibly can,' she said, giving me that look that suggested I do the same.

I'd finally settled on a navy blue dress, hopefully long enough not to gust up in the wind, flat shoes and properly blow-dried hair. Basically, I was channelling Princess Kate. She knew what she was doing. If she was ever worried about people speculating about her arse, she just threw her sister in the way. I also looked about 104. I don't know how French women get away with that aggressive plain-dressing thing.

Liz looked me up and down and sniffed and said well, it was better than making a spectacle of myself again (I had noticed that somehow having to be saved had become my fault), but Bettina leapt out of her seat, led me to the mirror and put a coat of red lipstick on me.

'That'll definitely help in the pictures,' she said. 'You look fine. Don't be nervous.'

'I'm not nervous,' I lied. Then I checked my watch for the seventieth time in the last half an hour. The press conference was at 10. It was show time.

Chapter Nine

'Hi,' I said awkwardly.

Seriously, the purple suit. It looked even worse in daylight. We were standing on the steps outside the mayor's office. Ultimate Man had given me a big fake smile and pretended to remember who I was. Even as we shook hands, he did it to the side so the photographers could get us, and he wouldn't meet my eye.

'So, thanks for rescuing me,' I said reluctantly.

'Sure thing!' he said, in a super-perky accent, which made me even more annoyed. Of course vigilantes have to be American. He probably wasn't really American. He's probably originally from Stoke. He mugged for the camera.

'Do you really like doing this?' I asked.

'Sure thing!' he said again, like a robot.

'*Really?*' I was surprised at my own surprise. I mean, who else but a weirdo would do this?

He paused then and looked at me, just for a second. I couldn't see much of him behind the stupid mask, but it did feel for a moment that he was looking at me properly rather than staring over my shoulder, wondering when he was going to be released from hanging out with civilians.

'The laundry can get pretty tedious,' he said in a voice so quiet and low that I thought I might have misheard. But there was no sign of mischief on his face as he firmly shook my hand once again, turned to the photographers and said, 'Hope you got your shot, guys!', saluted – yes, he saluted, the div-box – and vanished back into the building, leaving me standing by myself feeling like an idiot.

And that – which resulted in a stupid rictus grin photograph in the evening paper and the mayor making a big fuss about the police doing better and extended people making really rude remarks about my rear end for another three days before it died down and everyone stopped noticing – would have been that, I think, more or less.

Until it was my turn on the corporate party circuit.

We produce a horrible, tax-funded magazine every quarter which runs pap shots of horrible rich people pretending to say how fantastic everything is and picks up insanely overpriced house advertising from optimistic estate agents. You probably get one in your mailbox and think, 'Why don't they spend the money on giving us an extra bin pick-up?' and I would be hard-pressed not to agree with you.

Anyway, my job is to turn up and take comments from everyone along the lines of 'I love living in Centerton!' and 'Thanks so much for the delicious sponsored cocktails!' and 'I love the mayor so much!' as well as spelling their names correctly, and I would then put the anodyne remarks underneath the photos.

I didn't get any overtime, so my usual plan was to get the blondest, tallest women's names as quickly as possible, then partake in as much of the free fizz and canapés as possible. It wasn't the worst part of my job by any means.

Liz sniffed as I got changed to leave. She pretended to hate these things as she thought a) it was demeaning and b) she really felt she ought to be invited herself and was terrified of being mistaken for staff even though we were there as staff. But she liked them more than I did.

This one was at the museum, some kind of fund-raiser to save an impressive piece of sculpture from going overseas.

I'd seen it, and it was rather beautiful and huge; several pounding abstract horses. One piece of them that wasn't abstract however was their great big, exquisitely rendered in oxidated copper, penises.

The photographer had been instructed to make sure not to get any of the horse's special areas in any of the frames. He had confided in me that he would be getting nothing else. 'Ideally,' he said laconically, 'I'm going to line as many of them up as possible so that it looks like it's going in their mouths.'

'That's your night's work is it?' I said. I liked Hectorio: he thought what we did for a living was even more BS than I did. 'Yup,' he said. 'That, and I've brought a plastic bag for the canapés.'

'That's taking it a bit far.'

'You're joking, aren't you? Every dick out there thinks they're a photographer these days! Fricking smartphones. I can barely afford to eat!'

I had moved away before I gave Hectorio a chance to get onto his smartphones rant. They tended to take quite a long time. I was sure I'd hear it again before the end of the night.

I'd changed into a shortish black dress with a yellow collar. I looked slightly smarter than serving staff, slightly less smart than the guests (which was precisely what I was aiming for) and a bit like a bee (which I wasn't) but it was too late now.

'Well, make sure you spell the names right,' Liz had said for the billionth time. 'It's your only job; it should be easy. Last time you got Barina Von Furness all wrong.'

'Why do rich people have such stupid names?' I said.

'So you know they're rich,' said Bettina. 'Otherwise you'd mistake them for your common or garden drunks who happen to be wearing stupid dresses.'

Liz got ready to go home.

'Have a good time,' she said grudgingly.

'It's work,' I said.

'Yes,' she said a bit wistfully.

'You can go if you like,' I said. 'I want to go home and watch NetFlix.'

She shook her head.

'No,' she said. 'It's really boring really.'

'It is,' I said.

I arrived pretty early in the hope that I could get enough blonde women posing near to a gigantic horse's penis to go home early, but the place was already thronged. How rich did you have to be, I wondered, before the promise of an open bar didn't bring you in descending like an insect invasion?

Sure enough, the women were all stick-thin and tall, candy-floss-haired, air-kissing in a frenzy and competitively barking about after-school programmes. The men were muttering at the back. Waiting staff were floating in and out with champagne flutes.

To cover up for the fact that I didn't know anyone there – I was there to do a job, I told myself fiercely, it didn't matter if I knew anyone or not, but it still made me feel a little anxious, particularly when the women turned round and scanned me briefly, before making it incredibly clear that they knew I wasn't one of them and so they didn't feel the need to worry about it. I grabbed a glass and took a large sip, then glanced around the room. The whole thing smelled of money; of expensive cologne and new clothes and shoes which had gone straight from a car to a red carpet. I studied the huge horse sculpture more closely.

Yes, it was beautiful and everything, but this city ... On my way here, through an apparently nice part of town – from City Hall to the Metropolitan Art Gallery – I'd been asked for change three times, and spotted plenty of people bedding down in alleyways and stumbling up the road, pushing shopping trolleys full of old bags. Wouldn't all this money – this rich, insulated money – be much better off helping with that? Choosing to give their largesse to some big piece of metal with cocks on it – I wondered how many of them paid their taxes. If they paid their taxes, we probably wouldn't have as many cracked pavements, as many vagrants. If they gave their charity to a proper shelter for real human beings ...

Well, there was no point thinking about that. Their taxes, if they paid any, paid my salary too, and my job, however ridiculous, was to get their names into our stupid City Hall magazine. I caught Hectorio's eye – he was wearing a filthy old polo shirt which barely covered his belly, as if on protest at the glittering spectacle around him, and we approached the nearest blonde to the sculpture.

I listened to her wittering on through inflated lips about how much she adored to contribute to charity because that was just the kind of great person she was, although she didn't really like to talk about it.

Her job was something called a roving ambassador, which obviously I knew meant trust fund, but I nodded nonetheless and

44

made sure I was spelling all four of her double-barrelled names properly without my eyes glazing over. One ticked off. I looked around for the police chief; he was always at these things. He had a booming voice and a barrel chest and absolutely loved getting his name in the paper so he was a shoo-in. I checked him out chatting up one of the junior museum staff, who looked rather startled. Perhaps this was not the moment.

'The men in here,' whispered Hectorio loudly, 'have only ever had an orgasm over the bond market. The women in here have never had an orgasm at all.'

'Stop it,' I said, stifling a giggle. 'You're disgusting.'

'I don't think it's disgusting,' he said. 'I think it's heartbreaking, all of them desperately frotting up against one another. Not. A. Single. Orgasm.'

I looked around. Two blondes were furiously comparing how well their children were doing at school and how difficult it was to get genius training when their children were too bright for their schoolwork. Another woman was looking at someone's very expensive shoes as if she was hungry which, judging by the way her expensive sparkly dress fell off her sharp hip-bones, she obviously was. An elderly man had fallen asleep in the corner. I sighed.

'I'm going out for a cigarette,' said Hectorio. 'Hopefully, the demon that is tobacco will kill me and save me from the misery that is the rich at play.'

'You know tables for tonight cost ten thousand?' I said, leaving Hectorio shaking his head as he mooched off, astounded at the stupidity of the world.

I half-smiled, peering round the room to see who to pounce on next, but there weren't even any other gossip columnists there; they saved money by just using our pics, which was a real shame as a couple of other hacks to hang out with would have made all

45

the difference in the world. I loved journalists. I waved to one who looked familiar. He waved back, looking confused and I realised to my horror I didn't know him at all: he just looked familiar but not in a way I could place.

'Hi,' he said distractedly. 'Do I know you?'

I rallied fast.

'Hi, I'm reporting for "Around Centerton"!' I said brightly, taking out my notebook. 'Can I just ask you a few questions about . . . ?'

'Christ,' he said. 'No thanks.'

And he walked over to the other side of the room. I glanced in his direction and mouthed, 'You're-a-dick' under my breath. He couldn't possibly have seen me or lip-read, but for the tiniest moment his smooth face creased a little as if he had. It was odd. I moved quite close to him and started talking to somebody else while listening in. Where had I seen him before?

A portly-looking man came up and clapped him on the shoulder.

'Evening, Rufus!' he said loudly. 'Here to waste all your money on widows and orphans again? Or what is it tonight?'

'Contemporary art,' said the man. It couldn't be anyone I knew; I didn't know any Rufuses. Rufus sounded like a posh Labrador.

The drunk man leaned over to me.

'Excuse me,' he said. 'But aren't you Pantie Bumbum? That girl from the papers? Oh, Rufus, the funniest thing, you would not believe: this girl throws herself at Ultimate Man, right, jumps up on him, legs akimbo . . . '

Rufus stared at me suddenly and I had a very weird sense again . . .

'Excuse *me*,' I said without hesitating. 'I think there's somewhere else I need to be.'

And I walked very deliberately back to the other side of the room, fuming, which was exactly where I was standing when the bomb went off.

Chapter Ten

At first I thought it was a car backfiring; then I heard a ringing in my ears and smoke entered the room and I realised to my shock that it was an explosion. I couldn't hear properly at all, and immediately threw myself onto the floor – I didn't even know why – and fumbled for my phone.

I could hear slightly muffled screaming, and felt a fine dust come down and cover me from the ceiling. Instinctively, I rolled under one of the catering tables, where I nodded at one of the waiters who'd done the same thing. How could this have happened again? Was the entire city under attack? The screaming continued, and my hearing cleared a little. There didn't – so far at least – seem to be any further explosions. Trembling, I lifted the tablecloth a tiny bit to peer out. Women were crawling around on the ground wailing; many were running to the exit but they weren't, as far as I could tell, getting through it. There didn't (thank God) seem to be that much blood; the hideous vista of disconnected limbs I half expected to see didn't materialise. People were coughing; it appeared to be some kind of a smoke-bomb.

Suddenly, all noise ceased, topped and people froze –

everyone – where they stood, like someone had paused a film. For a second, there was a terrible silence. Then a heavy tread as footsteps entered the room.

It was him. The man from the bar. Frederick Cecil. My heart suddenly started racing; I felt as if people could actually hear it pounding. My mouth was completely dry. I knew my head was visible underneath the thick white draping of the tablecloth but I couldn't move now without drawing attention to myself; everyone else was completely and utterly still.

'Nobody move,' he said in the same polite, nonchalant tone he'd used before. I didn't even recognise the accent – English, but with a trace of something else? I'd tried googling him the last time, but nothing.

Oh God. This was utterly appalling luck. I was trembling. The man didn't have to shout or threaten. He was, simply in himself, a terrible threat. 'Don't worry. It's just us. Jewels, phones, etc., blah blah.'

Somewhere to my right, I saw a fat man lying on the ground looking furious and thumbing his phone. I glared at him, willing him to stop, not to draw attention to himself. His damn keypad lit up, for crying out loud. I could have hit him.

A millisecond later, something did. It was a simple cosh from one of the goons. Quick, efficient, and the man was lying there, completely unconscious.

'Anyone else?' said Frederick Cecil. 'So tempting, aren't they? You just can't resist those shiny, shiny buttons, even when your life depends on it.'

He walked up to the blonde I'd spoken to before. Her face looked hard and strained in fear; the tendons stood out on her neck. He towered above her and leant gently in to whisper something in her ear. I couldn't hear what it was, but she didn't like it, whatever it was. She leant back, pale beneath her make-up.

Frederick Cecil went behind her and unclipped the necklace quickly, easily. He had obviously spent a lot of time taking off women's necklaces. There was a practised expertise in his fingers that made me feel a little strange. His hands were large, but elegant; the hands, I supposed, of a thief. I remembered yet again his fingers gripping my upper arm; the gentle scent; the bruise.

He moved quickly around the rest of the people, whipping off watches and gewgaws and phones – all the bright, shiny things – and hurling them into a bag like they were nothing.

'Come line up, you plastic missies,' he shouted. 'You empty-headed vessels, who think that your salvation will come in these shiny trinkets, these earthly passing nothings.'

He snatched up a designer bag.

'Seriously,' he said. 'I'm interested. Did you long for this? Did you beg for it? Did you wait for it? Did you think it would fill in a hole in your soul, a part of you that cannot be fulfilled? Did it work? For how long? For a moment? An hour? For long enough to fuck an old man to get you another one? To forget the miserable child you once were? The desperate adult you have become? How long did it work for?'

I couldn't help it: I was mesmerised. He was crazy, obviously, but I was so engrossed by the way he was talking.

'Did it make you feel alive?'

He leaned in to a woman who was standing in front of him, trembling, the vein pulsing in her throat. He moved his face in very close indeed.

'Or does this make you feel alive? Aren't you more excited now? Can't you feel it? Aren't you living at last? For the first time?'

Then – and I should not have been surprised because of course he was a villain and this is what villains do, yet somehow I still was – he pulled out the shining knife. There was an intake of breath around the room.

He put it close to the woman's face. I could smell her fear.

'Come on. Isn't it nice to feel *something* once in a while?'

He was going to cut her. Where the hell was Ultimate Man?

Chapter Eleven

I felt around me wildly for something practical I could use. I wasn't being brave or feeling heroic because I was the only one who knew the hero was actually here; I just needed to cause a distraction until Ultimate Man could get his fricking ultimate shit together. Assuming he was coming. It was of course possible he had a very important photo shoot to attend.

I had one hundred per cent absolutely no doubt that Frederick Cecil could and would maim this woman without a second thought. He lifted the knife again.

'I am of course anti-violence, more or less,' he said softly to the woman stuttering in front of him, pupils wide, breath torn.

My hand found a fork and I grabbed it, my heart ripping in my ears, getting prepared to pounce. As to what I was going to do exactly I had no idea, but since I was the only one who knew that help was at hand, anything I could do to extend matters had to be useful, right? It wasn't even a big fork: it was a stupid pudding fork for stupid cheesecake.

I would not have mentioned, even to myself, that it was like looking at a snake in the zoo: horrible, disgusting and yet somehow hypnotising in a way that made me want to get closer to him.

But I told myself I was being brave.

Still crouching underneath the table, I moved my fist forward.

Suddenly I felt a strong hand over the top of mine. My head shot to the side: I was terrified, and bursting with adrenalin. The hand was wearing a pair of purple rubber gloves.

My breathing slowed down.

'Don't,' he growled. 'Don't even think about it.'

Chapter Twelve

'Go and help that woman!'

'First I have to stop the vigilantes,' he said.

It took me a split-second to realise he meant *me*. The cheek of him.

'You stay under here, you understand me? There's no room for heroics.'

'Right, like what you aren't doing,' I said, but he ignored me.

'Doesn't it chafe, that stuff you're wearing?' I went on. 'Because you know, it doesn't look comfortable.'

'Do I recognise you?' he said.

'You mean you don't?' I said. 'Obviously I too ought to dress myself in purple Lycra to remind people who I am. You know, in lieu of developing an actual personality or anything.'

'If you want to put everyone's life at risk here, keep talking,' came a low growl. I rolled my eyes.

Then he moved, and it was actually incredibly impressive.

He hurled himself out from beneath the table, hurtled past Frederick Cecil like a panther, threw himself off the back wall and turned around to face him. I couldn't work out what he'd done until I saw that he had the great knife in his hand. I had to admit it was pretty cool.

Frederick Cecil looked momentarily startled, and dropped the blonde woman. She crumpled in a heap to the floor.

'Oh, here you are again,' he said. 'Always so desperate to stop all the fun. Come on, admit it: things were incredibly boring until we turned up.'

I saw two of the men in dinner jackets lying on the floor exchange glances. I knew it! I knew nobody liked these fund-raisers really.

'Give everything back,' growled Ultimate Man. 'Now.'

Frederick Cecil looked weary.

'Oh goodness,' he said. 'You think you're on the right side, don't you? When you really don't have the faintest idea.'

'I've been threatened before,' said Ultimate Man.

Frederick Cecil blinked behind the mask.

'This isn't a threat. This is simply what's coming. The new world. The better world. It's coming, Purple Man.'

'It's Ultimate Man.'

'It is coming, Purple Man.'

His voice went even quieter.

'A great wind, a purifying storm.'

'Not on my watch.'

'You watch,' said Frederick Cecil. 'But you do not see.'

Then they all totally did some fighting.

It was a bit of a blur, and I covered my eyes some of the time, but quite a lot of it was Ultimate Man knocking people's heads together while simultaneously kicking other people.

To Frederick Cecil's credit, this time he did not run away when things were very clearly taking a turn for the worse from his POV, and there were a fair few large goons lying bleeding on the priceless museum rug.

He stared intently at Ultimate Man as if trying to work out the root of his technique. He showed absolutely no concern or even interest in the wounded men – presumably employees of his – who lay writhing under his feet. I couldn't help it. My fist punched the air. I had never been to a boxing match in my life, and had genuinely always believed I'd abhorred violence, but this was undeniably kind of exciting. Ultimate Man was just full-on duffing them all up.

'Take that, Frederick Cecil!' I couldn't help shouting.

The room froze.

Oh, I am such an idiot. An utterly unbelievable, chuffing, fricking idiot. Stop nodding. Anyway, immediately, he turned around and whipped the table cloth away from the table I was still cowering under.

He then crouched down and looked me straight in the face, curious, intent. Time stood still. Then his arm shot out like a cobra attacking and grabbed my wrist. Behind us, the noise of the fight continued.

'I thought I smelled you down here,' he whispered. 'Have you got your best panties on today? I do hope so! There's going to be paparazzi again, you know. I mean, I've got the phones, so I'm helping you out there, but those pap shots ... Don't read the comments. Nobody should ever read the comments; they're awful. Just awful.'

With a tired sigh, as if all this was too much to bother with, he hauled me to my feet.

'Oh, Purple Man,' he said in a singsongy voice. 'I've got your little frie-end. You know, the one whose panties you spread all over the internet?'

The punching noises ceased as Frederick Cecil whisked me round to face the back wall, where Ultimate Man had just kicked someone in the throat. Everyone stood and watched.

'Really? *Again?*' said Ultimate Man, looking annoyed with me. 'Are you doing this for attention?'

'What? I didn't do anything!'

'I think she likes being in the papers,' said Frederick Cecil. 'You shouldn't like being in the papers; it's a terrible habit to get into. You need to find your own self-worth.'

'I do *not* like being in the papers. Stop talking about me!' I said, flushed and struggling. 'Let me go.'

'Maybe she fancies Ultimate Man,' came a voice from the ground. It was the blonde who'd nearly been killed. I really felt I didn't require her input.

'I don't!' I said. 'He came and got me!'

'Oh, you're such a special hostage, are you?' said somebody else. 'Got a little taste of fame. She only works for the mayor's office. Embittered gossip columnist.'

'Hoi!' shouted Hectorio. 'Right, that's it. Every picture I take of you from now on is going to have four chins.'

This situation seemed to be deteriorating.

'Oh, for heaven's sake,' I said. 'Trust me, there's a million places I'd rather be right now and four billion people I'd rather be with. Take your filthy paws off me, you stupid mugger.'

Frederick Cecil looked amused.

'Sorry, I can't just now; good goons are expensive, and he's making it tricky for me to find them.'

'I don't want to have to save you again,' said Ultimate Man. 'I am actually a bit worried you're doing this on purpose. It's happened before. We had to take out a restraining order.'

I blew out a breath.

'Fine,' I said. And I jammed the fork in my hand into Frederick Cecil's leg as hard as I could.

He didn't shout out, but he did do some muttering under his breath. I think it was surprise as much as anything else, but those huge hands dropped momentarily from my arm, and I dived and rolled away from him. Then I realised I was on the floor, and as he made an angry shout and went for me, I squeaked and literally crawled away until I could stand up, and charged for the door. By which time, Ultimate Man had him almost in his grasp. He raised a huge hand, and through the gap in the doorframe as I made a hasty retreat, I saw Ultimate Man shoot me a quick anguished glance as he prepared to bring him down, and I ran through a phalanx of amassing, anxious-looking policemen preparing to charge.

Chapter Thirteen

I assumed upstairs rather than downstairs. All my instincts told me to run downstairs out of the museum. But I thought of how swift they were, how much bigger, how likely to catch up with me if they wanted to – it was of course also possible, I thought in my panic, that they might just be pleased to see me gone, seeing I was apparently a nuisance who got in the way of their fighting.

So I ran upstairs and hid in an alcove, while I heard a lot of thuds and noises and yells as the police went in with batons and some smoke came out, and then there were loads of complaining noises, which I took correctly to be a good sign, as some order was restored and people gradually started filing out, covering themselves in expensive coats but not putting the sleeves on – have you noticed that posh people don't put on their sleeves? It's because they never have to go outside in the cold. Sleeves are for the scum. I didn't see anyone being brought out under arrest. A bell went off and I kept hiding as the rest of the place emptied out: police and party-goers. Hectorio departed taking lots of pictures and cheerfully smoking indoors, presumably as he was being sent out anyway.

The policemen left, shaking their heads, with a few goons handcuffed and annoyed-looking. They hadn't got Frederick Cecil though; that much I could see. He must have had an escape plan out of the window. Ultimate Man too; presumably he'd gone racing after him.

Finally, the great echoing marble staircase of the museum was deathly quiet and still, and I could feel I was alone in the building. I straightened up. My heart carried on pounding, but I was calming down. Nobody had chased me. Nobody was there. It was safe. Or as safe as things seemed to be those days, which obviously wasn't very.

The lights had all been turned out. The moon shone through the great long windows, brightly onto the pale white marble stairwell. I gently took a step, and then another.

They say in life timing is everything. I think, for me, it was a little more than that. You could stroll past the right dress in the right hour of the sale. You could meet a man in the right year, or your best friend in the right decade.

This wasn't the right moment.

It was the right millisecond.

It was the only possible conceivable fraction of a second in the entire universe. No one had ever seen it before. And to my knowledge, nobody ever saw it again.

The museum is ancient and too big to update really. Anyway, as I crept down, I remembered that on the mezzanine there's a very old, long-forgotten line of telephone kiosks. The ones that look like they have giant helmets over your head. I was walking down past those when suddenly, something shimmered in the corner of my eye. I whipped round. I had an impression of speed – something like a whirling dervish, or the Tasmanian devil in those old cartoons – then it froze, and there, right in front of me, was a face. A panicking face.

Dressed half in a suit and half in a purple Lycra costume.

A millisecond later, the shirt had vanished and the costume had covered his head and face.

But it was too late. I'd seen him.

And not only had I seen him. I'd recognised him.

Chapter Fourteen

'Ah,' he said.

'I just met you,' I said.

'Did you?' he said, eyes darting past my face desperately.

'No, no, now I know,' I said. I knew now why he'd seemed familiar when I walked into the room. 'You're the dick I just tried to interview for the magazine. *And* you're the guy I saw in the bar. Before Frederick Cecil. And you're ... you're ... '

The suit really was very purple up close. His expression was one of complete and utter horror.

'I didn't think anyone was still here,' he said, his voice stuttering.

'Well,' I pointed out. 'In *Ultimate Man's Guide to Keeping Fit!* you do say take the stairs whenever possible.'

That had been a huge bestseller the previous year. DuTroy had secretly bought one.

There was a pause.

'Oh,' he said. 'I do say that, don't I?'

I nodded.

'But nobody ... nobody's ever caught me ... Right then.'

'I didn't mean to.'

'I mean *nobody* ... '

'Hey, don't sweat it,' I said. 'I am nobody. As you've already made abundantly clear.'

He took a step backwards.

'I'm sorry,' he said. 'That was rude of me.'

'I'm Holly,' I said. 'And you're Rufus.'

I put out my hand, but he moved back a bit and smoothed down his mask.

'Sorry,' he said. 'But I really ... I mean, it really has to be a secret identity.'

'That's okay,' I said. 'I don't know who Rufus is. So it's a total secret. Just change your first name. It's a stupid name anyway. You sound like a Labrador.'

There was a pause.

'Why do you have to have a secret identity?'

He sighed.

'Well, because I've got a dog and stuff. And I vote. I'm on the electoral register. So you could find me. And if the baddies found out where I lived ... '

'They'd do mean stuff to your dog?'

'He didn't ask to be a hero's dog.'

'Does he have a sensible name? Is he called, like, Peter?'

'He's called Puddles,' said Rufus. 'Jumping into the muckiest puddles is kind of like his superpower. Oh God. What a mess.'

He adjusted his mask one last time.

Suddenly, of all things, I felt slightly sorry for him. He looked so ... He looked so kind of *lonely* standing there, wearing a stupid purple suit, doing stupid photo shoots, getting beaten up, then going back to wherever he went back to, scanning the police radio and looking for even more bad guys.

'Why ... ?' I cleared my throat. 'Why do you have to do all this stuff? Can't you just secretly work for the CIA and go around assassinating massive terrorists and stuff?'

His eyes blinked behind the mask.

'Because I can't compromise like that. When they have you in that way ... No.' He shook his head. 'And of course they don't just want me to go on their murder trips. They want to experiment, to copy me, to train ...'

'Oh,' I said. 'Is it true, all that hero stuff? I thought they were just hamming it up for the cameras. Do you really have powers?'

He smiled a bit ruefully.

'Well, I used to be able to get changed too quickly for anyone to spot me.'

'So, are you an alien or what?'

'"What",' he said. 'Radiation accident.'

He held up his spandex clad arms, the tight muscles bunching. That was some radiation, I found myself thinking.

'Did it have to be purple though?' I said.

'My first one was yellow and black. I looked like a gigantic bee. Trust me, it was worse.'

I found myself smiling at him.

'I didn't mean to pull up your skirt by the way,' he said. 'That picture thing. I didn't mean it.'

'Oh! No. I didn't ... I mean, it wouldn't be a very Ultimate Man thing to do.'

'No,' he said. 'It wouldn't.'

He looked at me.

'Could you please ... possibly ... possibly forget we ever met?'

I thought of how much I wanted to be a journalist. I thought of what a gigantic scoop this was. I noticed how downcast and miserable he looked.

'You know,' I said. 'None of the pictures on the internet of the people who are supposed to be you are actually you.'

'I know,' he said.

'I mean, Ultimate Man ... you sound like a bra.'

'I know,' he said. 'All the good names were taken.'

There was a long silence. The moon shone down on the chequerboard floor of the great museum atrium; the marble steps glowed. It looked like the ball after Cinderella had danced away.

'Okay,' I said finally. I thought of having a by-line in the paper. Writing something real instead of a bunch of BS press releases. Catching a break. All of it.

Then I looked at his face.

'Okay,' I said. 'I promise.'

But he didn't look convinced. He didn't look convinced at all.

I walked down the stairs and out through the fire escape. The alarm went off again, but I didn't even care.

Chapter Fifteen

'Stop doing this!'

'I'm not doing anything, Gert! I was just doing my job!'

'Did you meet him again? Was he a nobber?'

'He's not a nobber,' said DuTroy from the corner.

'He might be a nobber,' I said. 'I don't know him well enough.'

'What's he like with the mask off?'

I paused. For a long time. Gertie was my best friend in the entire world.

'I don't know,' I said. 'I don't think he takes it off.'

'It must reek in there,' she said.

'That's what I thought.'

DuTroy tutted.

'Seriously, man, you girls are nuts. He's a genetically modified human!'

'Seriously? Do we evolve to stop sweating? That sounds great,' said Gertie.

DuTroy sat down and took us through it. I had already googled it though, but pretended I hadn't and in fact wasn't remotely interested. Developed superskills. Incredible strength. Unknown powers. Extraordinary speed. And a secret identity.

Until now.

I felt annoyed with him though. I had told him I wouldn't betray him. I'd given my word, even though I didn't particularly get anything out of doing so. I felt he should be grateful to me.

Although of course then I thought about Frederick Cecil, and the way he'd saved me – twice now. Well. Anyway. Something had happened and it was driving me crazy that it hadn't been acknowledged.

Despite 'Rufus's' obvious dislike of the press, he'd been fairly easy to track down. Plus, since the Frederick Cecil incident, I was staying in. I was staying in *a lot*.

Rufus Carter. Billionaire philanthropist. Inheritor of his deceased father's company and wealth. Supporter of museums, orphanages, wild elephants, you name it. Single and wildly speculated about. Sometimes not entirely flatteringly.

No connection anywhere. I really was the only person who knew.

He must be terrified of me.

I looked at my email. I typed it, then deleted it. Then typed it again.

Dear Rufus,

I stared at the screen, then sighed.

I am very sorry if

That didn't seem like a very good start.

I was emailing him, or rather the Rufus Carter Foundation, so

I had no idea if it would get to him or not. I wanted to apologise – he'd been handling a situation and I had made it a lot worse – and reassure him I wasn't going to blackmail him or betray him or anything.

Although it was wildly annoying having this terrific piece of gossip and not being able to do anything with it. Given that when Gertie told me she'd met this amazing guy at work called DuTroy but I wasn't to tell anyone she liked him, I'd told everyone which had led to him asking her out so actually it was fine in the end, mostly.

This was much harder.

I admitted it to myself though. Also, what if – for example – he wanted to unburden himself? Talk to someone, someone sympathetic, someone looking to break into journalism with a truly amazing story, someone who'd be fair and even-handed …

I looked back at what I was writing.

Dear Rufus,
I am very sorry if

I deleted the 'if'. You can either apologise or you can't; it's not conditional.

I am very sorry I caused you some embarrassment on Friday night.

Obviously embarrassment wasn't exactly the word I was looking for, seeing as he lost his prey because of me, then was unmasked, also because of me, but I had absolutely no idea who read his emails.

Hopefully our paths won't cross again.

Okay. I will admit it. Much as I hated to. This was one hundred per cent of a lie. Gertie, although I hated to say so, had been right the first time she saw him. He was hot. Tall, dark. Chiselled. Everything Gertie had always said about me not liking the handsome guy – well, I liked the handsome guy. Obviously he had a *lot* else wrong with him.

I wondered if he had a lie-detecting power. I thought about the look on his face when I was running out. It had been exasperated; resigned to getting a pounding . . . but had I been wrong in thinking there'd been a little smile in it too?

Probably, I told myself sternly.

I erased the last sentence and replaced it with:

'Hopefully if our paths cross again it will be under pleasanter circumstances', which I also deleted because it looked like I was flirting with him which I was obviously but I didn't want it to look that obvious. I tapped a pencil against my teeth, then left it with 'Hoping you are well', both kicking myself for being so mimsy about the entire thing, and also telling myself it was a relief not getting pulled into anything like this, and also reminding myself that he wasn't just super-handsome, he was a billionaire and I was a PR girl and he had a mansion and I had sandy, scruffy hair and about a zillion freckles and my last boyfriend had played the banjo really, really badly, so I had to get a grip.

So I went back to work and tried not to think about it and wrote boring pieces about subway improvements and museum repairs and he didn't get back to me obviously – why would he?

So I left it at that and tried to appreciate my life being boring – seriously, I'd had enough run-ins to last a lifetime – and my new colleague Nelson and I got into the habit of going to the grotty café round the corner to hide from Liz, and I have to say, after messing about with snake-mouthed supervillians and holier-than-thou heroes, his cheerful, country-boy attitude and the fact that he actually thought I was quite interesting and funny, rather than someone defined by their underpants, was actually quite refreshing.

I didn't really like being a walk-on in someone else's story.

Chapter Sixteen

It was July, and I was half watching *Don't Mess With the Dress* with Gertie, who took furious notes and shouted all the way through it, and half messing about on the internet. After the show, Gertie headed out, leaving me in again for what felt like the hundredth night in a row – she'd stopped asking.

Plus it felt weird that there had been no further – as far as I could tell – Frederick Cecil hold-ups since I'd started staying in. I knew this was superstitious nonsense, but I slightly felt like I was protecting the city simply by not doing very much. Gertie worried a bit that it was because the last time I went dating all sorts of disaster happened, but I was quite comfortable at home. Well, mostly. Kind of. In a 'I don't want to panic about my entire life passing me by' kind of a way. I sighed.

I went and fetched myself a Diet Coke, and when I got back, the webpage on my laptop was blank. I pressed a few buttons, and a cursor arrow – an actual cursor arrow, in actual green, like an ancient film from the eighties, popped up. I blinked.

As I watched, it started to type. It read:

>This is not junk mail

I looked at it suspiciously. That is exactly the kind of thing junk mail does.

I deleted the line, and a second later another appeared:

>Honestly not junk mail

However, I reckoned I probably didn't have a mysterious missing relative who'd died and left me $1,000,000 mysteriously trapped in a Nigerian bank account, so I deleted that one too.

The next one took me by surprise though:

>Holly, I promise: not junk mail, it flashed sinisterly.

I took my hands off my laptop as if it had turned hot.

'Shit,' I said out loud.

I gingerly pulled up a new window and googled 'how do you know you're being hacked?'

>YOU'RE NOT BEING HACKED, HOLLY'

I got up, swearing.

>It's okay. It's me

I leaned forward and typed warily beneath it:

WHO'S ME?

Nothing happened for a while. Then:

```
>I can't say. There's an email. Open it
please.
```

I looked at it. There were as far, as I could tell, four possibilities.

Firstly, that it was him: Rufus, Ultimate Man, whatever. Although he hadn't struck me as the super-geeky hacker type to be honest. All that messing about in the gym and marching around the city couldn't leave him much time for anything like that. People – like my brother Vinnie – who were good at computers didn't spend as much time jumping over cars in my experience. You could practise for one or for the other, but not both.

It could obviously be a new highly personalised marketing service that, when I pressed it, would tell me I was using the wrong brand of shampoo and that theirs was the only one that could make things right again between my split ends and me (at that point in time, I could probably have done with it actually).

Or it could be an aggressive hacker who liked my pants and was looking to spill up all my nude photos to the internet. I didn't have any nude photos, and even if I did, I couldn't imagine anyone wanting to look at mine rather than the vast arena of larger, rather more voluptuous ones available at the click of a mouse, but you never knew.

There was another possibility: that the baddie had got hold of me.

That it was Frederick Cecil.

I breathed in a little sharply. It was the kind of thing he would do – controlling, scary. Why was he trying to make contact?

Because he thought I was some kind of a pull on Ultimate Man;

that much was clear. He thought he came to my aid on purpose rather than just a massive example of bad coincidence and underpants. He was trying to track me down to pull me into his web.

I stared at the computer again.

>PLEASE, it blinked up.

That didn't sound a lot like Frederick Cecil. I hadn't thought of him as needy.

I looked at it. I looked at *Don't Mess With the Dress*, which was playing a new episode. Someone was having hysterics about a stupid white gown. I was twenty-six years old. This was my Friday night. I had got excited when I had gotten home, because there was some leftover curry in the fridge.

Since I had arrived in the fabled 'big city' of Centerton and got a job – in the mayor's office, no less! – I had been waiting for something exciting and different to come along which wasn't just me scraping to pay rent and hang out with my flatmate.

This wasn't exactly what I'd had in mind.

But outside in the warm summer evening, I could hear the sounds of couples and friends laughing and joking, sitting out in bars, giggling and chatting; the smell of the city, of perfume and taxi exhausts and cigarettes and bodies; all of it spiralling upwards; and me, tucked away in our tiny horrible rental, missing it. Missing everything.

I took a long pull of my Diet Coke. Then I opened the email.

Or to be more specific, I backed up all my files into the cloud, and pressed 'open'; then my eyes snapped shut and I jumped backwards from the computer as it started beeping furiously.

I opened one eye a crack.

On the screen, windows of operating code were opening

themselves very quickly, one on top of another. I swore mightily. Dammit. Hacked. Probably by some nine-year-old off his nads on Ritalin, picking me at random for kicks. He'd probably plant a virus which would bring down western civilisation and I'd get ten thousand years in prison from the government.

Rats. Finally, it slowed down until there was only one black box open, with the cursor flashing green again.

>Finally, it said.

There was a pause, then – this was retro; proper old school stuff:

>I needed a secure encrypted line, it said. >They don't check these old intranet pathways any more.

I moved forward tentatively.

>Who doesn't? I typed.

>The NSA. Or any organisation with three letters.

>Who is this?

>Seriously?

>Uh, no, I like wasting pixels.

There was a very long pause.

Chapter Seventeen

>It's me. Rufus. Who did you think it was?

>No one, I typed quickly.

>Why didn't you find me on Facebook like everyone else?

>I'm not everybody else.

I looked at this, in bright green, a low childish font, a blinking cursor. I couldn't even remember the last time I'd seen a flashing green cursor.

>No. No, I guess you're not.

So I suppose the email had got through. Well, either that or he'd found my mothballed Tinder account, which was just me in a stripy T-shirt smiling politely and saying I liked dogs, pies and airports, and had been read by everyone who'd clicked it as a straight-up request for an orgy.

>How did you track me down?

>You know if you don't swipe right or left, but instead turn your phone upside down and wiggle it, you get all the secret inside info?

I stared at the screen. It was as if he'd known what I'd been thinking. He couldn't though, right? I sat back.

>I'm kidding, came the typing hastily. >I'm sorry. This was a bad idea. I'm sorry for bothering you. It's just

The cursor blinked on in the corner of the screen, but there was nothing to indicate if he was typing or not. I waited. He wasn't. I sighed.

>Just what? I typed.

>Just. Sorry. This is stupid.

>????

>It's just Friday night and . . . are you doing anything??

>Yes. I'm out solving crime and saving lives. Hang on, isn't that your job?

There wasn't anything for a while. Then:

```
>Wanna come over?
```

I swallowed hard. I really wasn't expecting this at all. For starters, I'd kind of thought that he either swung the other way, or was completely smooth in the front, like an action man. There'd been plenty of speculation in the press I'd read.

I knew from reading everything about Ultimate Man that he had been a mortal but now had extraordinary powers after an industrial accident. Whatever. I just wasn't that interested. Also, if I had extraordinary powers, I reckon I'd have used them to live a life of comfort and ease and given a lot of money to vaccination programmes, not beat up pathetic drug-addicted muggers for kicks.

Or if I was being more altruistic, I'd work out why muggers had such awful lives that they had to hold knives to the throats of innocent tourists.

Or if I was being even more altruistic and had all the superpowers and everything, I might consider why the system was so skewed that some hedge fund manager could cheat a million people out of their pensions and life savings and still be considered an innocent tourist wherever he went.

Anyway. I may be a bit of a sad case stuck at home in the city on a Friday night, but I wasn't so sad that I hacked people's computers for dates.

I thought back to that first night in the bar; those bright blue eyes, that wide open face.

And I couldn't deny it. I had thought about him since. A lot. And I was excited. Quite a bit.

Soda wasn't cutting it. I paced up and down the little sitting room, went to the fridge and opened one of DuTroy's beers, drank a hefty swig and decided to call him on it.

Then I sat down and boldly typed:

```
>Sorry, not really a booty call type of a
girl.
```

The cursor blinked furiously and what came back was misspelled, obviously in his hurry to explain himself.

```
>No sorry dint mean that at all, sorry. Just
hanging out. Came our wrong. Sroy. Bye.
```

I am absolutely no good at playing hardball. I cracked immediately. I think it was 'sroy'. Plus I had beer. I decided to trust my instincts.

```
>It's okay, I typed. >It just sounded a bit ...
```

```
>I'm so so sorry, he interrupted me.
```

```
>It's okay, I said again. >Calm down. What are you
up to?
```

```
>Thinking about what to have for dinner.
```

I thought about the cold chow mein in the fridge.

```
>Where did you get to?
```

```
>I was thinking filet mignon.
```

79

>WERE you? With fries or without?

>Without. I need a lot of protein.

>Oh.

>But, you know. I could have fries. Like,
sitting near it. In case anyone wanted to
steal some.

>I thought if people started stealing, you
pinched their spinal cords until they collapsed in a heap in the floor.

>Oh yeah. What if I promised to make an
exception?

>What if I steal too many fries by mistake
and you forget your exception?

>I totally almost would never do that.

>You have perhaps no idea how many fries I
can eat.

There was a pause. I was contemplating it. And also wondering
what I could change into out of my pyjamas. Which I guess meant
I was probably way, way past the contemplation stage.

>Just something to eat? came the cursor.

```
>Hang  on:  you  infiltrated  MY  computer
and  hacked  ME  and  now  you're  playing  the
gentleman?

>I hope so. Outside in ten?
```

Ten minutes? Was he stalking me? Also was he *kidding*? It was Friday night! I'd taken my bra off and put my bobble socks on! This wasn't getting done in ten minutes! We didn't all change in phone boxes!

Chapter Eighteen

I pulled on my go-anywhere black dress, yanked a comb through my sandy hair, added as much mascara as I could lay it on – my mascara policy is if it's too much, you're halfway there – and just to make me look fancy, added some vampish red lipstick. Then I wiped it off again as it looked scary and vampish; then I put it back on again. Then I wiped it off. Then I put it back on and wiped *most* of it off, but left a kind of a blush. That would have to do.

I brushed my teeth, squirted myself with some of Gertie's incredibly expensive perfume because she almost certainly probably wouldn't mind, put on my black platforms and stopped to look at myself in the mirror.

A month ago, I wouldn't have said boo to a goose: it was most unlike me. I wasn't brave; I wasn't intrepid or adventurous. But here I was, going to eat steak with a man I barely knew; a man who looked rather campily fine in a tux and rather mad in purple spandex, but who also seemed ... I wasn't sure ... vulnerable somehow. Sitting at home alone on a Friday night, just like me.

*

On the street, I stopped and gasped as a black car drew up. It wasn't a limo; it was the kind of totally nondescript black town car with tinted windows you don't realise is really impressive and expensive until you get up really close. The front window wound down.

'Miss Phillips? Mr Carter sent this car for you.'

'Um, can you prove that?'

The driver was elderly, and actually wore a peaked hat. I had never seen a real chauffeur before. I was slightly fascinated.

'Would you like me to call him for you?'

Actually, on reflection I didn't want to sound like a girl who'd never been picked up in a car before. (I had never been picked up in a car before, unless you counted Buster Merrydew's '84 Ford Cortina, which I certainly didn't, seeing as he started feeling me up the second I got in it, which meant I was in it for about thirty seconds. Parents shouldn't let their sons be the first kid at school to get a car, not ever. It makes them utterly insufferable for the rest of their entire lives. But I digress.)

'No, don't worry,' I said, sliding into the back seat after a moment's fierce internal debate with myself as to whether it would be more egalitarian to go in the front. 'I'll be fine.'

The car slid through the summer night. I'd never experienced the city quite like this. The back of the car was done out entirely in black leather, soft as a kid glove. There was an armrest down the middle with two silver cup-holders and a discreet half-bottle of champagne in a built-in ice bucket down the central well. I rolled my eyes. The entire interior simply smelled expensive, like deep cigars and blotting paper. There was a glass wall between the back and the front, and I could barely make out the back of the chauffeur's neatly clipped neck.

I rolled my eyes again, worrying. Had I been taken in by the hopeless, insecure schmuck? Was this a method? I mean, was 'I'm just sending my car to pick you up' the booty call of booty calls, especially the champagne already on ice? I picked it up. It said Laurent Perrier. I had never heard of it, but gave it the eye anyway. Maybe he hoped the girls would be so squiffed by the time they got there they'd fall out of their dresses the second they stepped out of the car.

I looked at the back of the driver's head and considered asking him how often he was required to do this, then thought better of it, even though I was feeling a little like a high-class escort. Well, an escort.

We slowed down at lights and I saw a couple of hipsters give the car a scornful look through their beards. I had forgotten they couldn't see me. I looked out, a little wistfully, at the crowds parading up and down one of the pedestrianised streets lined with bars and restaurants. I should be with them, with normal people my own age, not going out on the weirdest dinner date of all time with someone who could throw people across rooms. I bit the inside of my lip anxiously.

We crossed the town bridge and I turned my head to look at the beautiful glistening city: so noisy, so full of bustle and people and fun and trouble, out there somewhere, beneath it all, pulsing at the crosswalks and the stop signs and the cars with the blacked out windows . . .

We left the city behind us and hit the motorway, the warehouses and buildings of the outskirts falling away rapidly. I felt excited and nervous all at once. I realised I didn't know where we were going; where he lived. Just as I started to speculate on whether or not I was being kidnapped, the driver took a sharp turn off into a tiny exit I'd never noticed before. The road twisted all the way round in a circle, heading steadily upwards, then turned off sharply towards a gravel way in front of a large gate which I wouldn't have known was there: it was under some shady trees and looked completely deserted.

But to my surprise, the gates suddenly slid open, soundlessly and quickly, and we passed through. I swallowed. Oh my God. Where was I being taken? Somewhere in the middle of nowhere? Some abandoned place? What was I thinking? Stranger danger was stranger danger however often they'd been photographed for the front of the newspaper.

I quickly texted Gertie, 'Going to Ultimate Man's house off the bridge. If not texted by the morning, send help!', then looked out of the window, my heart pounding. I tried not to think about how strong he was. What he'd done to Frederick Cecil's men. What the penalties seemed to be for crossing him.

The driveway seemed to curve on for miles. Where was this place? It couldn't be his home, surely. Trees lined the driveway, and in the distance I thought I saw a flicker of white, two eyes glinting in the headlights of the car; a deer, or something else.

The house came into view. It was beautiful: large, traditional stone solidly set; sash windows looking out towards the grounds. We were fifteen minutes from the city but it felt as if we were in the middle of nowhere. The chauffeur pulled up behind a fountain and in front of the heavy front door. He jumped out and opened the car door, and I felt slightly ashamed of my scuffed shoes. I prepared an anxious smile as the huge wooden front door, black with brass fittings, opened slowly. But it was another man, someone else who worked for him, opening the door to let me in. The chauffeur tipped his hat as I nervously walked up the steps and inside the huge house.

Chapter Nineteen

Inside, the house was large and dimly lit, and my feet echoed on the flagstone hallways. I followed the silent man down a long corridor. Somewhere, I heard a dog scampering about.

To either side were splendid formal rooms, and I noticed a large library. It was all utterly impressive, but oddly cold: I saw no family pictures, no coats hanging up, not even a television; none of the detritus of normal life being lived.

The house was like a museum, or even – given the chill – a tomb. I shivered involuntarily just as the man (the butler, I supposed – but seriously, who had a butler? Maybe it was a spare henchman, I thought gloomily) delivered me down a small flight of curved steps to a heavy wooden doorway where there was light showing underneath, and a distinct and comforting smell of garlic cooking, which happens to be my favourite smell in the entire world.

'Modom,' said the man, then, as I turned round, he seemed to fade away into the shadows, continuing on down the staircase.

I stood for a second, feeling nervous – but again, also a certain amount of excitement. This wasn't your common or garden Friday night. That didn't smell like chow mein. I took a deep breath, steeled myself and knocked on the door.

There was a slight pause. Then the door was pulled open.

'Uh, you don't need to knock on the kitchen door,' came the deep voice.

I stood there, slightly taken aback at the sight of him. So far I had seen him in a smart suit, a tuxedo and – I didn't really like thinking about this again – tight purple spandex. Seriously, why did it have to be purple?

But here he was, in a huge kitchen with a large central island, a butler's sink – which made sense, what with the butler and everything – and a huge oven and long table. It was softly lit, and he was standing by the stove with a huge pile of chopped ingredients, gently cooking the onions and garlic up. The radio was playing something quietly I couldn't identify.

'Hey,' I said, suddenly incredibly nervous. Tonight he was wearing, of all things, a soft, old-looking Breton shirt and a pair of thick-framed black glasses. He was still a big man, but not quite so oppressively muscular all over the place; his shirt was boyish, untucked over a faded pair of Levi's and some old black Converse.

'You look ... off-duty.'

'I am sometimes off-duty,' he smiled. 'I'm glad you came.'

He didn't say I looked nice or anything, but I didn't mind. That would have made it too date-like, whereas I didn't know what this was.

'Nice pad,' I said. 'Is it yours?'

He smiled, surprised.

'Well, kind of,' he said. 'It used to belong to my parents ... '

He trailed off and turned back to the cooking, and I figured not to ask any more.

87

'Okay,' I said. 'Well. It's nice.'

He sniffed. 'I don't go in about half of it. Freaks me out a bit. But the kitchen is nice. Which you'll find out if you want to step across the threshold at any time.'

I moved forward into the warm room; unlike the rest of the house, this seemed cosy and lived in. And he was right: it was a nice room. Along the back were large windows which looked out, as far as I could make out through the gloom, onto a walled garden lined with neat rows of labelled herbs. There was an open fire crackling away cheerfully at one end as the evening cooled, with comfortable old faded armchairs pulled up in front of it; also full spice racks and a large dresser full of cups and plates. His laptop was open on the countertop; it was larger and heavier than most, and obviously where he'd been contacting me from.

'You cook a lot?' I said.

'A bit,' shrugged Rufus. 'You hungry?'

I suddenly realised I was. It was late, and the nerves of the car ride had served to make me feel quite highly strung. Now, as he handed me a glass of red wine, I realised I was starving.

'I changed my mind about the filet mignon,' he said. 'Is that okay?'

'Yes,' I said. 'Because I am not one hundred per cent sure what filet mignon is. What are we having?'

'It's nothing special,' he apologised. 'Just a puttanesca. I like it pretty fiery ... Sorry, I'm being very boring talking about cooking.'

'How did you hack into my computer?' I said.

'Sorry about that too,' he said, pushing his glasses back up his nose. 'I ... I'm not very good at making friends.'

'That is a terrible way of going about it,' I said. 'I mean, people get arrested for less.'

'I know,' he said. 'It's just . . . '

He chopped up a set of olives ridiculously fast. 'Well, you know,' he said.

'I do not know,' I said truthfully. 'Tell me.'

'Well, people don't know who I am.'

'Nobody knows who anybody is,' I said. 'Unless you're famous, and that looks rubbish: everyone just stares at you all the time.'

'Yes, I realise that,' he said. 'I don't think I'm actually famous. As a normal.'

'Do you actually say it like that?' I said. '"Normals"? Like we're all some kind of lesser civilian species?'

'I don't mean it like that,' he said quite sharply. 'I don't mean it like that at all. I would love . . . I would love to be like you.'

I narrowed my eyes at him.

'Yeah, totally. You would totally love to have flabby bits and no fighting abilities and to run like an idiot, and . . . I mean, I can't even skip.'

'You can't skip?'

'Not everyone can skip, okay?'

He flipped the olives in expertly, and they sizzled in the pan as he cut up some tiny lethal-looking peppers. 'Everyone can skip,' he said gravely. 'Seriously.'

'I'm totally over it,' I said. 'More or less.'

He smiled.

'Really, how did you grow up as a small girl unable to skip?'

'With some difficulty,' I said.

He smiled again.

'How did *you* grow up?' I said. There was a bit of a pause.

'Quickly,' he said with a tone which made it clear that that conversation was over.

The food smelled astonishing. He took a loaf of bread out of the oven and I stared at it with unavoidable avidity. I realised he was smiling at me.

'What?'

'Nothing,' he said. 'You just looked so hungry.'

'Yuh-huh,' I said. He grinned, then tore a bit off the corner, slathered it with salty butter and handed it to me. I took it happily, then dropped it immediately: it was scorching hot.

He caught it before it hit the ground.

'Oh God, sorry,' he said, placing it carefully in the bin. 'I didn't realise.'

'Seriously?'

He shrugged. 'Yeah ...'

'So back to us boring normals,' I said, 'who had to invent the oven glove. Why are we so hard to meet if we don't know who you are?'

He shrugged.

'Because I go out a lot at night. I can't make plans, not really, and I can't keep the ones I do make. I let people down. I'm mysterious apparently. Everyone thinks I'm having a secret affair or up to something.'

'Well, you are up to *something*,' I pointed out.

'And they might put two and two together; that could happen.'

'Oh yeah,' I said. 'Plus doesn't the purple like totally get in your tumble-drier and stuff?'

'Sometimes.'

'Hmm.'

'Plus, I can't have ... I can't have anyone close to me. You know. Just in case.'

'Because of Frederick Cecil?'

'There's a lot of Frederick Cecils.'

There was a moment's pause, then we both spoke at the same time.

'So why . . . ?'

'Shall we eat?'

The pasta puttanesca was rich, spicy and utterly delicious. Maybe having asbestos hands made you a better cook. I let him refill my glass and enjoyed eating at the large table, the fire crackling behind us as he threw a couple of logs on it.

'So let me get this straight,' I said, twirling the pasta on my fork. 'You're telling me basically you have no friends at all?'

'Well, I wouldn't go . . . Well. No. Not really.'

'Could you not have a dual identity?' I said. 'It sounds rubbish. Whereas if everyone knew you were Ultimate Man, they'd all want to be your friend.'

He winced, and I realised this was precisely the problem.

Then he shrugged. 'I've started now,' he said. 'And now . . . even tonight. Even to have one night off – which is absolutely mandatory to keep my effectiveness – even now I'm thinking what if someone's in trouble? What if someone's about to jump off a bridge? Or there's a warehouse on fire? It took all the effort I have just to turn the police scanner off just for one night. I couldn't walk away, I don't think.'

I thought about this.

'Doctors do,' I said. 'Firemen do. People put their lives on the line to save people every day and still manage to find some friends to go out with. What makes you so special?'

There was a long pause.

'Because you are special,' I said eventually.

'I didn't ask for it,' he said in a low voice, putting down his fork. 'I didn't want it. And now I have it, I don't really have any choice.'

I looked at him. The black lashes framing his blue eyes were long, and the sides of his eyes drooped a little downwards. There was no stubble on his face. I wondered if he grew any.

'Well,' I said, trying to perk him up a bit. 'At least you get a lovely kitchen!'

It didn't work: he didn't change expression at all.

'And you're a very good cook,' I said with my mouth full.

'You think?' he said, finally smiling. 'I never get to cook for anyone.'

'I do think,' I said. 'This is awesome.'

He smiled again, revealing beautiful white teeth.

'I thought,' he said, 'when you found me on the stairs. I thought that this was the end for me, that it was the worst thing that had ever happened.'

He looked up at me, his blue eyes staring straight into mine, and at that very precise exact moment when I had decided that I was actually, after everything, going to kiss him; that in fact I thought (and the wine agreed) suddenly it was actually a tremendous idea, he said:

'But it's so nice to find someone I can be myself with. It's so nice to finally make a friend.'

We did the washing up side by side – which was obviously some kind of a novelty for him – then he made coffee with an absurdly complicated gadget and took me up a floor to show me a large drawing room with big floor-to-ceiling windows. Ahead were the grounds, rolling down from the house in an Elysian paradise: lawns, fences, gravel paths and a wood on the far side around a lake. It was glorious.

And there, beyond it, a row of lights twinkling. We were in total silence apart from a gentle rustle of the wind through the trees from a far-off open window and the occasional distant hoot of an owl, but the lights and the planes and helicopters swooping above it made it as if we could hear the honking cars, the backing-up trucks, the garbage lorries, the glass bottles being put out, the shouts and fights and hawkers and buskers filling the streets; everywhere noise and life being played out.

I said so and he looked at me inscrutably in the near dark and said, 'Well, of course I *can* hear it,' and I was taken aback that maybe he meant it literally, but of course he did; and I felt, suddenly, how very, very strange he was.

He looked like a man – he *was* a man – but there was something else there, something I didn't understand at all. The logs crackled in the grate. The fire had been burning all night, even though we had only come in for a couple of minutes.

He almost certainly had no idea that the fact that he was rich was as strange to me as the fact that he could lift up a truck with one hand.

He offered me something brown from a decanter. I looked at it curiously.

'It's brandy,' he said. 'Or there's whisky. I think.'

'Can I have tea?'

'No,' he said. 'I haven't got any tea. Do you want me to send someone out for some?'

We settled instead on another glass of red wine down in the kitchen, and his face lost the brooding look it had had staring out over the lake and the water to the great, bustling city beyond.

'You're not worried about crime-fighting on a hangover?' I said, indicating his glass. He squinted. 'What's a hangover like?' he asked quite earnestly.

'Seriously,' I said. 'Wow. I mean really. Wow.'

I looked at my own glass balefully and mentally reminded myself to take paracetamol before I went to sleep. Not that he'd have any. I realised then I'd considered staying the night, and felt myself blush. Of course I wasn't staying the night.

'You can stay if you like,' he said.

'*What?*' I said.

Now it was his turn to flush bright red.

'Sorry,' he said.

'Seriously? What? You can do that? You're psychic! I didn't know you could do that,' I said in a panic, trying not to think of the absolute worst things I could possibly think of.

'I can't ... I mean, just a tiny bit. When something beams out strongly from the surface. I mean, not ... I can't read your innermost thoughts or anything. Just ones that pass through strongly, like fish floating to the surface. And I don't have to ... Sorry, I did it without thinking.'

I stood up. He stood up too, immediately good-mannered, also without thinking about it.

'Seriously, can I block you from doing it?' I stuttered.

'Yes – yes, you can. It's like Facebook. I'll just up your privacy settings.'

'I mean it, don't you dare. Don't you ever *dare*.'

He shook his head.

'I won't. I promise. This is another reason I don't have any friends.'

'Have you been in there before?'

My face was burning as I tried desperately not to think about Frederick Cecil and the strange hypnotic spell he'd cast.

'It's okay,' he said, moving towards me. 'Honestly. I can block it. Would you like me to block it?'

'Yes!'

'Okay. Right. Excuse me.'

He placed his hand on either side of my head. I gazed furiously at the floor.

'Sorry,' he said. 'I have to look you in the eye.'

'Do you really?'

'Yup.'

Reluctantly, I lifted my head. His eyes were ridiculous: a bright metallic blue, like a brand-new car, or the sky at twilight in high summer. His hands were huge and strong, but rested gently on the side of my head. It was hard to stare into his eyes, very difficult in fact, particularly while trying not to think about anything. I finally rested on thinking very hard about camels, and managed to return his gaze.

'That's not what a camel looks like,' he said finally. 'That's a cross between a dromedary and a cartoon you saw once.'

'STOP IT!'

He pressed a tiny bit harder on the side of my face, his hands strong and warm, and I felt as if a curtain had descended, unfurling in my brain – a warm sensation, as if someone was tucking me in with a blanket. My thoughts went slightly fuzzy, then cleared again, but this time I knew – I somehow just knew, deep down, that they were private and safe.

'There you are,' he said. 'I've sealed you off.'

'What if you've just done witchy-woo stuff that's persuaded me that's what you've done?'

He let his hands drop to his sides.

'All life is risk, Holly.'

'Okay.'

'Seriously, do you want me to show you what a camel looks like on Google Images?'

'No, you're fine,' I said. 'Right, I'll make you a gigantic cake if you tell me what I'm thinking of right now.'

'A gigantic cake,' he said straightaway.

'No, stop – hang on, I haven't started yet.' I paused. 'Now I can't think of anything but cake.'

'Would you like some cake?'

'Well, yes, but that's not the ... '

Sure enough, he had a large fruitcake, made, he said, by one of his staff.

'Did they just make one of everything?' I said.

'I eat a lot,' he said. 'I need the calories. No, I didn't get what you were thinking of apart from cake.'

'Oh yeah,' I said. 'It was just another type of cake.'

'Not even an inkling.'

He cut me a slice. It was delicious. We sat back down by the fireside.

'So how did ... I mean, how did you get here? To this house, I mean? All by yourself?'

He grinned. 'See, if you hadn't insisted on the shutters being down, I could have just beamed you all the boring childhood stuff.'

'That's the stuff I like,' I said, mouth full of cake.

'Also, didn't you ever look me up?'

'Yes,' I said. 'But the internet said you were going out with Miley Cyrus, and were also a robot and the Antichrist, and were a thinly disguised lizard, so I pretty much gave up after that.'

So we sat, the lights of the city twinkling in the distance, and he told me in his own words what I knew already: the orphaned boy; the terrible powers unleashed on him as the entire family were caught in the lab explosion which killed them, but gave him abilities beyond mortal dreams.

'I'm surprised you're not more tortured than you are,' I said when he'd finished, staring into the flames, clutching his glass. He gave a half-smile.

'That's because you haven't got to know me.'

He looked at me. I was warm and woozy by the fire.

'Do you want to stay over?' he asked again. 'In the spare room?' he added a little too quickly, in my opinion.

'Really? Have you got a spare room?' I said. 'Only, the house feels a bit poky.'

'Yes, there's ... oh!' he said. I grinned at him.

As I headed up to bed, I thought, Well, I might as well ask him. I might as well know.

'Do you ... I mean, do you have girl or boyfriends. I mean, can you ...?'

He looked at me in a very deadpan way.

'Goodnight, Holly,' he said, and I felt dismissed.

'Aren't you going to bed?'

He shrugged.

'I don't sleep.'

'At all?'

'No.'

'You're awake *all the time*?'

'No,' he said. 'From time to time, I get knocked out.'

Chapter Twenty

The next morning, he'd gone before I woke up – or rather, he was at the gym, his butler said, which could have been in the house. Probably was.

I'd slept incredibly well on fresh white sheets in a white-panelled room, with views out the back of the property, a whole forest of trees keeping the house a secret. It was beautiful. And I'd woken up without a hangover, which made me think that in fact it was the extraordinary quality of the wine which had saved us both rather than any heroic recovery skills on Rufus's side.

I felt a bit weird going down for breakfast alone, except for staff – particularly when I saw they'd left everything out for me. But the fruit smoothie was delicious, and the chauffeur drove me back, and I felt incredibly relaxed and happy until I walked up to the apartment and Gertie started screaming at me like a banshee and I realised to my horror that I hadn't had a mobile signal at the manor, and I had been feeling so dreamy and cheerful in the back of the town car that – I know, I know – I had forgotten to turn my phone back on (this has never ever happened to me since smartphones were invented), and that basically she'd tried to get hold of me and couldn't and, well, this was the long way round of finding out that there was a policeman in my apartment because they thought I'd been kidnapped by Ultimate Man.

I looked at the policeman for a long time.

'Ah,' I said.

'You said she was wearing a red skirt,' he said to Gertie, looking at me as if I couldn't talk.

'That's right,' said Gertie.

Of course, I was still wearing it then. I sighed.

'This isn't what it looks like,' I said.

'Why didn't you call me?'

I didn't know how to explain about the pasta puttanesca and the fire and the sense, the absolutely one hundred per cent sense that I had left behind everything about my modern daily life – the holes in my tights and being jammed up against sweaty armpits commuting and overpriced noisy bars where I promised myself I would eat salad at lunchtime tomorrow – that everything that was familiar to me had gone, and that had apparently temporarily included my girlfriends.

'I'm sorry,' I said, genuinely feeling bad. I had completely forgotten how nervous and worried I'd been on the way to Rufus's place, how unexpected it all was.

'When you didn't come back ... I called and called, you know. Then I phoned the police and they basically implied you were being a bit of a slut.'

'Oh, that's good,' I said.

'You know, with the staying out and stuff. They asked if you'd done it before and I said ... '

'Never mind.'

Gertie still looked upset.

'I'm so sorry,' I added.

'Well, then I mentioned Ultimate Man, and here they are.'

I looked anguished.

'I really wish you hadn't done that.'

I really did. Partly because obviously he'd asked me not to mention it, at all, ever, and partly because I wasn't looking forward to trying to convince people I hadn't slept with him. Also, it's not the kind of thing that wouldn't get around. I shot Gertie a filthy look, which was immediately misinterpreted.

'Miss, have you been harmed? Are you all right?'

'Of course I'm all right,' I said. 'He's the good guy, remember?'

The police officer gave me a long look.

'He's a vigilante, ma'am. As far as we can tell, he does exactly what he feels like doing, whenever he wants to do it. So we can't presume on his good nature too far. I've had to scrape up some of the people who got in his way.'

'You mean muggers,' I scowled.

'I mean citizens, ma'am.'

'Anyway, you're back now,' said Gertie, who still hadn't smiled or asked me about it or done any of the usual things at all.

'So Ultimate Man wasn't busy last night?' went on the humourless policeman. 'I mean, busy in a "crime-fighting" sense.'

'Nothing happened,' I muttered crossly. 'We ate some pasta; that was all.'

I sounded unconvincing even to myself. The policeman stopped stabbing at his little smartphone suddenly.

'Wow, he left the city undefended?' said DuTroy, sounding startled.

'Well, it still seems to be there,' I said, indicating out of the window.

'Dang,' said the policeman. 'I can't get a signal. Have you got a Wi-Fi connection?'

I nodded.

'Sure. It's called GertieDubose Wi-Fi and the password is "soinlove". Try not to vomit while you're typing it in.'

We waited a second while I attempted not to consider why I was helping a policeman to type up a report which basically said I was a dirty stop-out, and I also wondered why they weren't leaving now I was clearly back. No crime had been committed; no damage done. They were just being nosey parkers, I could tell, wanting to sniff around, asking me what I'd seen at Ultimate Man's house and whether he lived underwater or something.

The other policeman looked up at me.

'Could you tell me Ultimate Man's real name, miss? Just for our records?'

I looked at him. Could they arrest me? Could they?

'I'm afraid I don't know it,' I said, trying not to let my shaky voice give me away. He nodded, not sounding terribly surprised.

Then the other officer cursed and said, 'Nope, that's not working either.'

DuTroy glanced down at his phone.

'Mine's gone too.'

'Great,' said the policeman. 'We're never going to be able to file this report.'

'What a shame,' I said. 'Not being able to file the report about the absolutely nothing that didn't happen today. How will you manage? Thank you – seriously, thank you for coming; I am so sorry for wasting your time, and sorry, Gertie. But I think we've cleared it all up, don't you?'

'I just have a couple more questions about Ultimate Man,' said the policeman.

'Well, call him,' I said.

'Have you got his number?'

I realised I didn't. He had mine but all I had was those mysterious emails and, I realised, glancing quickly at my laptop, the address had never actually appeared on my computer, but that didn't matter, as all the messages had disappeared anyway.

'Um, he totally said he'd call me,' I said. There was a pause.

'Bet he did,' said the policeman on his way out the door. I would have wanted to slam it after him if he hadn't been wearing a truncheon on his belt.

Chapter Twenty-one

'Ugh,' I said, heading in to make coffee. 'I can't believe you just did exactly what I asked you to do.'

'Well, that's what happens when you don't report in,' said Gertie, still cross. 'I call the police to come round. You're lucky it wasn't the fashion police too.'

'I like this skirt.'

'Oh, that's why you're wearing it two days on the trot.'

She squinted at her phone and looked cross.

'This is annoying, I need to post on Facebook that we've found you,'

'You said I was lost on *Facebook*?'

'You were lost.'

'Gertie, my *mother* follows you on Facebook.'

I glanced at my phone. Sure enough, it was vibrating ominously. 'Holly!'

'I'm fine, Ma.'

'But Gertie . . . '

Gertie was looking shamefaced on the sofa, stabbing frantically at her phone.

'I'll take it down,' she muttered.

'But where were you?'

'I was out seeing a friend.'

'What kind of a friend?'

I put my hand over the receiver.

'What did you type exactly? Did you mention his name?'

'No! What do you take me for?'

'Someone who panics and puts stupid things on Facebook.'

I uncupped my hand. 'Just a friend, Mum. Nothing to worry about. Gertie must have been having an otherwise boring evening.'

'Hey. You ungrateful, spoilt FIEND!'

She had a point.

'Well,' said my mum. 'I hope you're being careful.'

I am twenty-six years old. Which, to be fair, you wouldn't necessarily realise if you overheard me talking to my mother on the telephone. Don't get me wrong: I love my mum. She didn't have it easy in the slightest. The fact that Vinnie and I are more or less functioning adults (well, sometimes I think together we'd make one very successful person) is totally down to her.

Here's the thing though: when I was young, I remember her as being the bohemian divorcee, bit of a woman about town. Then as soon as I became an adolescent – and Vinnie's unusual character traits started to emerge – she suddenly turned into this disapproving nun, forever pursing her lips and worrying about stuff.

I realise now she didn't want me to turn out like her – pregnant, abandoned, on her own with a small child, no help and no prospects. And she must have been frantically worried about Vinnie. I see that now; it was just at the time I assumed she'd gone mad.

Anyway, we kind of got through it more or less. But I'd quite like to hang out with my old mum from time to time. From what I remember, she was great fun.

'Yes, Mum,' I said, slumping with my coffee against the doorframe.

'Vinnie wouldn't do anything like this.'

How would you know? I thought crossly. He sees you about as much as he sees me. At least I call you.

'I mean, don't embarrass your brother. He has a tough job; he needs to concentrate.'

When I managed not to get pregnant in my teens, she eased off the accelerator a bit with me. Not her precious Vinnie though.

'Anyway. I need to call him. My internet isn't working,' she said crossly. 'I need to check in with my bridge club.'

'Has Peaches knocked it out of the wall again?'

Peaches is her ridiculously fussy dog. She wears a different bow in her hair every day and only eats roast chicken.

'Oh, probably,' she said. 'I thought it just worked like magic through the air now.'

'Yes,' I said. 'But you have to plug the magic in to start with.'

'That's disappointing.'

'Oh, only for now,' I said. 'I'm sure they'll beam it down from the sky any day.'

'Well, now would be good,' she said. 'Because I haven't got any.'

Suddenly there was a loud honking noise outside – louder than usual – and I leaned over to the window to see. Outside on the busy street, a van had jerked to a stop in front of a guy who was standing right out in the middle of the street, staring at his phone in consternation. The van driver was screaming at him, but he barely seemed to notice. I glanced around the street. Everywhere people were standing stock still, frozen to the spot. As the lights had turned to red, I suddenly had the oddest sensation: the world had been put on pause; everyone had stopped.

Then the lights turned green again and the traffic ground on and people started to spill out of coffee shops and offices, all of them prodding at their devices gormlessly, some of them glancing up at the sky or pacing slightly from side to side as if that would make a difference.

'I don't think,' I said suddenly. 'I don't think anyone's phone is working this morning.'

Gertie came and looked down with me.

'They're like headless chickens,' she observed. 'Look at them.'

'Well, that's not right,' said DuTroy. 'I mean, one carrier might fail, but not all of them, not at the same time.'

'Maybe they're all with the same company.'

'I'm not on the same company as my mother,' I said. 'She got on a really stupid price plan because they advertised it with a dog that looks exactly like Peaches, so she can send it to me and say, "Look at this dog which is much uglier like Peaches, can you believe it?"'

I turned on the TV. The local newsreader was looking distracted.

'And earlier today, in the town of . . . '

She glanced off-camera, and her very thin face with straight blonde hair suddenly lost its usual expression of calm hauteur, and took on a look of molten fury.

'*Cue!*' she whispered. Nothing happened. She looked back down the camera with a reassuring smile. Still nothing happened. 'Excuse me, ladies and gentlemen,' she said. 'We're just having a few minor technical difficulties. Let's go over to Sondra for the weather.'

Sondra plastered on a tight grin which only vaguely overcame her panicky mask at the weather station. Where the little temperatures and sunshines usually went on her board was nothing at all, just flashing green lights.

'Um, we're having a few technical issues too!' she said anxiously. 'Nothing to worry about. We can probably pretty much say that today's weather will be exactly like yesterday's, more or less.'

'You could probably say that every day,' observed Gertie, standing beside me staring at the TV. 'I don't really see the need for weather forecasts at all.'

'Yes, but what's up?' I said. 'What does Twitter say ... oh.'

'No Twitter,' said DuTroy grimly. 'What on earth are forty billion rabid liberals going to masturbate about all day?'

DuTroy had quite strong feelings about Twitter.

I blinked. No internet. No internet. How? I tried not to let worry overtake me. It must be temporary. We still had TV. And the telephone. It was just a temporary blip, like all those rolling blackouts we had last year.

But the weird thing was, as Gertie changed over to a national news station looking equally puzzled, my entire instincts were to look it up on the internet. Someone must have a periscope or a blog update or a newsflash or something which told us what the hell was actually going on. Someone somewhere must know, and the way the world worked was that they told everyone. Then we were all reassured and kept on in our little bubbles that everything was going to be okay because someone, somewhere, knew what the hell was going on.

Because nobody seemed to have any idea what was going on.

'News is reaching us of a wide loss of internet coverage,' came the man on the screen, who was, of all things, listening to a telephone live on air and obviously repeating what he was hearing.

'It is not yet understood what is causing the blackout, and people are advised not to panic.'

'Not to panic?' said DuTroy scornfully. 'Mankind lived successfully without LolCats for about fifty thousand years; I think we can all make it through a morning.'

I nodded, but I wasn't so sure. Since high school, the internet had been part of my every waking minute, part of my every move. My phone functioned like my right hand. I had a closer relationship to it, I think, than any man who'd ever been in my life. Even now, my hand was ruthlessly scrabbling for it; flipping it over, although my brain knew it would be useless, just like when I looked at it to check the time, then forgot the time ten seconds later. I didn't quite know what to do with myself. I felt itchy, awkward, anxious. And if I felt like that ...

Sure enough, there was more noise outside the apartment. Two hipsters were yelling at each other, which looked a bit strange considering one of them had a gigantically curled moustache and the other had a scooter parked by the kerb. So you would think: peace-loving, slightly nerdy guys working on artisan juice bars and stuff? They were fighting. They were actually fighting. Punching and kicking and yelling about lost screenplays and cloud back-ups and all sorts of stuff.

'Go down there!' said Gertie to DuTroy. He looked horrified.

'No chance,' he said. 'You know I'm not Ultimate Man, right?'

'I just thought ... '

'Hey!' DuTroy leaned out of the window and shouted, none too politely. 'Can you keep your disagreements to yoga class, please? Or there's water coming down.'

Fortunately – and to DuTroy's great relief, I was sure – they looked up and separated, taking him at his word and ambling off in different directions, hurling insults at each other as they went.

But the next thing I heard was a smashing window. Then another one. Then more curses and shouting.

'Oh my,' I said.

I couldn't remember the last time I'd answered the telephone to someone who wasn't my mother. If everyone had to actually start using their telephones again ... as telephones ... well. This was dramatic. No, I had to stop being stupid. It was only for a few minutes. Like a power cut.

Gertie and I looked at each other.

'It's only the internet,' I said, trying to sound more reassuring than I felt. 'I'm sure they'll have it up again in no time.'

She swallowed.

'What if they don't? Who are "they" anyway?'

I thought of all the press releases I did, all the facts and figures I found and relied on every day, the constant electronic updating of social media and websites and services and bookings and ... well, I'd be out of a job for starters.

'Not even the Kardashians can break the internet,' I said soothingly. 'And they tried so, so hard. It's going to be all right, I promise.'

'Can you really promise?' said DuTroy, his face hard suddenly. 'Can you really promise supply lines aren't going to break down? Do you know how much stock the average supermarket holds?'

DuTroy read a lot of apocalyptic magazines. He was pretty up on this kind of stuff.

'Well, can't they just phone up and ask for all the same things as they had last week? Like the weather?' I said. 'How did they used to do it?'

'What about the banks? What about the stock market?'

'I don't have any stocks,' I said. 'They're only for rich people.'

'Don't be ridiculous,' said DuTroy. 'You have a salary and a pension and a bank that provides all that stuff to you, and it might suddenly stop doing it any second.'

'No, it won't,' I said.

'The last time there was a panic, back in 2008,' said DuTroy. 'We were twenty-four hours away from the banks closing.'

I glanced out of the window again. No way. Yes. There was someone queuing up at a cashpoint. Then another person joined the queue. Then another. Then another. I glanced back at the television. The rolling stock-ticker had stopped.

'Shit,' I said. 'No. Surely not. You're being ridiculous. Some grown-ups will sort it out.' Gertie looked scared. Across the road was a little convenience shop which normally had people popping in and out of it all day long. Today there was a large queue which looked antsy and restless. People still couldn't stop fiddling with their phones, even though nothing was happening.

'There you are,' said DuTroy. 'Look, it's starting already. Here's the thing:you don't even need anything terribly bad to happen. As long as people panic and start fighting and getting anxious with each other, the city can still completely break down without a shot being fired. Until the shots get fired.'

'You're enjoying this,' I accused him. DuTroy read a lot of zombie comic books. Gertie was clinging onto his arm, I noticed.

'Not at all,' he said grimly. 'Just telling you what's going to happen.'

'Well, and then in ten minutes everything will switch back on again and civilisation will all be fine,' I said. 'And won't we all feel stupid?'

'I hope so,' said DuTroy. 'You go fill the bath with drinking water. Just in case. I'll go to the cashpoint, just in case money's still a thing.'

We both watched him go.

'This is ridiculous,' I said. 'It's nothing.'

We turned back to the television. A man was smiling inanely.

'And if you have any reports of internet coming back on in your area,' he said, 'Do contact us . . . I mean, call us. Call us on . . . Hey, does anybody know the phone number for this place? Anyone? Can you get it up on screen?'

There was a pause.

'Oh,' he said. 'Apparently you have to type it into a computer to get it up onscreen. And the computer won't speak to the other computer.'

'Hang on,' said Gertie suddenly. 'I thought the whole point about the internet was that it was invented to work if everything else fails. It was for nuclear war, wasn't it? It can survive a nuclear war. It can't just be turned off. You couldn't turn it off if you tried. That's the whole point about it.'

'There we go,' I said, still trying to persuade myself that everything was all right. Everything else that had happened – last night, dinner, Rufus – had gone from my mind completely. Instead, my brain was churning with exactly what was going on. I was trying not to be scared, but somehow it felt like inside me was a slow tolling bell – that tiny peep you sometimes get through the cracks that the only difference between our lives and the lives of people in some ghastly hellhole where they will kill you for nothing is negligable; that our entire society is only propagated by us willing it to be so.

I heard a commotion coming from next door. It was a single mother and her young, very shy, bespectacled son, who barely spoke when we passed in the hallway. They never made a sound. She worked long hours and although we said hello on the stairs, our paths never crossed apart from that.

Now there was the noise of yelling and things being thrown. DuTroy returned, frowning.

'It's getting mean out there on the streets, man. Everyone's shouting.'

We listened to the noise next door continuing, and got up.

'Should we do something?'

It was hard to make sense of the incoherent yells, but I gently knocked the door none the less.

'Sare? Sare, are you there? Is everything okay?'

The noise broke off, then the door opened just a tiny fraction on the snib. Sare's face poked out.

'He's ... hello. Have you got internet? Have they fixed it? Is it back on?'

'Not yet,' I said. 'I'm sure it will be any second. Why?'

There came the crash of something breaking and an angry shout. She glanced back nervously.

'What's wrong?'

'It's Eli. He's ... he's not pleased. He was playing Neverwinter. Apparently his team are ready to storm the acropolis and ... well, it won't go.'

It was impossible to believe that the little shy boy who couldn't say boo to a goose was in there breaking up the apartment.

'Do you want me to have a word with him?' said DuTroy.

'No, no, he's fine,' said Sare. He didn't sound in the least bit fine. 'I'm sure they'll turn it on again soon. Won't they? Won't they?'

'Of course,' I said as Sare closed the door hurriedly, the shouting redoubling as young Eli obviously discovered that we weren't the people there to fix the internet after all.

I stood in the corner of our sitting room, thinking furiously. But it wasn't Rufus I was thinking about – he could get muggers in a headlock for sure, but that wasn't quite the same thing as reconnecting the millions and millions of devices there were in the city via some complicated computer network absolutely no one understood.

'Maybe this is it,' said Gertie, running over to the window. 'Maybe this is Skynet.'

'Of course it's not Skynet,' I said. 'What are you doing?'

She was staring up at the clouds; it was a heavy day, as if the clouds were full of rain that wasn't ready to fall, pregnant.

'Looking for the drones,' she said. 'First they immobilise us, then they send the drones to zap us.'

'Why would anyone want to do that?' I said. 'And we're not immobilised. Cars still work. The phones still work.'

There was a massive smashing noise outside. A car alarm went off.

'Cars aren't Wi-Fi,' I said.

'No,' said DuTroy. 'But the people driving them are looking for it. Plus ... the traffic lights.'

Gertie still looked unconvinced.

'But if you call anyone ... will they come?'

'Of course,' I said.

'How would they find you without Google Maps?'

I looked out of the window again. People were marching aimlessly up and down the road, staring at their devices, glancing secretively at one another. I didn't like it. I didn't like it at all.

Everyone needed to be home, huddled close, waiting for everything to get better again, waiting for everything to get right.

'For an apocalypse,' said DuTroy, looking out too. 'It's going pretty much textbook so far.'

'It's not an apocalypse!' I said, indicating the television, which was now showing old *Friends* reruns. 'If it was the apocalypse, would they show old *Friends* episodes?'

'That's exactly what they'd do,' said Gertie. 'Also, look at it. It's a show about a bunch of people having great lives and a terrific time without any Wi-Fi. Do you think that's a coincidence?'

I did not think it was a coincidence, no.

Chapter Twenty-two

I had made myself cut down from staring at my phone to once every fifteen minutes, willing those four little semicircles from coming into view. Instead, I was sitting in my bedroom. My mother hadn't called again. I don't think she'd noticed too much. In fact, although you'd expect the phone to spring to life, it hadn't, and I was shy to call people we knew; I think we all were.

I'd stopped phoning anyone except Mum, really. And anyone else you spoke to, well, you just kind of assumed they knew what they were doing; that they were in command of all the facts and you could take the situation from there. Calling someone up and saying 'I have no idea what's going on' … it felt a little strange. I didn't want to hear that everyone else had already got it sorted or discovered a different network or something. Well, I did want to hear that – of course I did. It was just a little difficult to make the first move. And obviously everyone else felt the same.

I tried not to think about Just In Time; about the ordering system of supermarkets and shops. About production lines and food lines and gas lines that relied on computers talking to each other to work. I had been twelve at the turn of the millennium and remembered people talking about planes dropping out of the sky, and the world stopping working and everything falling apart. It hadn't happened. The worst didn't happen.

I thought of global news reports. Sometimes the worst happened.

I looked out of the window. It was getting dark. We had tried phoning for pizza, but couldn't get through. We then tried to laugh and said no wonder everyone wanted pizza on a night like tonight. We didn't let ourselves think that maybe the sat navs couldn't find the delivery apartments, and maybe the pizza people couldn't get their card-readers to work and maybe some of them hadn't come to work at all tonight and maybe the shift system had broken down. We told ourselves they were very busy indeed.

You could barely see the stars above the lights of the city. The lights were still on. It was reassuring. I looked up. Perhaps there was a huge shower of green zeros and ones which were all up there, trying to stream down, like in *The Matrix*, but they weren't getting down and they weren't getting in. I bit my lip. How? Why? The companies must be going crazy trying to fix it, but they couldn't. Why?

I recollected – suddenly – as an image came into my head unbidden: Frederick Cecil, standing in the middle of a room, pouring jewels into a bag, smiling politely, saying thank you, saying … what did he say? Something about funding something.

This wasn't an accident. This wasn't an error. Last night, Rufus was off. Somebody knew. And somebody had planned something.

I cursed again Rufus's absurd lack of giving me his number. It was arrogant and stupid, as if I would simply wait around, hanging on for a hero to turn up. It showed he didn't even care enough:

everything had to be done at his beck and call, in case some girl called him up in the middle of crime-fighting to moan about her shoes or something, which also went to show that he didn't know me at all.

Which he didn't. I told myself to calm the frick down and went and stood at the window, looking, pondering.

In the distance, I could hear shouts and yelling. Probably a trivia night gone horribly wrong. I heard a shot ring out. Maybe not. Or no, maybe it was a car backfiring. Yeah. I swallowed hard. DuTroy had gone out. Gertie had begged him not to but he said he had a night planned with the guys and she said how could he know how to meet everyone without 95 dsm and texts zipping back and forth between them and he'd said the normal way, just getting there and they'd be there too at the agreed place and she'd wrinkled her nose and said that never happened, and he'd looked concerned but he'd gone anyway.

'Otherwise they win.'

'But we don't know who "they" are,' she'd whispered. 'If the internet isn't there to tell us.'

'This totally isn't Skynet,' said DuTroy mostly to himself.

'I'm glad you're so sure.'

I tried not to get worried in the apartment, but we'd put the latch down, just in case. Couldn't be too careful. I looked up again at those misty stars.

The name flashed up again in my head. Frederick Cecil.

But what was he planning? And while everyone was wailing about the money and the diamonds or, in Rufus's case, beating up his minions, did nobody even ask what the long game was?

I wished I could contact him too. But presumably everyone wanted that. Just to know. Just to know what was up.

I looked at the phone. It rang. I nearly jumped out of my skin. I hate it when it does that. It should never do that. The nicest thing about my adult life is how the phone has almost entirely gone out of fashion: that anti-social, loud, intrusive, rude, demanding bell is nearly outlawed from public life; people who use it on the bus or the subway are becoming like lepers, looked at as pathetic by the young or plain insecure by everybody else.

I gazed at my phone in loathing as I normally did. Then my heart started beating as I realised I didn't recognise the number. I didn't even recognise the area code. Could it be Rufus? Surely he'd want to know I was all right; it wasn't even possible he couldn't have heard about it.

The nasty little worm in my mind whispered, What if Frederick Cecil could tell you were thinking about him? But I banished it immediately. For a start, I had my psychic blanket on now, so even if he could do what Rufus could do – which I thought was unlikely; Frederick Cecil was unusually clever and twisted, but he seemed one hundred per cent human as far as I could tell – Rufus had pulled that curtain over my mind so he couldn't have heard me even if he had once been able to.

It rang again. I looked at it carefully, then – hearing Gertie's steps in the hallway – tentatively picked it up.

'Hello?'

My voice felt strange, as if I'd forgotten how to communicate with anybody.

'Hey there.'

I didn't recognise the soft tones at once; it took me a moment to place them. Then I realised: it was Nelson, from the office.

'Nelson! Hi.'

I couldn't help it. I was a bit disappointed it wasn't Rufus, and a bit relieved it wasn't Frederick Cecil.

I mean, seriously, Rufus – major incident here? And you're the hero and everything? Any time you want to check in on the girl who just spent the night at your house is totally fine by me.

'Oh hi, Nelson!' I said more cheerily than I felt. A lot more cheerily than I felt. 'How are you?'

'Well,' he said, not sounding in the least bit cheery. 'Well, you know, things seem pretty weird. Uh. Does this happen often in the city?'

I wanted to be reassuring, but I didn't know how.

'Not really,' I said. 'But I'm sure they're fixing it. Or trying to fix it.'

'Right,' he said. 'Because there's a massive fight going on outside my building. Two buses crashed into each other. Loads of people are hurt. I went out to help but ... Then an ambulance came and people started throwing stones at it.'

'Why? Why would they do that? Because someone couldn't get his NetFlix stream?'

'No, because the traffic lights went off.'

I went quiet.

His voice trailed off as we both thought the same thing.

'So, uh, is there work tomorrow? is what I wanted to ask you,' he said. 'I mean, it feels like everything is going to shit – I mean, it's only Wi-Fi, right? But everyone's going bananas! I saw two women fight over a chicken.'

'What?'

'A dead chicken. A frozen chicken. There was a run on the supermarket. I mean, really is there any point in going to work?'

I hadn't thought about it. I had absolutely no idea how we would attempt to spin this. I had absolutely no idea what was going on. And even if we got some kind of a press release together, how was I going to send it to the ten thousand people on the mailing list? Carrier pigeon?

'I really don't know,' I said. 'But I think we'd better go in. Just to ... well, you know: Keep Calm and Carry On.'

There was a pause in which I was delighted that I had said absolutely the lamest thing I could think of.

'Holly ...'

I blinked. Nelson saying my name out of working hours or our lunches felt oddly too personal or informal, as if he had no right to my name, which was of course utterly ridiculous.

'Yeah?'

'Holly ...' His voice sounded strangulated, nervous. I didn't like it. I didn't want a great big guy like Nelson to be scared. I didn't want anyone to be scared. I wanted everyone to join me in pretending everything was going to be fine again in five minutes flat; then it would be.

'Do you think ... do you think they'll be able to fix things?'

He sounded like he was genuinely asking me, as if I might have the solution.

'Totally,' I said.

'Because ... because it looks like it's getting completely out of control.'

'I'm sure it'll be fine,' I said, like I'd been saying to Gertie. I don't know when I felt I'd become the person in charge of fake reassurance; I wasn't the least bit good at it.

'Yeah,' he said, not sounding in the least bit convinced. 'I just ... I just wish someone would fix it.'

'So do I,' I confessed. 'I like to believe there are grown-ups in charge.'

There was a short pause.

'See you tomorrow then!' I said as breezily as I could muster, which wasn't very.

So. There wasn't anyone around I could depend on then. Nobody who knew ...

Then Mum rang, just as I was thinking it.

'Go check on your brother,' she ordered.

Chapter Twenty-three

'Right,' I said going back into the sitting room. 'I'm going out.'

'No!' said Gertie. 'You can't! The town's full of looters!'

'What are they going to steal?' I said. 'Computers they can't connect up or phones they can't connect up? I'll just stay clear of food shops.'

'Seriously, no,' said DuTroy, who'd come back in looking terrified.

'Look,' I said. 'If there's anyone who has the faintest idea what's up, it'll be Vinnie.'

'Your little brother Vinnie?'

'No, Vincent Van Gogh. Yes, Vinnie. He's a tech genius. He'll know about this.'

'He might have caused it,' said DuTroy.

'He's not an *evil* genius. Just a really, really unusual one.'

There wasn't really a word for Vinnie when we were little. He was just odd, and different. It wasn't until he was grown up Mum realised there might be a label for him, and by then it was too late: he'd already been to university on a scholarship, aced everything and been offered an incredibly successful job which paid him a fortune before anyone had time to tell him he might be disabled.

It was only a few blocks to Vinnie's apartment complex, but it was stepping into a different world.

We were down a cruddy little old brick alley, where no one picked up the rubbish properly, and the street cleaners never seemed to get down and a lot of people thought it was a usefully quiet place to have a fight or a screw or a piss or a drug deal, or sometimes all four at the same time.

Walking across Centerton to where Vinnie lived was an education in itself, even in oddly quiet streets. I realised the normal gantry signs – Slow down! Don't drive and text! – were out, presumably including the ones that told you when there were accidents ahead.

I passed two bankers screeching abuse down their phones in a panic which made them sound like fighting birds.

As if on cue, I heard a loud crunching noise followed by an alarm. Oh my lord. I hastened my steps. There were people lurking. Normally I try not to judge people lurking. But these people were lurking in an especially lurky fashion, as if they were just waiting for the sun to go down when they could unleash . . . well, I didn't know what to think. I mean, the phones were working. You could ring the police. But the city was uneasy, as if was holding its breath and just waiting: waiting for the time to come when they could let it out.

The faster I walked, the worse things got. It was only the internet, for goodness' sake! It was only Wi-Fi. Nothing happened in the last couple of hours; you haven't missed that much. If we didn't all check our phones like dogs check their bowls . . . I smelled something burning. BURNING! Just because someone couldn't get into LolCats.

Someone hissed at me from an alley. I started to run.

You know what Centeron is like: the posh streets and the rough ones can often be nearby. Vinnie didn't live far from me at all, but I never saw him.

Vinnie's building used to be art studios built in the twenties. They have huge, clear north-facing windows and intricate brick-work. He never asks me over, obviously. He never asks anyone over. I hadn't bothered to ring: he doesn't answer the phone. He's scared of the ringer, so he's just always done without.

I rang the bell. It made a noise, but the video phone didn't come on. I waited tentatively, glancing behind me every so often. Where was he? It wasn't like he went out. But I was worried that the change in things and the difference in losing his computers – just change in general – might have upset him. I tried again. He hated the buzzer so much it felt like cruelty, but I really felt like I needed him.

After what felt like an age, a shape turned up in the hallway. The front door was a beautiful double door with silver handles and embossed windows, and I could see it come towards me without knowing who it was. I felt nervous.

There was a pause as whoever was on the other side bent down to the peephole. Then, very quickly, the door was unbolted and opened a tiny crack.

'Quick. Get inside.'

Chapter Twenty-four

Vinnie locked the door very carefully behind us and hushed me as we padded up the luxuriously carpeted ornate stairwell. I was so jealous of his living arrangements it wasn't funny. And even though I realised and understood he needed his space and etc., etc. and was a bit different, I still couldn't help taking it personally; he was my brother after all.

'Seriously,' I said. 'Let me move in. I'll sleep in the post box corner.'

All the mail boxes were ornate polished brass. He still got post for the last four tenants, mostly council tax bailiff summonses.

'This is my house,' said Vinnie, not turning around. 'My house, Holly.'

'I know,' I said. 'I was only teasing you.'

Once when drunk, Gertie psychoanalysed me to say she reckoned the reason I was so sarcastic was because I'd come from a family where everyone had to say precisely what they meant all the time, every second of the day.

Vinnie, as usual, was dressed in a pressed white shirt and pressed blue jeans. A laundry service delivered seven of these items, plus underwear and pyjamas, every week and picked up the old ones. He never had to meet anyone.

'I don't think you realise how serious this is.'

'Well, obviously I do,' I said. 'Because you've let me over your threshold.'

His apartment was totally bleak. Well, I mean, awesome if you liked that kind of thing. Basically no furniture. One white sofa. Huge spotless picture windows looking over the whole of downtown Centerton. A stainless steel kitchen. One telescope. Decades' worth of *Railway Magazine* organised into folders perfectly on a bookshelf. And acres of space. That was about it. Okay, probably more awesome than bleak.

'I could just roll up a futon in the corner,' I said. He looked at me sternly.

'This is my house, Holly.'

I padded through into the kitchen.

'Got any coffee?'

It was a stupid question. He drinks Tang. It took mum two years to get him onto the diet stuff to at least leave him with some teeth.

I poured myself a glass of water.

'So,' I said. 'Did you notice anything strange?'

He blinked.

'The Wi-Fi is down. Yes. I know.'

'So what are you doing?' I said.

'Waiting for it to come back.'

'Can't you fix it?'

'I'll try.'

I stopped suddenly.

'What's that noise?'

He smiled then. He didn't smile very often. In fact, if you didn't know him really, really well, you wouldn't have realised that was what it was at all.

'Hang on, I recognise it.'

I moved over to the one busy area of his apartment: his massive black sinister-looking computer equipment, three screens and various blinking boxes.

'You know, this set-up is totally what an evil genius would have,' I complained, but he ignored me.

I realised how I recognised the sound. I'd heard it as a child, when we went to bed. We shared a room then. Wasn't brilliant, to be fair. But it was a kind of hiss, followed by a brr, followed by a loud cracking noise.

'OMG!' I said. 'It's dial-up! You've still got a dial-up modem!'

I darted over and sure enough, there it was, plugged into an old phone line.

'I haven't heard one of those for years.'

'I had it filed away,' said Vinnie.

'Course you did.'

The machine made a long beep and, slowly, one of the screens started to warm up. Vinnie sat down. I ran to stand beside him – not too close.

'Okay,' I said. 'When there's no internet, what's on the internet?'

Chapter Twenty-five

'Okay, go to Google News. No, hang on. Go to BBC-dot-com. They'll tell you the same stuff, but in a much more reassuring way.'

But there was no going anywhere. The screen stuttered a little and then, very, very slowly, line by line, a picture started to appear.

'It should be Google Seek,' said Vinnie.

'What's Google Seek?' I said.

'Oh, there's a secret Google for people who are too smart for regular Google.'

'No, there isn't!' I said hotly.

'Yes, there is, Holly.'

I couldn't see what it was, but it wasn't Google. Or Google bloody Seek, which I wouldn't believe in if Vinnie had never once told a lie in his entire life.

I held my breath as the two of us stared at the pixels descending one at a time – this couldn't have been what it was like back then, was it? Was it? What on earth did we do? Lived life, I suppose. Left the house. Went outside and looked at things instead of through a lens of a camera, or into a little box.

The image – I could see it was an image, a picture coming through – slowly continued to download, line by agonising line.

'It's weird, isn't it?' I said, just to break the silence. 'Because everyone I know says the world was fantastic in the nineties.'

'Ssh,' said Vinnie. 'It's coming.'

But in fact all we could see at that moment was hair: slowly, a fine blond kiss-curl being filled in, row by row. We stood back a bit to get a better look. But I didn't need a better look.

I knew. I knew it straightaway.

'Fuck,' I said.

Vinnie looked at me; he didn't like swearing.

'Sorry,' I said.

'What is it?' he said.

'Sssh,' I said.

It came down further, to the top of a mask. Then it stuttered, and stopped. I could see something just behind him.

'I know that guy,' I said.

'You can't know someone just from that.'

'I do. It's a bad guy, Vinnie. The guy who did all those robberies. He's behind this,' I said instantly, ice chilling my bones. This wasn't a small blackout, a meltdown, a temporary failure. This was sabotage. It was my worst fear. He was doing it on purpose.

I thought of his implacable face; the way he let his henchmen get beaten; his casual indifference to pleading and terror and bargaining.

'We are so screwed,' I said quietly. My first instinct was to get a cab and get out of town; go and hide under the bed at Mum's until this entire thing had blown over. Drag Vinnie there if necessary, which it would be.

'Maybe it's a frozen page ...'

Vinnie stopped talking as suddenly some letters – some

ridiculous, white, nineties font interspersed with lime green, with little lights flashing around them – began to appear.

'Greetings, snails,' it said. Flash flash flash. The lines of words revealed themselves painfully slowly. I swallowed hard. The thing was, what wouldn't he do, this man? I had looked into his eyes; I had felt the iron grip beneath the soft skin, the skeleton within.

'No more,' said the letters. 'No more.'

Chapter Twenty-six

'What is that? What does it mean?' said Vinnie. He started rocking in his chair, which was rarely a good sign.

'Sssh,' I said. 'Want some Tang?'

He nodded, and I fetched him some; it always calmed him down. I wanted to touch his shoulder, but of course he didn't like that at all. When he was little, he would scream and scream and scream and my mum would try and hold him and cuddle him to make it better and it only ever made it worse.

'Who is he, Holly? Who is he? Who is he? Who is he?'

'He's the thief that did the museum. And all the nightclubs. He must have been raising money to bring down the internet.'

There was a pause.

Vinnie shook his head.

'No. It wouldn't work like that.'

'What do you mean?'

'You don't need money to do this. Just ... just ... '

He looked at me.

'When he took the things ... did he just take wallets and jewels and watches and handbags?'

'Yes,' I said. 'Things of value. Wallets, jewels, phones ...'

'Phones?'

'Uh-huh. He took everyone's phones.'

Vinnie nodded a lot, his head bouncing up and down.

'Phones. Yes.'

'What?'

'All the phones. Jewels are no use. Watches are no use. Wallets are no use. Phones are what he needs. All the information in all the phones; all the digital footprints; every little step; everyone connected to everyone else in the city. Did he take them on the street? Did he take them at the welfare exchange?'

'No,' I said. 'Bars, nightclubs, museum benefits.'

Vinnie nodded again in that funny jerky way.

'Connected,' he said. 'He needed the interactions. He needed all the connections. The whole web.'

'The well-connected,' I breathed. 'The robberies were just a smoke-screen.'

The picture shifted very slightly. There was something there, I knew it. Something just behind him. Something I thought I knew.

'No,' said Vinnie, leaping up.

'What?' I said.

'It's self-destructing. He's sent a very slow-moving virus in to my machine. Enough for us to get the message then ...'

Vinnie pulled out all the wires from his machines, and the screen stuttered and froze, with just his face on it, then, line by line, it began to degrade. I stared at it. There was something, something in the frame that had snagged my attention. Something. A blur. I saw a blur in the top left-hand-side of the frame.

'Can you enhance that bit?' I shouted, pointing at it.

'No,' said Vinnie. 'One: because it's trying to give my computer a virus; and two: because it doesn't work like that. Pixels
are pixels.'

I stared at it very hard.

'I think,' I said. 'I think I know where he is.'

I rang Gertie.

'Have you fixed it?' she said breathlessly. 'There's a platoon of
policeman on the road. They have *riot shields*, Holly. *Riot shields*.'

'Because there's no internet?' I said. 'The internet goes down
and it's the end of days? What's happened to us?'

I could hear the panic in her voice.

'Listen,' I said. I wasn't looking forward to this bit. 'You know
your pink cardigan?'

There was a long pause.

'My cashmere pink cardigan?'

'Uh, yeah,' I said.

'The one that I got specially from that awesome sample sale
and I couldn't believe it and they don't make that exact shade
anywhere else in the world and it was the best day of my life and
you said can I borrow it and I said absolutely over my dead body
and you said well can you at least leave it to me in your will and
I said no?'

'Uh, yeah,' I said again.

'Is this about we're all going to die and you want to wear it just
once?'

'Not exactly,' I said. This was scarier than what was going on
in the streets. 'Um, can you check if it's in your wardrobe?'

I'd meant to give it back. I'd only borrowed it because I was in
a rush and it was the second day Nelson was there and it looked
so pretty – seriously, it was a shade of soft off-pink which gave you

133

this radiant skin and made you look eighteen. I had totally meant to return it before Gertie had even noticed it had gone, without ketchup on it or anything. I was basically sure I had.

I heard the phone being dropped clunkily and Gertie dashing off. I closed my eyes. Tell me I'd given it back. Tell me I had.

Gertie's voice was cold as ice.

'It doesn't appear to be in my wardrobe,' she said.

I swore vividly under my breath.

'I'll explain later,' I said.

'Holly!' screeched Gertie. 'I swear to God you get that cardigan back or the last remaining two weeks of life on this earth will be a living hell for you!'

Chapter Twenty-seven

The cardigan. Which I had left in the office. Because I am a careless idiot who doesn't look out for her friends' things. That precise tone of soft rose-gold that you couldn't find anywhere else.

I'd seen it in the background of the shot.

I couldn't believe it. I couldn't believe he'd have gone there.

And was it coincidence?

Frederick Cecil was in the mayor's office. More specifically, he was in my office.

Which made sense, I suppose. It was a large building; all the radio telescopes came from out behind it; it was dead centre, so your coverage would work. It made perfect sense. I knew that. Did anybody else? Did he?

Where was Ultimate Man? What was he doing? Did he even know? I looked at Vinnie's useless computer. Great way of getting in touch that had turned out to be. Nineteen levels of encryption on an email doesn't help when there's no sodding email.

'I know where he is.'

'Call the police,' said Vinnie promptly.

We did, but they'd given up answering.

'Shit,' I said. 'They've all gone. Shit.'

Finally, a bored-sounding woman came on.

'What is your emergency?'

'I know who's doing this!' I shouted.

'Yes, ma'am,' came the voice. 'You're the four thousandth call on this today. Can I put you on hold please?'

After ten minutes, I hung up in frustration.

'This won't do it,' I said. 'I'm going out. Find a policeman to listen to me. Are you coming?'

'Don't, Holly,' said Vinnie. 'Please don't. Don't go out. Don't.'

'Are you coming? You could protect me.'

'Don't go out, Holly.'

'It's okay,' I said. 'You stay here, okay?'

'Don't go out. Don't go out.'

I knew though that once I did go out, he would be fine. I'd seen it happen with Mum a million times. He'd be so upset, then she'd leave the room and it would be as if she'd never been there.

'Don't go out,' said Vinnie again.

'I'm going to find a policeman and come back,' I said. 'I'll be on the phone. I'll phone you. From a phone box.'

'No phones,' he said. 'Don't phone me, Holly.'

I shook my head.

'It's all right: I don't know your number. I don't know anybody's number. Working phones aren't actually that helpful right now. Anyway. Just sit tight. I'll be back, I promise.'

I could still hear him muttering, 'Don't go out, Holly' as I padded down the pristine hallway. I hoped it wasn't some kind of hideous portent.

Chapter Twenty-eight

Outside, the streets had, after the first spasms of violence, fallen eerily quiet. There were no more sirens in the air. There were no people on the street. It felt like the entire city was holding its breath, as if this was simply the first smite upon the people, an opening salvo in a war they wouldn't understand and couldn't control. Everyone waiting for dark.

I looked up at the sky and suddenly cursed Rufus turning off his ability to see into my mind. Because if he could have read my mind right now, right at that moment it would have been screaming, 'Hey! Idiot! Come and find me and I'll show you exactly where Frederick Cecil is.'

I wondered if he was in other people's homes now, other people who'd figured out what to do, who'd fixed up their old telephone lines, blown the dust off their old modems. But would anyone know except me?

Finally, I saw a police car with an officer in front of a stalled tram, which had just come to a stop in the middle of the road. Obviously information was no longer getting through and it had just abandoned ship; everyone was gone. I darted up. There were four other people around him, drawn from shuttered shops and noisy, intimidating bars. Everyone was shouting at him.

'I know where the bad guy is!' I shouted.

'Wait your turn please, ma'am,' he said.

'What, does everybody know?' I said, confused. But everyone else was demanding that he contact their relatives, or fix their computers, or all sorts of other non-cop-related business, and nobody listened to what I was saying at all.

'I know where he is!' I shouted again. The policeman turned to me with a weary look on his face.

'Who's that, ma'am?' he said.

'Frederick Cecil!'

'Who?'

'The baddie! The bad guy! That bad guy!'

'What are you talking about?'

'You know? The bad guy who's threatening the city?'

I felt like I was stuck in a nightmare, hollering at a policeman who didn't seem able to understand a word I was saying. I'd forgotten we were the only ones who'd seen him. But he must know the name.

Still no recognition from the cop. Ultimate Man was right, I thought. Frederick Cecil definitely needed a more badass name.

'There's no point hollering at me, ma'am ...'

'Oh, there is,' I said. 'At City Hall. Right now. There's a bad guy and he's taken down the internet and I can prove it.'

'That's impossible, ma'am.'

'Have you got any internet?'

'I'm sure it's just an outage.'

'It's sabotage! Deliberate!'

One of the women standing beside him started to yell.

'Oh my God! It's terrorists! We're under attack!'

138

'We are!' I said. 'That's why we need to stop him!'

'Don't cause panic,' said the cop. 'Nobody can "take down" the internet, lady. That ain't how it works.'

'It's them terrorists!' yelled somebody else, and everyone started getting very worked up.

'Ma'am, if you start a riot, I'm arresting you,' said the cop seriously.

'I'm not trying to start a riot. I'm telling you there's a baddie, he's done this and I know where he is! Why can't you listen to me? Can't you radio someone?!'

I realised I was screaming.

'LISTEN TO ME!'

The cop raised his radio.

'We got an inciter going on here ... request back-up. Request back-up!'

'What? What are you talking about?'

Another woman started having hysterics in the street.

'Stop screaming – I'm trying to help!'

The screaming woman redoubled her efforts.

'We're under attack!'

More and more people were being drawn close by now, staring at their phones as if they could magically bring them back to life; shouting at the sky.

'You have to listen to me!' I yelled. 'He's at City Hall! I know he is! It's a big bad man who's turned off the Wi-Fi and ... Nobody is paying attention!'

The cop took out his handcuffs.

'I've asked you to stop, ma'am,'

'You are kidding me,' I said. 'I'm helping you! I'm being a good citizen here! Everyone! Get to City Hall!'

Nobody moved.

Chapter Twenty-nine

Actually, the jail cells at the metropolitan police station weren't as bad as I might have been led to believe. They were full of hipsters for starters, who weren't causing trouble, just complaining that they'd lost drafts of their screenplays.

Anyway, it was a cell with a bench, which wasn't bad, and a woman made me some toast, which honestly wasn't bad either. I managed to make my phone call to a furious Gertie, whose tone indicated she thought jail was the least I deserved for taking her Very Special Cardigan. I wasn't sure I should have called her after all. I couldn't even tell her about the mayor's office, in case she went.

'I'm sure they'll let you out eventually,' she said stiffly.

'Gertie, this is my one phone call ...' I started. Then I stopped. Walking into the room was someone I had given up expecting to see.

'Actually, I'll call you back,' I said, handing the phone to a surprised-looking policewoman.

Oh God. Why couldn't he have worn a suit? Seriously. A nice navy blue suit, to go with his eyes. Those black-rimmed glasses that really, really suited him. Maybe even a tie. But no. It had to be the purple. Always with the purple.

'Oh wow,' said the policewoman at the desk, obviously very impressed. 'Hi, Mr Ultimate Man.'

Mr Ultimate Man. Tremendous. Maybe he could rescue the Queen of England and be Lord Ultimate Man. My heart leaped a bit though. Couldn't help it.

'GET ME OUT!' I shouted. 'There's still time!'

He turned towards me.

'Can you let her out please? I know she sounds a little unhinged, but ... '

He nodded towards me.

'Ru ... Ultimate Man!' I hissed. I hated not being able to call him by his name. Also I was suddenly incredibly embarrassed that I was locked up in a cell and he'd had to come and get me. 'I'm fine!'

'You look fine,' he said. 'Are you going to squeeze through those bars or what?'

'Hahaha,' I said. 'Where were you?'

He looked at me, then glanced at the policewoman as if to say 'not in front of her'.

'I tried to explain,' I said sullenly. 'They wouldn't listen.'

'And did yelling help?'

'Yelling did not help,' I said, rubbing my wrists ruefully. Handcuffs hurt, like, totally a lot. They pinched a bit of my skin when they were putting them on and nobody even apologised or anything.

'Are they going to charge you with anything?'

'Oh no,' simpered the policewoman. 'Not now you're here. Now, I've always wanted to ask you ... those muscles. Are they all yours? Can I have a squeeze?'

An older, male policeman walked in the room and the woman jumped back. His body language wasn't quite so acquiescent.

'You,' he sniffed.

'Hi,' said Ultimate Man in his booming Ultimate Man mid-Atlantic kind of a way. 'Nice to meet you.'

The cop grunted.

'Whatever,' he said. 'Why are you here?'

'To get my friend out of jail.'

'You're his friend?' whispered the policewoman. 'Oh my Gawd! What's he like without the mask?'

'Annoying,' I said, still cross it had taken him so long to get here.

'Oh my God, is he like your boyfriend?'

'Hahaha. No.'

She looked at me.

'No. Ha. What was I thinking?'

'Um, excuse me,' I said, offended. 'I haven't had a shower.'

She nodded as if to say, 'in your dreams, baby'.

The men were still talking.

'Are you going to bust her out or what?'

'No, no, not at all ... Is there bail? Because, um. I don't have ... '

'I didn't know you were a friend of his,' said the cop. 'We might have to hold you a bit longer.'

'Why?' I said.

'Because anyone who knows him usually ends up in trouble,' he sniffed. 'Or hadn't you noticed?'

I shot a look at Rufus, who looked slightly embarrassed.

'So what was it you were trying to get across?' said the cop, taking out his notepad. Ultimate Man turned his focus on to me. It was weird. I could tell that if he could, he'd get in my mind. But of course he couldn't; we'd sealed it off. Instead, I just had to take it on looks.

'Nothing,' I said staring at the floor, desperate to get out of there so I could talk to Ultimate Man. And I sensed that he didn't want me mentioning Frederick Cecil. Not to a bunch of cops. 'I just got a bit upset.'

'Losing a bit of computer power is absolutely no excuse for shouting at a police officer.'

'I know.'

'What were you shouting about?'

'I can't even remember now. Um, I needed to get on to Instagram.'

The cop sighed.

'Great friends you've got,' he said to Ultimate Man.

'Yeah, she's more of an acquaintance really,' he said.

'This is worse than the last one,' said the cop.

'Excuse me?' I said.

Rufus didn't say anything.

'Can we go?'

'Apparently.'

The policeman looked at me, as if trying to assess how much of a daft idiot who didn't know what she was doing and shouted if she got locked out of her social media I was, and then obviously decided that yes, yes, I was. He sighed.

'Fine,' he said. 'I'm going to give you a caution.'

'I'm cautioned,' I said.

'Shut up,' he said. 'I have to read it out. Seriously. You talk a lot for someone on the other side of those bars.'

I sat down on the bench while he droned on about rights and responsibilities, and Ultimate Man looked at the clock anxiously. Finally, I grabbed the pen and signed the piece of paper they gave me. The cop looked at me.

'I don't want to see you in here again,' he said. 'Modern life is difficult. I get it. They're fixing it. We're unbelievably busy with the signal outages. It's a lot harder for a lot of other people who don't have public tantrums.'

'I know,' I said as meekly as I could.

'Keep her out of trouble,' he said to Ultimate Man.

'That's a full-time job, sir,' said Rufus, almost pulling me by the elbow in his desperation to leave.

Chapter Thirty

'Come on,' I shouted, the second we were out of there. 'Come on!' He stood there, looking severe in the afternoon light, and I could have kissed him. From gratitude, obviously. But we needed to go.

'Where are you going? I need to keep tracing it. You've really wasted a lot of my time, Holly.'

'Are all your devices wireless?'

'Well, I need to use the most up-to-date technology, keep on top of the police scans, the CCTV; of course they're all state-of-the-art, untappable fibre-optic . . . '

'Yeah yeah yeah,' I said. 'Well, hooray for me, I figured it out.'

'How?'

I didn't want to tell him I was a bit lazy about taking clothes home from the office.

'No time,' I said. 'Never mind.'

There were no taxis, and very few people were out on the street either, and the ones who were you didn't want to go anywhere near. Most were still at home, terrified of the forthcoming apocalypse.

But I knew what was up. It was four miles or so to the mayor's office and the subway didn't appear to be running. We could make it, but it was going to be tough.

'Come on,' I said. The afternoon had grown hot and I was puffing already, but there wasn't time to worry about that. 'Hurry up!'

He stopped, looking absurdly purple in the bright sun.

'Want to come my way?' he said.

I blinked.

'Does this involve liberating those touring bicycles?' I said. 'Because I haven't got the right change ... '

'No,' said Rufus. 'No, I was thinking ... '

He indicated rather embarrassedly down an alley. And then I saw it.

'No way,' I said. 'Absolutely no way.'

'I think she's rather beautiful.'

'I think she looks like something Prince humped in 1985.'

The huge motorbike was well hidden behind a dumpster, but once he brought it out, it glowed in the light. It was vast – and bright purple.

'Oh lord,' I said, covering my eyes. 'You know what, maybe the world can just end and he can rule it if we don't have to go out in that.'

Rufus looked upset.

'I think she's rather awesome.'

'She? Has she got a name? Is it Chantelle? Is there a naked lady spray-painted on the front?'

'Fine,' he said. 'I'll meet you there.'

Hurt, he walked towards it. I sighed and charged after him.

'No, wait for me,' I said. 'Have you got a spare helmet? Ideally with, like, a tinted visor so nobody will recognise me?'

'You don't even need to come,' he said sulkily. 'If he's really in the mayor's office, I'll find him.'

'I do need to come,' I said.

I did. I needed to see that bastard's face when Ultimate Man pounded him into the ground; needed to banish the thought of him for ever, get him out of my mind and out of my dreams.

I looked apologetic.

'It's a lovely bike thing,' I added as an afterthought.

'You don't mean that,' he said. It looked like something a teenage boy would doodle on his chemistry book during a long boring afternoon among the Bunsen burners.

'Does it matter?' I said, as I heard someone throw a brick through a window of a computer shop, and a bunch of young men laughing, cackling and capering; and I remembered once more how thin the layer of civilisation appeared to be. 'Give me the helmet!'

Chapter Thirty-one

I had never been on a motorbike before, let alone a ridiculously huge one like this. I had to stretch my legs incredibly wide to get over the top of it, rolling my eyes the entire time.

'Do the girls like this?' I shouted, but not even a superpowered eardrum could hear me over the sound of the enormously revving engine.

'Hold on,' he said. 'I mean it.'

I tentatively put my arms on his waist.

'No,' he said commandingly. 'I said, hold on.'

And he grabbed my arms and locked them tightly around his waist, pulling me up against his back. I could feel his taut six-pack muscles underneath my fingers. I balled my hands into fists, then jerked back instinctively as the motorbike shot off with the most tremendous noise I had ever heard.

Thank goodness Rufus had told me to hold on. My hair streamed behind me from underneath my helmet; I sensed flames too, coming out of the exhaust as we barrelled down Fourth Avenue at the most ridiculous speed.

Parked and abandoned cars were whizzing past so quickly I

couldn't believe he had time to register them coming; I closed my eyes and, when I opened them again, we were jumping a light and dodging a huge truck with a phone company's name written on the side of it. We cut corners, skidding round at a ridiculous pace with great squealing noises, and so nearly hit almost everything that I ended up like a child on a fairground ride, closing my eyes and simply waiting for it to stop.

Closing my eyes, however, had the strange effect of me becoming less aware of the road – I couldn't even think about it – and more and more aware of how closely pressed I was against his body. The long muscles of his back as he leaned from left to right, completely – it seemed entwined – with the machine; my legs beneath his legs; my entire body pressed against him; my hands now white-knuckled tight in front of him; and I became a little less stiff and a little more trusting: I bent when he bent – far further than I would have dared or thought possible; moved when he moved; gradually found my body entwined with his and the great powerful machine; realised what he felt as the wind rushed past us; and gradually opened my eyes as the exhilaration of ploughing through the city at extraordinary, suicidal speeds and a great joy overtook me, and I wanted to shout out loud.

And then the journey was over, and he helped me down, and I was slightly out of breath and a little pink in the face.

'Sorry you had to endure that,' he said.

'No,' I said. 'No. It ... Actually, it was fine.'

The mayor's building was supposedly closed for Sunday. Of course there was a security guard on watch and some people came in and worked, but Rufus wanted to do this slightly more stealthily, and naturally I agreed. I glanced up at all the satellite systems on the roof. How could it not have occurred to anyone to check them? Then I blinked as I looked closer.

'There's people up there,' I said.

Ultimate Man was looking rather more closely.

'They're wearing police uniforms,' he said.

'But the police wouldn't come here!' I said. 'We've just left them behind.'

'I wonder if they're fake back there to convince everyone it's all under control,' said Rufus. 'It's looking that way.'

He took a large gizmo out of the motorbike and held it up.

'What's that?' I said.

'Gizmo,' he said. 'Shh.'

He focused it on the top of the building.

'Something is happening up there.' He grimaced. 'Come on. Let's go for a closer look.'

He bounced up to a low window, quickly jemmied it open.

'That isn't very sci-fi,' I complained. 'Can't you ride the bike up the steps?'

'They'll have someone on the doors,' he said. 'Do you recognise the security guard?'

'I thought it must be someone they only have on weekends,' I said.

'You don't work weekends?'

'Some of us have a work/life balance.'

He gave me a hand up, and we quietly moved out of the small sluice room we'd ended up in and out into the corridor.

'No more stupid questions,' he whispered to me.

'What about intelligent, perfectly reasonable questions?'

'This is why I don't have a sidekick.'

We carefully ascended the stairs – I remembered him, frozen in changing, that tiny, tiny half-instant I must have caught him in at the museum – and I smiled to myself, then I pointed out my office to him.

'You're sure?'

I nodded. I hoped the cardigan was still there. Would definitely up the odds for me surviving today.

'What's the code for the office?'

I felt for my pocket. Of course I didn't have my entry pass. I'd left it in my bag at Vinnie's.

'Ah,' I said.

To Rufus's credit, he only stiffened for a second before very carefully unscrewing the keypad panel and shorting the circuit out with minimum fuss.

Two men were there immediately, dressed as security guards. They looked nothing like security guards. Our security guards were fat and a bit sleepy because they normally worked two jobs, and Rodge had a great big droopy moustache which used to get coffee on the ends.

These guys had shaved heads and big Adam's apples and strong jawlines and looked like they wanted you to think they were hired killers. Also, I think they were hired killers. They looked terrifying, and the huge guns they had around their waists looked more terrifying still.

I suddenly realised a massive advantage of Ultimate Man's ridiculous suit: they had to blink while they were looking at it, in case they didn't quite believe their eyes.

It bought time.

'Hey . . . ' said one, reaching for his belt, but it was too late. Neatly and rather regretfully I thought, Ultimate Man threw them each against a wall and knocked them out. It took less than a second.

'Wow,' I said, then remembered to add, 'I'm against violence.'

Ultimate Man didn't say anything, just grunted.

'Shall I take one of their guns, just in case?'

'No!' he said, striding down the long corridor. 'I thought you were against violence.'

'Just in case, I said!'

'Have you ever shot a really big gun?'

'No.'

'Medium?'

'No.'

'Teenie-weenie little gun?'

'I'm against violence.'

'Okay, well, good. We're not starting now then.'

Close to the office in the corner, he shushed me as we drew closer. We'd met another couple of guards en route and Ultimate Man had despatched them as cleanly and efficiently as he had the first two. Now we were at my funny little office, so close to the roof; so tucked out of the way.

I glanced behind Rufus. There was nobody in there, but hooray, I could still see the cardigan. I nodded.

'What did you do? Smell him?' said Rufus.

'I have good detective skills,' I said. He glanced at me through his mask and I felt smug.

'Is this your office?' he said, looking at the sign on the door.

'Yeah, all right, whatever,' I said.

'Did you leave that cardigan on the window frame?'

'Just find the bad guy, okay?'

Rufus pushed open the door and entered carefully, quietly rendering unconscious the guard who'd been standing just behind it. The funny little fire exit door was straight ahead. We both looked at it.

'Stay here,' said Rufus. 'He's dangerous. Worse than dangerous.'

'I'm not staying here!'

I felt my face grow hot.

'You are,' he said. 'I don't want to have to knock you out as well.'

'This is because I'm a woman!'

'It's not,' he said. 'It really isn't. It's because you're a human. And I'm not, precisely. And that thing upstairs. It's an alligator in tailoring. I would no more let a human up there than I would let a baby.'

I blinked. I was frightened, but adrenalised too.

'You have to stay out the way,' he said. 'You have to.'

'Okay,' I said reluctantly.

'If you disobey me, you could kill us both.'

'OKAY! I said okay!'

'I don't know whether to believe you or not.'

'Well, you could lift that psychic screen. Just for a second.'

He shook his head. 'I can't. I can't ever do that now. Not ever.'

I blinked.

'Really?'

'Really.'

I snatched the cardigan and hugged it to myself, the soft cashmere feeling somehow comforting against my skin, then I hid in the cupboard. As soon as I started to hear the noises from up above, I understood why. In fact, as soon as Ultimate Man left and went upstairs, I realised I was completely terrified, that the bravado I was showing was only when he was there. I didn't want to confront Frederick Cecil. Didn't want to see him at all. I was a coward and I couldn't help it.

The crashing and shouting went on overhead for quite some

time. I stood in the dark, wondering how on earth I'd got here. Then I remembered that all sorts of people had got locked in the stationery cupboard at the last Christmas party, so it wasn't really that strange.

Then I heard footsteps banging down the stairwell. Was it Rufus? It had to be Rufus, didn't it? He was the hero. He'd have won. He'd have tossed Frederick Cecil off a roof or something and I for one would be glad to see him go. Well, maybe not off a roof – it was pretty tricky, this anti-violence – but far enough. Maybe just unconscious on the ground, with his aftershave and designer suits, ready to be led off to jail.

The footsteps grew closer. I wanted to cry out but didn't dare, just in case. In case it wasn't ... My mouth was dry, I realised, and I was horribly nervous all of a sudden. No. Of course Rufus would win. He always did. He always ...

BANG

The door flung open. I could barely see after the darkness of the cupboard. I screamed.

'Oh fucking hell,' drawled a voice. 'This isn't the exit.'

Chapter Thirty-two

There was a momentary pause.

'YOU!'

He stared at me through the mask, that lizard look in his green eyes.

'Frederick Cecil!' boomed a voice louder than I'd known Rufus could speak. It resounded round the room.

'Come back and fight like a man!'

'Not likely, freak!' mumbled Frederick Cecil. I shrank away towards the back of the cupboard, as if that would save me. He sniffed once, then *bang*, he slammed the door on me again, and I heard footsteps charging down the corridors and out towards the door.

I swallowed hard. I realised I was shaking. There was quiet for a long time; I couldn't have said how long. Then finally, the door opened again, slowly, and I nearly fell into Rufus's arms.

'Didn't you realise he'd gone?' he said kindly. There was a small cut above his left eye but apart from that he looked completely fine.

'Yes,' I nodded. 'He opened the door by mistake.'

He frowned.

'So did you trip him up or grab him or anything like that?'

I shook my head.

'No . . .'

'Oh yes. the anti-violence thing,' he said. 'Just as well I didn't let you up to the rooftop.'

I shook my head.

'It wasn't that,' I said quietly, wringing my hands. He waited patiently.

'I'm scared of him,' I said. 'I am so, so scared of him.'

Ultimate Man nodded.

'But I'm here,' he said.

'You won't always be here,' I said.

He shrugged.

'Yeah, sure I will be . . . Did he see you?'

I nodded.

'Yes.'

'Okay. Well, he's gone now. Don't worry.'

'He won't come after me?'

'I foiled his stupid plan.'

'What did you do?'

'Um, have you got a PhD in space engineering?'

'I swapped it for a Family Guy DVD.'

'Well. Anyway. Satellites. Reversing. Cable virus. Etcetera.'

I looked at him.

'You fixed that just now?'

'Yeah. That's why I took so long. Done now.'

We looked at each other for a moment longer.

'So, um, do you want to come out of that cupboard, or are you pretty much set on staying there? If you stay the night, you'll be early for work.'

I blinked and realised I still hadn't moved.

'Oh,' I said. 'Um.'

I also realised that I didn't want to move; that it was comfortable here in the cupboard: nobody could scare me or hurt me or change the world I was living in.

'I'll be ... Actually I might just stay here a while.'

'In the cupboard?'

Out of the open windows, I could hear cheering.

'Have you turned the internet back on?'

'Why don't you come out of there and find out?'

'I can probably ... '

Actually, I could already feel my dead phone in my pocket filling up with messages and bleeping its little head off. I snuck a glance at it. Most of them just said 'test test test' and 'my internet is down'. I put the phone away.

'So,' I said. 'I suppose there's lots of places you need to be right now?'

Ultimate Man shrugged.

'Not really.'

'Don't you have people-rescuing to do?'

'I do,' he said. 'I'm on a job right now in fact. It's called "Getting Holly out of the cupboard".'

'I'm not stuck in this cupboard!' I said hotly. 'I'm just ... I'm just hanging back. You know I am not at all as brave at hero stuff as I always assumed I would be.'

'Hmm,' said Rufus. 'You know, me neither.'

'Well, that's comforting.'

We stood there a moment longer. Then, tentatively, Ultimate Man put out his hand.

'What's that for?'

It was ridiculous, this crippling, overwhelming anxiety I felt. It

157

wasn't like me. Okay, so I wasn't super-brave. But I was a coper, wasn't I? I could handle things. Even bad things, like that guy who Ultimate Man had just chased out of town. So why was I being so pathetic? I felt awful for wasting his time.

'Look, it's okay; just go,' I said. 'I am totally all right here. Nothing to worry about. I'll just . . . finish tidying up the cupboard, then I'll be fine.'

'I'm afraid, ma'am, it's part of the hero's code. No one gets left behind. In a cupboard.'

We were at a stand-off. Then, slowly, he took a step forward.

'What are you doing?'

'Well, you seem awfully fond of that cupboard.'

'Mmm?'

'I thought I might join you.'

'You can't come into my cupboard! Two people are only allowed in at Christmas parties! And anyway it's my . . . '

It was too late. He was already in there.

'Yeah,' he said. 'Nice. I like the smell of marker pens.'

'You're blocking out the light,' I said ungraciously. 'Your shoulders are too broad.'

We looked at each other. His body was very, very close to mine in the dark.

'I could go out with you. Or we could just stay in here.'

'I thought they'd been trying to get you to come out of the closet for years,' I said, trying to smile.

'I have never understood what that means,' he said.

'It doesn't matter.'

He looked at me. He was so much taller than me; I felt like burying myself in his chest. Which was better than what I'd been feeling just moments before.

'If I took your hand, do you think you could step out with me?'

158

I blinked. My heart was still racing, although I was no longer sure exactly what the cause of that was.

'Can you stay with me?'

'Yes.'

'I mean, every second?'

'Oh. No. But we could probably go get something to eat. If you like.'

His hand found my hand in the dark and he took it. Even through his gloves I could feel his strong fingers. My hand was dwarfed in his. I let him take it. He squeezed– rather too hard – and I very gently squeezed him back.

'Okay,' I said.

'Okay,' he said. 'Let's try it on a count of three.'

And I tried to leave all my dark thoughts about Frederick Cecil behind me in the dark of the cupboard; felt Rufus's strong grip; stepped out into the light with him.

Chapter Thirty-three

We passed the groaning guards in the hallway, Ultimate Man shaking his head. 'Seriously, the job description for these guys totally blows.'

'What was he doing?'

'Proving a point,' said Ultimate Man, frowning. 'Unfortunately, he refuses to let on as to what that point is.'

'This doesn't make any sense,' I said. 'It must be something else. Are you sure he's not just trying to get people to change broadband suppliers?'

Ultimate Man smiled at that. Then he went quiet for a bit.

'Well,' he said. Then, 'Hmm.'

We got to the back door of the mayor's office. There were already people massing around the front, police cars and whatnot. We could see them through the windows. We stood at the back door. He looked down at our interlocked hands.

'Can you ... Do you think you'll be okay to let go now? I don't think you'd like it if we got papped.'

I blinked. 'Seriously? There's paps?'

'I probably didn't hide the motorbike well enough.'

'Oh,' I said.

'If it's worth anything,' said Rufus softly, 'I think you're strong enough. I think you're more than strong enough. I couldn't have found him without you. I think you did brilliantly.'

'I should have tripped him up.'

'You absolutely shouldn't have,' said Rufus fiercely. 'That was a dumb thing to say. You're very lucky he didn't kill you.'

'Are you sure he won't come back and finish the job?'

'I think I made my message perfectly clear. Frederick Cecil will never succeed in Centerton while I'm here, okay?'

I nodded.

'Yes.'

And then – much to my disappointment – he unfurled his fingers, and my hand, feeling strangely empty, returned to my side.

'Come on,' he said. 'I was serious about being hungry.'

'Hang on,' said Ultimate Man as we reached the door.

'Are you going to change?' I said eagerly. Obviously he didn't want to walk down the street in costume.

'Yep.'

'Can I watch?'

'Can you what?'

'Can I see you do it? C'mon, I only saw half of it last time.'

But then someone shouted, 'Hey, there's Ultimate Man! Did you turn the Wi-Fi back on! Thanks, man!' and he turned round to acknowledge it mildly and I glanced briefly at my phone and when I looked up again he'd gone and instead, out of an office was walking a smartly dressed man in a suit. With black-rimmed glasses.

'Where do you hide the glasses?' I said suspiciously.

'I don't know what you mean,' he said serenely, and I tried to

161

see if there was a slight smirk at the corner of his mouth, because I couldn't tell exactly.

'Also the tie is a nice touch,' I said. 'Adds to the trickiness level.'

It was ridiculous, really, but suddenly there we were: a slightly scruffy post-police cell girl and a clean-cut rather metrosexual young gentleman, walking through streets which were suddenly thronged, full of people laughing with relief, texting each other with wild abandon, uploading pictures of the sky onto their Instagram accounts and liking everyone's statuses, even though everyone's statuses were just 'HOORAY FOR THE INTERNET!'. We are all in blissful ignorance, I thought. And then I thought, Maybe that's what Frederick Cecil wants us to think.

Chapter Thirty-four

Out on the street, shops were opening up, people were talking to each other in cheerful relief, debating what had happened and how funny it had been. Nobody mentioned the panic, the looting, the fires, the palpable sense of utter tension and horror which had been there, on the streets, in the buildings, in the bars.

There would be a few heavy heads too, not just mine. I wondered how I was going to explain this to my mother. So far, about the only thing I hadn't disappointed her on was 'staying out of jail'. Maybe I'd just skip that part and tell her about Vinnie winning some new award or something.

Rufus waited until we were out in the crowd.

'What?' he said. 'Really, what was it? What made you realise what was up?'

I shrugged.

'I'm just hyper-aware I guess. After everything that happened. Anything to do with ... that guy. I just paid attention.'

'Well, it worked,' he said. 'Well done.'

I grinned with pleasure. 'Thanks. Vinnie helped.'

'Who's Vinnie?'

'My brother.'

'Does he know about me?'

'No,' I said. 'And he wouldn't care if he did. But Frederick Cecil . . . I mean, aren't your spidey senses tingling?'

He rolled his eyes.

'Peter's got nothing to do with this.'

'You know him?'

'We meet at, you know, trade conferences and so on.'

'I do not know!' I said. 'Tell me. You guys have conferences? With, like, stands and stuff?'

He cut me a sideways glance as we passed a pretzel vendor, and I realised I hadn't eaten since breakfast and was utterly starving.

'Cor, the food is bad in prison,' I lied, eying the cheese pretzels longingly. Rufus looked awkward.

'Um,' he said.

'What?'

'I don't . . . I don't have my wallet.'

'Oh God!' I said. 'I didn't mean. I didn't expect you to pay. I was just saying do you want a pretzel?'

'Um,' he said. 'Sure.'

I walked towards the stand, then turned back.

'So hang on, you manage the glasses but not the wallet?'

'Something like that,' said Rufus. A smile played on my lips.

'You are *weird*, man. What do you want on your pretzel?'

'Whatever you like is good.'

'Well, I like cheese.' I said.

'It's very bad for you.'

I looked at him.

'Thanks for that, I didn't know,' I said.

'Yes, it's high in salt and saturated . . . '

He looked at me.

'Oh. Are you doing that thing?'

'What thing?'

'That sarcasticky thing.'

'No, I totally wasn't doing that,' I said.

'Good.'

He squinted.

'Are you doing it again?'

I walked up to him.

'Look,' I said. 'When you had that lab accident, I know it changed you physically. But it couldn't actually have done anything to your sarcasm detectors. There you're on your own. That's your fault.'

I bought two pretzels then, out of sheer defiance, two hot dogs too, and handed him one. He took a bite.

'Oh, that's good,' he said.

'See? That wasn't so hard,' I said, passing him an iced tea.

We walked on under the sunshine; it was a beautiful afternoon, looking to turn into a gorgeous evening, warm, with a gentle breeze stopping it from being that oppressive city hotness where the buildings act like giant radiators and every breath feels sopping wet.

Here, in what often felt like a difficult, dangerous town, the blossoms were coming out in the city parks, old people were playing chess in the paved squares, the hoboes seemed to have vanished and the pathetic town trees that lined the pavement all winter were doing their best to bud and flower. It was rather lovely.

'Tell me,' he said quietly, in that very low voice he had, and I suddenly had to remind myself that actually this wasn't a date, that standing very close to someone didn't always mean you were in a relationship since the 1800s, and I remembered even faster as we walked past a building site and a trowel fell from the scaffolding. Rufus caught it deftly and placed it gently on the ground without either looking at it or breaking step.

I swallowed. Today seemed like a dream now. A silly panic over nothing, already fading into the distance. A power outage. That was all.

'Vinnie used his old dial-up connection,' I said. 'It's what they used to use before ... '

'I know.' He shook his head 'I had all my top technology, all my latest development tools and guides – I had absolutely everything working on it. And I couldn't get it. It never even occurred to me to go retro.'

'Yes, we're awesome,' I said.

'What was it?'

'Well, with the old modems, the pictures come through really slowly. Like, line by line. And it didn't work very far or very fast. But I could tell from ... the curl. There's a curl on the top of his hair.'

Rufus squinted.

'What do you mean? Like in his hair?'

'You know, like where his hair is at the top? That ... kiss-curl?'

It was a ridiculous word to describe it. And I was full of embarrassment that I'd even ever noticed.

'A kiss-curl?'

'It's a kind of ... oh, I don't know. But it was him. There was no internet, but if you got into the old internet ... It was a picture of him. I swear. A threat. And I was rushing out to tell the policeman because somebody – that is, you – who might know where to find him, didn't bother to leave me any way of contacting him. You.'

'I thought we could communicate on that computer programme.'

'Uh-huh.'

That time I think he got the sarcasm.

We sat down on a bench by the river. There were sailing boats on the bay, the sun glistening on the water.

'What on earth does he want?' mused Rufus.

'Well, he was probably just testing it. I mean, you keep that up, you keep up with the panicking and the internet and hold the city to ransom like that,' I said. 'It's awful. I mean, the whole place was falling apart. Even though we're now all pretending it wasn't and we were all cool and it was fine. Another two hours – one nightfall and it would have got incredibly violent. Loads of people would have died. Awful.'

'I agree with you,' said Rufus. 'Why didn't he issue a ransom demand though?'

'Maybe he was doing that. Maybe that's what he was doing on the dial-up. But it was too slow to come through and then we got there.'

We pondered this as I spotted a van parked up by the side of the scrubby park.

'Do you want an ice cream?'

'You're buying me a lot of food,' frowned Rufus.

'I'm buying me a lot of food,' I explained. 'To help me recover from the terrible ordeal of my terrible day. With you, I'm just being polite.'

'Oh okay,' said Rufus. 'No, thanks.'

We sat watching the boats, me licking my ice cream and occasionally offering him some. Rufus shook his head, grabbing a runaway dog which was bounding away, fruitlessly pursued by its old lady owner, its lead bouncing in the wind.

'Here you are, ma'am,' he said. 'You need to keep a stronger hold.'

'Thanks!' said the old lady. 'I'd like to keep a stronger hold of you!'

I looked at both of them and rolled my eyes.

Rufus sighed.

'I'm going to have to go and find him.'

'How?'

'I don't know. There doesn't seem to be any trace of him anywhere. Do you know any more than you've told me? You've been closer than most.'

I shook my head.

'He smells of cologne,' I said. 'Have you got superpowered sniffing skills?'

'I don't,' said Rufus. 'Otherwise the smells in this city would have felled me long ago.'

I looked at him. His eyelashes were long and thick behind the glasses, which I wasn't sure even worked. I wondered if it would be rude to ask to try them on. Probably. His body was less absurdly intimidating in a suit. I suppose that's why people wore suits after all: to cover up their imperfections. The fact that he didn't actually appear to have any didn't detract from the effect at all.

Apart from the dark glossy sheen of hair on his head, he appeared to be completely hairless; nothing protruding from his shirt cuffs (I had always rather liked a hairy forearm; it seemed to me a good glimpse of something animalistic and sexy underneath a well-cut suit) or beneath his shirt, not even a stray eyebrow hair. He looked like he'd had them painted on. It made him look absurdly metrosexual, as if he was doing it all on purpose and spent hours a day looking in the mirror.

A child's cry rose in the air.

'Be right back,' he said, and he was almost instantly, lost pacifier duly found and, he explained, sterilised.

'Your breath sterilises pacifiers?' I said.

'Uh. Not all the time.'

Oh but he was the strangest, strangest thing. I found myself still staring at him, even as he looked up.

'And when I've found him again – when I find him, he won't be expecting it; he won't be the instigator,' he carried on, as if nothing had just happened. 'And then we'll see what he's getting at.'

He looked out over the water, planning. I turned back and looked over the city. Both of us were quiet for a second.

'Well, this is the weirdest date I've ever been on,' I said, just to break the ice. He turned, startled.

'But this isn't . . . this. Oh. Sorry. Are you . . . ?'

'Oh,' I said in return, remembering once more him telling me how much he only wanted a friend. 'I didn't mean it like that. I was only making a joke.'

I thought again of the policewoman's disdain when she'd suggested I might be his girlfriend. It had stung, I couldn't deny it.

'Do you ever say anything serious? Anything at all?' he said.

'Not if I can help it,' I said. 'It seems to me everything in the world is serious enough already.'

He looked at me.

'I never thought of it like that.'

'That's because you are so very dark and brooding,' I said. 'Good for you!'

We were silent a little longer. Then he stood up.

'I'd better go,' he said awkwardly.

'I know, I know,' I said, holding up my hands. I knew I'd said completely the wrong thing. I stood up too.

'Friends, I know.'

The sky was starting to turn pink just behind us, the light turning more golden, softer on us. He looked straight at me in that discomfiting way he had. Then he put out his hand to my cheek.

'Holly,' he said. 'I'm ... You have to know. I'm not built that way.'

'Are you sure?' I said.

There was a slight pause.

'It's ... it's for the best,' he said. And he very lightly cupped my cheek in his hand. Then in the very next instant, he was gone. I don't mean he walked away. I mean, he was gone.

Chapter Thirty-five

A millisecond later, before I'd even blinked, he was back.

'What?' I said. I was cross with myself and felt dizzy, and the day had given me too much to take in.

He gave me a small piece of paper.

'What's that?'

'Oh,' he said, looking slightly embarrassed. 'It's my telephone number.'

'You wrote it down on a piece of paper? You didn't, like, beam it directly to my phone or anything?'

He shrugged.

'Seemed easier. Less traceable.'

I looked at it. 'Well, is that a 1 or a 7?'

He frowned. 'Do you want it or not?'

'Yes please.'

I took it and looked down smiling.

'So do you have, like, a bat phone? Is this the bat phone?'

'No.'

'Is it purple though? Is it?'

He looked at me.

'I thought . . . I mean, I thought it would be quite cool to have a purple phone.'

'Did you?' I said.

'Yeah, well, anyway . . . '

'Thanks,' I said finally. 'But honestly, am I only to ring it in the event of a terrible emergency which threatens the entire city?'

He looked at me.

'You can ring it whenever you like,' he said, those eyes as blue and open as the sky, and I wanted to curse him again for making me feel like an awkward teenager, for reading far more into his words than I knew he ever wished to say. And I knew for a fact it wouldn't do me the least bit of good.

Chapter Thirty-six

Gertie eyed it for a long time.

'I thought you'd be pleased,' I said. I'd added a bottle of wine in with the cardigan, just to be on the safe side.

'I want you to dry-clean it.'

'I don't have nits or anything.'

'Don't take my stuff.'

'GERT!' I shouted to her departing back. 'How about we pretend absolutely none of that ever happened, just like the city is pretending with the whole Wi-Fi thing?'

It was true. People were more or less just pretending it had never happened. It did occur to me, somewhat despondently, that if humans didn't pretend that terrible things weren't really happening all around all the time, day after day, nobody would ever get out of bed, but I decided to forget about thinking like that.

The papers, of course, were all about the blackout – with, I couldn't help noticing, an undercurrent of jubilation in good old-fashioned physical media – and thankfully utterly no mention of the mayor's office, except more or less giving the impression that the city had fixed the problem itself. So it was business as usual as I slipped into the office the next day: bigging up the mayor's office. Ignoring the terrible things which appeared to be happening to our town.

Nelson was already there. He looked up, embarrassed.

'Hi there!' he said, grinning cheerfully and going pink at the same time.

'Hey,' I said. I had completely forgotten about him, but seeing him reminded me of how scary it had felt and how scary it had been at the time. I sighed. Vinnie hadn't wanted me to go over when I let him know I was fine – of course. And Gertie and DuTroy had taken themselves off for an early, cardigan-wearing evening. And of course I wasn't even thinking about how I'd made a fool of myself in front of Rufus. So I was feeling a bit lonely and fed up. But Nelson at least seemed pleased to see me.

'Ha, I guess I got a bit panicky there at the weekend, huh?' he said in such faux-casual tones I could tell he'd totally been rehearsing it the entire time. 'I mean, totally, it was fine; I was pretty cool about it in the end.'

'I could tell,' I said. Poor guy: he was sweating, even in the air-con. 'Don't worry – everyone was terrified.'

'Really?' he said. 'Because now everyone seems totally fine.'

'Yeah, they're faking it,' I said. 'Well, some of them are faking it and some of them have the memory of goldfish and haven't the faintest idea what they were doing. And the rest of them were just drunk.'

'Oh,' he said. 'Good.'

He glanced up, rubbing his eyes. His hay-fever seemed bad too.

'Did you have a nice weekend?'

174

'Did I have a nice weekend?' I mused. I thought about it. 'Apart from that. Do you know what? Let's not go into it.'

'Pretty quiet?'

I opened up some new initiative from the parks department and sighed.

'Mine was very quiet,' said Nelson in a low voice. Then he looked up at me nervously, and I got a very odd sensation that I knew what was coming.

'You know, I'm new in town. I mean . . . '

He flushed a deep red.

'If you ever wanted to show someone round . . . if you weren't too busy or anything . . . I mean, I don't want to intrude.'

I thought about it. I'd already had quite a few ridiculous things that weren't dates. I might as well have something that looked like it was.

'Sure.'

'Dating the guy you sit next to and will have to sit next to for the next two years?' said Gertie. 'Are you sure that's wise?'

She was talking to me again. Or, well, she was talking down to me again which wasn't exactly the same thing.

Now I was torn. On the one hand, it felt absolutely great just to be having a normal conversation again about normal stuff, like dating.

On the other hand, Gertie was being really annoying.

'I mean, seriously, was Ultimate Man really not for you?'

'He . . . he doesn't date. He's like, I don't know . . . covered in weird tentacles or something. Anyway, it doesn't count.'

'Under the mask he's all tentacles?'

'Yes. Can we drop this?'

'DuTroy, you know Ultimate Man is all tentacles?'

'Cool!' came the voice from the next room.

'So you're going to date your workmate? Oooh.'

'We're not dating! We're just going out to see the city.'

'You and a man going out the two of you together doing things. Sounds like a date.'

'Yes, well, I thought that the last time a man invited me over to his house and cooked for me and I will tell you that was so not a date it was … What's the opposite of a date?'

'Visiting your grandma in a home?'

'Yeah. That.'

'That *would* have been cool though,' mused Gertie. 'Dating Ultimate Man.'

'Like when I did it before and you called the police?' I said.

'Excuse me!' said Gertie.

'I know, I know. Thank you,' I said. 'And also, shut up.'

'What was he like? I never really got the chance to ask.'

I smiled ruefully.

'He was … He was sweeter than you'd think,' I said.

Gertie frowned.

'Oh no – I assumed he was very sweet. I was rather hoping he'd be a bit manly or powerful. You know, all the good stuff.'

'He made a good puttanesca sauce.'

Gertie smiled.

'Oh, I know: I've got his cookbook.'

I rolled my eyes.

'Fine. Okay. Forget it. You know far more about him than I do. I'm not going to tell you any more.'

'Is there any more?'

'That's not the point.'

We looked at each other.

'Sorry,' she said.

'That's all right,' I said. 'Turns out a radioactive guy with weird powers who wears Lycra isn't the one for me after all.'

There was a pause.

'Did you find out his secret identity?' she asked quietly. I knew she wouldn't be able to help it. I thought for a moment. She would absolutely bust a gut if I told her it was the guy she'd spotted in the bar; the one she already thought was super-hot. It would be a good way of making it up to her for Cardigangate too. And it wasn't like I was even going to see him again. It would be funny to slag him off every time he turned up at benefits and stuff.

'Neh,' I said.

'I wish DuTroy was a bit more dynamic like that,' she said briefly. I looked at her. It was *so* unlike her to diss him in any way.

'No, you don't,' I said shortly.

'No, I probably don't,' she said, and immediately changed the subject.

'Okay, you might as well book the boring boy. You are definitely going through a good patch though.'

'Maybe I am,' I said. 'I should probably strike while the iron's hot.'

'It's probably because I'm out of commission,' mused Gertie.

'You think that,' I said. And we smiled at each other, friendship restored.

'But I'm locking my cupboard!' she yelled after me as I left the room.

Chapter Thirty-seven

I was oddly not too nervous about meeting Nelson.

Well, maybe a bit – obviously I was a little anxious. It was a date. I'm not dead.

But after all the thrill and adrenalin and disappointment of everything that had happened recently, this definitely came down the list. And it would be fine: Nelson wasn't a weirdo who dressed up and ran about in a cape every night because of some unexplored parental issues from being injured in a lab. He was a real, proper, nice boy. Who I should be far more interested in, if I had the least bit of sense.

Plus I liked his country ways and good manners. Before this whole nonsense started, I'd had enough of men who had taken me out and interviewed me to see if I was easy enough or the right size or hot enough for them and called those dates and then acted all unconcerned when I suggested paying my half of the bill then let me pay it anyway.

I had had enough of those.

Nelson might be a clumsy klutz but he was a sweet clumsy klutz, who appeared to have absolutely no interest in furrow-browedly saving the world, which at the moment was enough for me.

It was another beautiful day the following Saturday (we had studiously ignored each other, and not eaten lunch together all week (which passed without incident, thank goodness). I had started to notice more things I liked about him: his slightly shambolic bulk, which at first I'd thought a bit messy, now seemed comforting and solid; he also had the loveliest soft brown eyes, and soft curly hair which I rather liked. I didn't know why I hadn't thought he was good-looking at all; I thought I could see what Liz could see.

So by the time the weekend arrived, I was quite excited. Still stung by that policewoman's snide comments, I put on a cherry patterned dress I'd always thought was a little fancy to wear out, as if I would pair it with a red hat and stilettos in an eighties movie (I did not).

I did though put a nice red lipstick on and a big pair of sunglasses, which I felt gave me a touch of je ne sais quoi.

'Oh hi, Joan Collins,' said Gertie, who was in her sweatpants even as the sun came blazing in.

'At least I'm making an effort,' I said to Gertie.

'You look beautiful whatever you wear, babe,' said DuTroy, kissing Gertie.

'Oh *bleargh*!' I said. 'I am *so* out of here.'

Nelson had asked me to pick the venue, somewhere nice and touristy, and I'd instantly thought of Centerton Tower.

I hadn't been up the Centerton Tower since ... well, since I was a child, I think. It was the kind of thing tourists wanted to do when they came to Centerton, and I just tended to let them get on with it, doing funny perspective photographs and putting quarters in the penny-stamping machine, that kind of thing.

I suppose I felt it went with hats with supposedly humorous slogans on them and bum bags and tennis shoes and shorts and slightly confused people with huge cameras squinting in the sun; going to matinees of things; getting in the way and eating dinner at 5 p.m. in the afternoon at places that had pictures of their food in the windows. If I ever save up enough money to go absolutely anywhere, I swear I won't eat in places which are just full of other sad tourists chewing sadly on picture menus in the windows (I probably will though). All of this, of course, says far more about me than it does about Centerton tourists.

When I first moved to Centerton, of course the idea of doing anything touristy was just rank insecurity. In case anyone who saw me would instantly know I didn't 'belong'. In fact, of course as I stayed there longer and got a job and started to feel more at home. And discovered that nobody really belonged. There was no such thing in Centerton. Native Centropilitans disdained their hometown and talked a lot about Italy and Paris and 'KL' and were basically busy being a bunch of the most terrible kinds of entitled pricks you can conceivably envisage.

The tourists you could spot by their hats, obviously. And the rest of us were all from smaller towns, smaller cities, other places, who had all turned up nervous and weirded out and ready to work our heads off, so there really wasn't much difference between us after all. But by then I'd been there too long, and there was always a new cocktail bar to try out or shopping to do, or extra jobs to cover just to make rent, so the idea of seeing the things the city was famous for just got further and further away.

Nelson, though, was totally delighted when I suggested the

idea and couldn't believe I'd been working in Centerton for years and had never even been inside.

He wasn't, thank goodness, wearing a hat when he turned up – I had been worried. In fact, I realised I had been worried about his choice of weekend wardrobe. It had occurred to me briefly that he might be one of those guys who just can't dress themselves, who look totally fine in a weekday suit and tie; then it hits casual time and they're getting down with their mum-waisted jeans and white sneakers and socks and tucked-in shirts and paunches you hadn't noticed were there and weekend earrings. Please let him not look like that, I avowed. Seriously I wasn't a clothes snob – I don't know what the problem with a white T-shirt and some Levi 501s is –but dating one guy this month who wore a purple Lycra fricking catsuit was probably enough without having to deal with one of Go West as well.

Thank goodness he approached in an open-necked check shirt – yes, a little safe, but it could be so much worse – and chinos (perfectly acceptable) with plain boots. Suits are so dangerous for men. At least with women in the office you can get a hint, but with men, they can look fine all week – then its double denim all the way from here till Sunday night.

He waved unselfconsciously, his large arms flailing and the sun glinting off his glasses. I smiled back; I couldn't help it. Considering how crippled with awkwardness Rufus seemed to be at absolutely everything, and how ridiculously cool some of the other losers I'd dated were, Nelson was such a refreshing change.

'You look nice!' he said. 'Different from the office.'

Huh.

'Good different?'

'Yes,' he said. 'Not that you don't look lovely, of course, you know, every day – not that I think about you like that when I'm looking, although of course if I was but I'm not ...'

'Calm down,' I said.

'Okay,' he said. He glanced up at the huge tower, ninety storeys high and the tallest building in the world when it was built. It wasn't so much its height that got people now, but rather its exquisite, no-expense-spared gilding and art deco styling, surrounded as it was by every new building in Centerton, which were tedious ugly glass boxes, as if someone was trying to rebuild the city out of Minecraft blocks, or felt we all had a desperate desire to look at other people's unused exercise equipment through their gigantic windows. All glass above, cruddy filthy mean streets below.

I mean, there was loads more money in the world now than when Centerton Tower was built. But every corner, every angle had been thought about, decorated, made deliberately beautiful by people who cared about it, not thrown up in a tearing speed by people who didn't live here to act as money boxes for other people who didn't live here. It made me sad.

'You seem sad,' said Nelson mildly, as we watched the beautiful old-fashioned pointer follow the floor numbers of the lift.

'I am,' I said. 'Look how beautiful this is. And all the new stuff is horrible.'

'Maybe it's just beautiful because it's old. Maybe at the time they thought it was really overdone and cheesy.'

'Hmm,' I said. 'And do you reckon we'll think these new buildings are gorgeous in eighty years' time?'

'They won't be here in eighty years' time,' said Nelson. 'They're horribly built.'

I sighed.

'I liked it when life was simpler,' I said as we gave our tickets to a man in an old-fashioned hat and red coat who opened the lift doors for us.

'I think there are simpler places than Centerton,' said Nelson mildly.

'Where are you from?' I said as the lift started clunkily to ascend.

'You wouldn't have heard of it,' said Nelson. 'Lots of wheat.'

'Sounds awesome,' I said. 'Why did you come here?'

He blinked.

'My ... my uncle died. He was raising me, him and my aunt.'

I looked at him.

'Why?'

'My parents died. When I was a baby. I don't really remember them.'

'That's awful.'

'Oh, I don't know. Losing them when I knew them would have been awful. Being sent to an orphanage, or a family that didn't love me – that would have been awful. But, you know. You don't miss what you never had. And Uncle Al and Aunt Maisie were great to me. I mean, absolutely the best.'

He had gone quite pale, I noticed, and was staring at his feet. His hair was gelled down too much. But in a funny way, it was rather touching that he had gone to too much effort rather than too little.

'It must have been awful to lose your uncle,' I said softly.

He nodded.

'Yes. Yes, it was. It was my aunt who wanted me to get away ... make something of myself. I would have stayed. But we needed the money too.'

The lift dinged. He looked up and smiled awkwardly.

'And there you are. My entire life story in one lift journey.'

'Very good, sir,' said the lift operator in the hat. I smiled.

'Well, it is quite sad. But I see what you mean. Do you have pictures of your parents?'

There was a slightly strained silence.

'Not really,' he said, and I felt awful for going so far.

Given that it was after the summer holidays, the crowds were gone – back at work and school and college – even though the weather was still heavenly, and we had practically the entire observation deck to ourselves.

The structure was long and thin up to this point, the eightieth-floor viewing deck. Above us, stretching overhead, was the infamous Revolving Restaurant, haunt of tourists and putative seduction love nest of Liz. It loomed overhead like a vast flying saucer, a set of circular steps leading up to the velvet rope that stopped simple tourists not ready to commit to turning round slowly with a seafood chowder.

I suddenly felt ridiculous to have lived here as an adult for so long and never been up here. What was the point of a tall city if you spent all day on the shadowy grounds and dingy nightclubs? It was noisy; the wind blew quite harshly, but the view itself was exhilarating: I wanted to lean out as far as I dared over the balustrades, to the corners where the carved brass gargoyles sat, protecting this city.

'Wow!' I said. My cherry-red skirt was already blowing around my legs, and I felt giddy and happy, despite Nelson's sad background; just to be on a date at the weekend, with a proper nice guy who told me things about himself and didn't behave all weird and chiselled and terrified of intimacy and stuff. Nelson never even needed to know that I'd spent time in jail.

I looked at him. The wind didn't even ruffle his hair as he focused carefully, looking through one of the telescopes, surveying the city. From up here, you couldn't hear the wail of the sirens or the shouts of the early-morning loaders or the late-night glass recyclers or the bin lorries or the taxis honking or the people shouting. From here, it was serene and beautiful; even the glass box towers simply caught the light and glinted and reflected back until the city shone all the way up to the park at the top; even, on a lovely day, through the brown and muddy rivers we sat among. I watched the boats come and go, and the tiny toy aeroplanes queue politely to land in the distance, and felt like Centerton was the world, and we were in the very centre of it, and it was a toy set to us.

Looking out, I could almost understand what Frederick Cecil thought, what Rufus thought, that this was a city you could hold in the palm of your hand. So small. Did Rufus, I wondered, think like this all the time? Is this what he saw everywhere he went: a tiny snow dome he could shake up at will? A box of lego; a child's toy to fix? An absurd power? And why was I thinking about Rufus again?

'Hey!' shouted Nelson. 'Come here – I can totally see the most gorgeous roof garden!'

I took a deep breath and smiled. Down in the city, with its dangers and wars, that was crazy. But up here, it was wonderful.

'I would love to,' I said, and I peered and followed his finger where he was pointing, and sure enough, to my absolute surprise, at the top of one of those utterly bland and featureless glass buildings, towering up from the street without any eye-catching or redeeming features at all, at the very top, someone had ridiculously built a perfect – absolutely perfect – little white clapperboard country house, complete with green shutters, a front door – this is twenty storeys in the air – a weathervane and a chimney. It was completely astonishing. It sat there, looking perfectly at home, among a water tower and a ventilation shaft. It got even stranger: it was fenced in all around with, yes, a white picket fence, and inside there was grass, flowerbeds, what looked like a herb garden and – no, it couldn't be.

'Are those chickens?' I said, dumbfounded.

'I think I'm going to love this city,' said Nelson gleefully.

'Someone has a country house retreat in Centerton. Amazing.' I shook my head.

'I think it's wonderful,' said Nelson. 'Everyone should do it.'

'Get a bit noisy with the cockerels,' I said, but I was still delighted I'd seen it. I hoped a plump lady who baked a lot lived there. In fact, a bit of me slightly hoped she had no idea she was in Centerton at all.

After that. we had to look everywhere. Nelson wanted to know every area of the city; wanted to glance into the theatres, where the stagehands and the understudies sat on the roof in the sunshine, sharing cigarettes; wanted to zoom in on the tennis courts in the little parks, and horses pawing impatiently on the ground in the big ones. He was just delighted with everything. From here, you couldn't make out the graffiti on the corrugated doors, or the discarded needles in the gutters.

But I found I didn't mind. His exuberant happiness about everything, his optimistic nature – I wondered if it came from such an unusual and difficult start. Regardless, it was absolutely refreshing, particularly when he said, 'I am totally starving! I sure could do a hotdog!' in a way that didn't involve lecturing me about my health, or explaining in great detail why they were almost totally sure they were allergic to gluten.

In the end, we did something even more ridiculous than I could have imagined: another six storeys up Centerton Tower was the Revolving Restaurant Liz had suggested on Nelson's first day. I had only ever imagined it could be tourist trap, overpriced idiot fodder. We looked at each other wickedly, and dived inside.

It might have been all of those touristy things, but it was also tremendous fun. Nelson frowned at the drinks menu – though not the prices, which were a disgrace to all living things – but I pointed out you could hardly come up the Centerton Tower and not have a martini and he concurred, so we ate terrible 'gourmet' hot dogs, and got lost coming back from the toilet (the toilets were in the middle, and did not rotate, which was probably a wise choice on behalf of the builders) and giggled, and stumbled and then ate some awful fried chicken and an even worse Caesar salad, and in the weirdest of ways, the terrible overpriced food didn't matter in the slightest – in fact made it even funnier – and we vied with each other to order the most ridiculous desserts, which is how I ended up with a ridiculous mound of about nine different flavours of ice cream, whipped cream, fruit, sprinkles and – to top it all off – a cherry and a sparkler.

We both burst out laughing, and then impulsively, Nelson grabbed the cherry off the top of the dessert and popped it into my mouth, and as its ridiculous sweetness burst on my tongue, I found myself looking up at him, suddenly realising it was hard to tell what colour his eyes were against the shifting shades of the sky; the restaurant was empty, for everyone had gone. He looked at me, kind of faux-casually and said:

'So, I mean, this will probably sound really forward and everything and totally out of place and I don't want to … I mean …'

He had gone bright red and was stuttering.

'But I just wondered if … I wondered if you were dating anyone?'

'Um,' I said, even though it was a perfectly normal question.

'Oh, you are,' he said. 'I knew … I mean, I thought not. I hoped not. But, you know, of course you're dating someone. I bet he's . . . Well, it's none of my business.'

He was stuttering all over the place now, and I felt awful for him.

I blinked and swallowed carefully, looking at him. He smiled, a sweet, hopeful, endearing smile, and I thought, Do you know, this might just . . . This could . . .

'No, no,' I said, putting all last remaining thoughts of Rufus firmly out of my head. There was no point in thinking about someone who was completely unattainable. I might as well be thinking about a Jonas brother. Seriously. Okay, not a Jonas brother. Someone famous and attractive.

I realised I was distracting myself and looked back at Nelson's sweet, sincere face. The large, comforting bulk of him and everything he represented. Safety. Stability. Things I had had absolutely no experience of lately. I looked at his unusually wide mouth. It didn't seem to go with the mildness of the rest of his face. I liked it.

'I'm not dating anyone,' I said, and he looked pinker than ever and said, 'Well, you know, wow, I mean, wow, that's good. I mean . . . '

I didn't say anything and just waited for him to stop talking. Which he did, staring me straight in the eye. I looked back at him and looked down at my hand, which I started inching forwards . . . just a little . . .

A sudden burst of thunder split the sky. Up here, it felt incredibly close and was incredibly loud. I jumped and turned around. Without us even noticing – we had obviously been wrapped up in food and chat and ice cream – the weather had changed utterly: clouds were scudding in from the bay, ominously coloured, with a yellowish tinge like a bruise, and CRACK – an enormous fork of lightning bolted through the sky.

'WOAH!' I said. I'm not usually frightened of storms, but being right up here in the middle of one ... well, I wasn't sure about that. I felt very exposed and stood up quickly to see what was going on.

Suddenly he was at my back.

'Are you all right?'

He felt reassuringly solid beside me; his height and his heft belied the soft goofiness of his nature.

'Um ... '

He tentatively put a hand on my shoulder.

'Excuse me?'

A waiter came bustling up. I noticed we'd stopped revolving.

'I'm afraid during thunderstorms we normally evacuate all visitors.'

Nelson frowned.

'Well, sir, I believe this tower has stood through plenty of thunderstorms in the last eighty years or so.'

The waiter nodded.

'It certainly has, sir.'

He was trying to out-sir Nelson, I noticed, with a sarcastic Centerton sir rather than Nelson's proper country-boy sir. This would be totally lost on Nelson, obviously. Had he not been there, I would certainly have pointed out that you don't get to sarcastically sir people when you work in a *revolving restaurant*.

The little man went on:

'Unfortunately many of our visitors have not, and we have known it cause a little hysteria from time to time, which is rather more dangerous for our visitors than our lightning rod.'

CRACK. An enormous bolt seemed to land three feet away from us, and I can't deny it: I jumped. Nelson looked at me.

'I see.'

'I'm fine!' I protested, but actually, although watching the storm was rather thrilling, I couldn't truly refute that I'd rather be watching it from about seventy-nine storeys below where were at that moment.

We turned to go. And it's then that I saw it.

Chapter Thirty-eight

It was so dark outside with the clouds that at first I wasn't sure. Then the city lit up again with the lightning, and I knew.

'Look!' I shouted and tore towards the window. 'Look!'

Nelson blinked, took off his glasses, rubbed them with a napkin, which even in my panic I couldn't help noticing made them even more smeared, then poked them back on again and ran to the window.

Just below the restaurant was another, quieter viewing platform. I'd guessed correctly that it was used for parties and private functions: it was prettily done, with ivy wound round the old iron balustrades which leant over the sides.

Standing up on one of them, on the other – on the *wrong* side – was the figure of a young woman.

Her feet weren't on the ground; instead she was propped up on the metal bars. Her hair streamed in the wind of the storm. She looked like one of the carved figures in the lobby, the beautiful brass goddesses holding up the doors; or the wooden figurine on the prow of a ship. She was beautiful. And she was three hundred metres up in the air.

*

'Oh my God!' I screamed, glancing around. All the waiting staff seemed to have disappeared.

'There's a jumper! She's going to jump!'

I ran down the ornate central staircase which connected the two levels of the restaurant in the middle, where the room didn't rotate. A waiter came up to me.

'Excuse me, you know we're evacuating the building?' he said fussily.

'There's someone out there!' I hollered at him. The lightning flashed and rolled again.

'Where?' he said. 'I don't see anyone.'

I glanced back at the huge windows. We'd moved round again; I could no longer see her. I ran across the empty floor, tables rattling, knives and forks dancing.

'Nelson!'

I couldn't see him. This damned revolving room, so confusing. I heard his voice from somewhere.

'I'm going to get the police!' he shouted, and when I turned my head, he'd gone.

'Where is she?' said the waiter.

I couldn't remember where we'd been, where we were, but I had seen her; Nelson must have too, if he'd ran for the police. The waiter was staring at me crossly as if I'd had too many martinis at lunch, which I also had.

'You're sure it wasn't one of the statues?' he said, pointing to the gilded ladies holding up the pointed corners. I blinked.

'No!' I said, then made once more for the grand circular staircase, which was no longer where it had been a moment before. It was like diving through a maze.

Downstairs, I went to the French windows which opened onto the private terrace. It was locked.

'Can you open this?'

The thunder was growing louder.

'I don't think so ...'

'THERE'S SOMEONE OUT THERE!'

I stared at him and gave him the look the mayor gives people when they interrupt her at council meetings. It worked. One of the waitresses came forward with a bunch of keys and fumbled the lock open.

'Do you want me to call the police?' she said timidly. I nodded, although I assumed Nelson was on it. I paused.

Then I felt at the bottom of my bag. There it was. The silly little scrap of paper. I took it out with fumbling fingers and thrust it at her.

'Call this,' I said.

The door banged open in the wind and the storm; I hadn't realised how thick the glass would have to be up here to protect the building from the elements. Even without the horrendous weather, I imagined it would be mad up here, all howling wind and roaring noises. I could feel the building sway.

I was immediately drenched, of course; the rain hurled itself against me and I couldn't see in front of me: too wet. The ground beneath my feet was only wrought iron, with small gaps like an ornate balcony, except high; far too high in the air.

I couldn't look down. I told myself once more I wasn't afraid of heights, but I couldn't reach out to the balustrade. Instead, I hugged the building as the wind, it felt, tried to hurl me off; tried to bodily pick me up and dump me elsewhere. I bit my lip and gritted my teeth, even then thinking, Was it possible? Had I seen something? But Nelson had seen it too, right? It wasn't just me going crazy.

193

With my back to the glass wall – the outer wall didn't move, I realised; it was just inside, although it was still intensely disorientating seeing it move through the doors. Why on earth hadn't they just switched the damn thing off? – I edged very, very slowly around the building, feeling like the biggest idiot on earth. It was hanging out with Rufus, I knew it. I suddenly thought I had bloody superpowers as well. I'd totally normalised doing ridiculous things for people. It was his fault really. Who on earth did I think I was? I was showing off, that's what I was doing. Trying to get Nelson and Rufus to think well of me, when in fact I would just make things worse. What if I made her jump? My heart was pounding so loudly. Only the fact that I was as scared of going back – against the window – as going forward kept me steady and inching on.

After seven windows, looking straight out over the eastern river, I saw her. My insides seemed to turn to water. It was her. She was in the same position: hair flying out behind her; hands on the railings. I swallowed hard. Was it a waitress, maybe? A disappointed tourist? She seemed young; I couldn't see her face.

'Hey!' I shouted, but the wind tore the sound from my lips. I didn't want to approach her; she was on the other side of the barrier. It must be taking all her strength to hold on; I was terrified of startling her and her simply letting go.

'HEY!'

Round this side of the building there was more protection from the wind. I waved and yelled desperately, but I still couldn't get her to turn. The storm was moving towards the north, and here there was rushing clouds, still with that odd, yellow, unhealthy tinge.

'Please! Please let me help!'

But she wouldn't turn her face.

'Please don't jump!'

I was nearly at her now, nearly there. She was incredibly thin; there was nothing to her. I held up my hand.

'Please! Please can you ... please!'

She still wouldn't turn around. I gripped the barrier, terrified to move closer in case something worse happened.

'Look,' I said. I had to holler over the sound of the storm to make myself heard. 'Look ... whatever you think it is ... whether it's your job or a man or something ... if it's something in the world outside yourself, you are so young, you can't ... you won't believe things will get any better ... I mean, when I moved here ...'

I didn't think I was being particularly useful. The rain was filling the sky, pounding on the building. It felt like we were at the end of the world up there.

'Okay,' I started again, desperately wishing there was someone – anyone, even that snitty little waiter – around who might be more qualified than me to do this, where the stakes weren't quite so high.

'Okay. I won't pretend to understand your problems. Or what you're going through. Everyone has their own shit to go through; I know that for fact. And I am so, so sorry about yours. And I just want to know: is there any chance – any chance at all – you might consider giving it one more day? Or maybe just the afternoon? To think it over? To find someone more qualified to talk it over with? Just a little longer? Hold on? Hold on just a little ... we're all, sometimes, just holding on.'

I inched a tiny bit closer. She hadn't moved. Did that mean she was listening? Did that mean it might be working? If only this goddamned storm would pass over; if only she could see a tiny ray of sunlight in the sky ... That would help, oh yes. It would really help.

'Just a . . . '

I took another step. Too far. It was too far.

She started; her entire body seemed to move in the air. I screamed then, I think, and lurched forward as she moved, as her body shimmered in that strange, broiling light, and instinct made me reach out and make a grab for her slender arm, but my hand didn't close on anything; instead, it passed through nothing but air, totally empty, and I definitely screamed then, because I heard myself inside my head, and threw my arm over the side, all fears forgotten, to see if I could catch her plummeting; but my brain couldn't catch up with my hands, because all the way down I could see . . . I could see there was nothing there, no one below me, no figure at all, nothing.

Chapter Thirty-nine

'WHAT?' I screamed down into the abyss. Then I drew back and – once again, standing there, leaning out from the terrace, there was a figure, the same figure, the young girl: shimmering, holding on, hair streaming out behind them.

My brain couldn't understand at all what I was looking at: a monster, or a ghost. I shook my head, again and again; went to touch the figure, which once more vanished, and I realised – I realised that this was a hologram, a trick of the light, nothing real, a manifestation of a malicious spirit, and I took a step backwards and turned round; but the wind was blowing too hard for me to return, and when I turned forwards again, even though I didn't want to see the horrible scary apparition which had appeared on the ledge, with plummeting hair and no face, I knew that I had to, just as somewhere deep down I realised who I was looking at as I moved onwards, coming round the other side of the tower: the real flesh and blood apparition in front of me.

'Frederick Cecil,' I said, gasping.

His skin was as bad as ever; his eyes still glinting in that careful way through the mask.

'You rang?'

'What? What the hell were you doing? What was that?'

He glanced down.

'Well, nothing. It was a light show. Why are you upset?'

'Because I thought I'd killed someone.'

'I know,' he said. 'I knew your basic decency would get you out here. But isn't it wonderful now you knew you didn't?'

'Can you save the evil villain routine? It's very boring.'

I was unutterably furious; all that adrenalin with nowhere to go was spilling out as rage. I glanced around, just as lightning struck the building and fizzed and buzzed as it was absorbed. I jumped.

'Jesus, fuck.'

I started to inch round. Where the hell was Nelson and all the waiting staff? And the police, come to that? It was as if the entire building were deserted. As if . . .

Suddenly I heard it. Beneath the roar of the wind in my ears, which was immense. An evacuation alarm.

'Storm is getting a little ratty,' said Frederick Cecil. 'Everyone's gone. Except for us.'

Then he glanced up. On the top of a roof of the restaurant was parked a helicopter, sleek and black; a wicked-looking thing. I closed my eyes.

'You know,' he said. 'I wasn't sure it would work. Wasn't sure it would pull on your bleeding heartstrings enough to get you out here.'

'How did you know the restaurant staff . . . ?'

I thought back to that jumped-up maître d', wondered what he wouldn't do for a half-decent tip once in a while; the terrified waitress.

'Oh,' I said.

'It was hardly complicated.'

'But you don't want me.'

'I don't,' he agreed. 'I want that chap who seems to turn up whenever you're around. This seemed simplest.'

'I'm the bait.'

He nodded. 'I don't know what it is about you ... '

'I wish people would stop saying things like that,' I said. It was true. The idea that Rufus only paid me the slightest bit of attention because I accidentally knew his name was Rufus. It really stung.

'Anyway, yeah, you're right. He's not that interested in me.'

'That's why he breaks you out of jail.'

'He didn't break me out of jail. He bailed me out of jail. Quite a lot of difference. Anyway, it won't work. He's really not that fussed.'

'Really,' said Frederick Cecil, that nasty grin splitting his face again. 'Then what's ... ?'

He handed over his phone. At first I couldn't tell what I was looking at. I squinted.

'Oh,' he said. 'It's a camera on the outside of the building.'

I looked at it carefully. A murky shape was ... Oh my God. Ignoring the wind finally, I ran to the side, but I couldn't see a thing.

'Oh, he's a long way down,' said Frederick Cecil, taking back his phone. I bit my lip.

'Also why is he climbing up the side instead of breaking into the building and taking the lift?' I said. We looked at each other.

'I know, what a show-off,' said Frederick Cecil. 'I mean, the lifts are off obviously, but there's a fire exit. Ridiculous man.'

He heaved a sigh. 'Right, well, anyway, we'll have to wait until he's here to get him in the helicopter.'

'This is stupid,' I said. 'Can't you guys just call each other up? Or flame each other on message boards?'

He flinched.

'I want him on my territory,' he said. 'This time I'm prepared.'

'Oh for GOD'S SAKE,' I said. 'You can't beat him. And now you're kidnapping me again!'

'What do you mean, again?'

'After that time in the nightclub.'

'That was you? Is that why he's interested in you?'

I sighed. So much for me thinking I was an important pawn in this game.

'Look,' I said, glancing down the side of the building. Couldn't he fly up or something? Where was his hover pack? 'Whatever is going on between you two – don't tell me, did your mummies fall out in their sorority or something? – this is really nothing to do with me.'

'I know,' nodded Frederick Cecil. 'You're expendable.'

'I am not expendable!' I said. 'Shut up! Seriously, I mean it, can't you just go and snog or something?'

He looked at me.

'What? Your plastic boyfriend?' he said.

'Oh, screw you,' I spat, throwing myself into the hideous rain which bounced across the metal grating floor, oblivious now to the high winds; I was used to them and all I knew to do now was hurl myself at the heavy glass door around the other side, even though of course I knew before I even got there that it would be locked, and it was, as I heaved and pushed and pulled to absolutely no avail.

I gritted my teeth.

'WHY AREN'T YOU ONE OF THOSE HEROES WHO CAN FLY?' I screamed internally at him, but he still wasn't there, and me pounding on this door wasn't doing a single thing; Frederick Cecil wasn't even moving, I could hear the sirens now, but they were a way off across town, and I could already tell they weren't going to get to me in time. If they even knew I was up here. Which they didn't. God knows what Nelson was doing. I grabbed at my telephone, knowing even as I did so that it was too late. It was too late to call for help.

Chapter Forty

Frederick Cecil didn't run or chase me. He just began to move slowly, taking his time, knowing his prey. The rain was easing off now. I could see in the far distance a tiny hint of the sun coming back, breaking through the clouds a long way off as the storm passed us over. I looked behind. That ridiculous, horrifying hologram was still there, shimmering in the new light. It was remarkably convincing. What kind of twisted idiot would even consider such a thing?

Well, this twisted idiot, the one slowly advancing on me right now, a stupid grin on his face.

I turned round. Then I saw it. Of course. When he set off the fire alarm. That would have set off the fire escapes. Obviously they didn't go all the way down the building. But they did go up and down the restaurant complex where we now were, perilously perched, the entire edifice nothing more than a little box on top of a huge pole – or at least that was how it seemed, when you were desperately clinging to it with all you were worth.

I grabbed the ladder and hauled myself up it, my fear of heights swamped by my greater fear of what was coming for me, and I threw myself hand over hand, as quickly as I could.

Sweating, I glanced down. Frederick Cecil was still standing there, unhurried, looking at me without the remotest concern, as if I was a bug he was about to brush off his sleeve.

'Thanks,' he said. 'The helicopter's just up there. You can get in it if you like and I'll wait for Ultimate Man.'

Damn. I'd forgotten. I glanced up at the sinister black helicopter. It had landed perfectly on top of the restaurant's hexagonal roof, a space that seemed too dainty for it to inhabit. I glanced around the roof from there. There must be another way back in, otherwise ...

Frederick sighed theatrically.

'You can go down the hatch, but you can't get out of the restaurant again. So you'll run round and round and it just turns into Tom and Jerry. I mean, you're welcome to, but it will simply tire you out and I might have to ... '

The rest of what he had to stay vanished in the wind. I had reached the top of the ladder, already spied the hatch and dived straight through it.

Chapter Forty-one

Inside, being out of the wind and the rain had an instantly disorientating effect. The alarms had quietened now, and the dark restaurant was empty and eerie. I stepped sideways and accidentally knocked into a trolley full of dirty plates; the noise made me jump in the air. The entire restaurant was deserted.

I was panting, looking around. There must be a way out he hadn't thought of. There must be. I edged towards the kitchen. I glanced back up at the trap door; I had locked it, but I didn't know what else to do. I could hear his heavy tread coming now on the roof, and my heart pounded in fear. I dived out towards the lifts, but they had stopped and the fire exits were all now locked.

The idea that that little prick of a head waiter had actually locked fire exits made me white with fury.

I threw some chairs at the glass, but they were made to withstand that kind of thing, and I couldn't have crawled through them even if they had broken. I tore round the entire stupid dining room again, upstairs and downstairs, looking for something – anything – that would mark a way out. Above me, I could hear buzzing noises. He must be drilling through the trapdoor. Rufus, where the *fuck*? Where the *fuck* was he?

I tried to see down the side of the building, but I couldn't. How long could it take him to climb a fricking ninety-floor building anyway?

BANG! There came a gun crack. He must be shooting off the lock. I dived towards the large, greasy kitchen, its abandoned stations. In the cold store? No, that was stupid. Could I hide in a fridge or an oven? High risk. I looked around and pulled open a cupboard door at random. It was a waste disposal. I looked down it. Where did it go? Was there a rubbish chute all the way to the bottom? Surely not. Could I fit down it? It would be tight, but . . . could I?

'Well, you could try.'

While I was going crazy, tearing about like a trapped animal, Frederick Cecil wasn't breaking a sweat. He stood, smiling tiredly in the kitchen doorframe.

'Come on,' he said. 'I'm almost getting hungry enough to eat here. Not quite, obviously.'

I looked around wildly. The knives were out of reach. But there was a large red button that said 'Do Not Press' on it that clearly had something to do with the revolving element.

I banged it instinctively with the flat of my hand. The machinery cranked into action. I was right. I charged out of the side door, back into the body of the now once-more-Revolving Restaurant.

I charged around the moving space like a guinea pig on a wheel. Frederick Cecil leaned in the kitchen door, looking complacent. I didn't care. All I had to do was draw this out. Frederick thought he could wait for Rufus, and beat him. I wasn't sure about that at all. I thought all Rufus needed was a shot.

There was a noise. A squelching, exhausted, stopper noise. I looked up. A palm, with something in it, jammed itself on the side of the window. Then another. Then Rufus's shattered face, filled with pain, appeared. He looked like a bug on the side of the glass. It would not stop moving. I stopped and looked at him and we rotated, staring at each other. I pointed out where the door was, and he gasped and started to move sideways. I moved with him, trying to keep half an eye on Frederick Cecil – except, when I turned back to the kitchen, he'd gone. I heard a buzzing noise from inside the kitchen. What the hell . . . ? What was he doing?

'You have to punch the door out!' I screamed at the top of my voice, miming it. 'Punch the door!'

I tried to run to it. And as I did, I realised something. The Revolving Restaurant was speeding up. Whatever he was buzzing with in the kitchen, Frederick Cecil had done something to the mechanism.

Now the room was moving faster and faster, spinning at top speed, making ominous groaning noises. I got dizzy, staggered backwards as it continued to build, and it felt like the entire structure would simply spin off its axis, going too fast, that it would topple off the tower altogether. Inside, all the tables were falling over, crockery crashing onto the ground, knives and forks flying.

The entire thing whomped as it turned round and round again; Ultimate Man had stopped moving now. The momentum simply wouldn't allow it. Instead, he had grimly fixed those eyes in the mask on me. At first I thought he was trying to tell me something. Then I realised it was an old dancer's trick: he was trying to stop himself getting dizzy by focusing on something straight ahead. I hoped to God it was working.

206

'FREDERICK FRICKING CECIL!' I screamed. 'STOP IT! STOP IT AT ONCE!'

'Wait!' he shouted from inside the kitchen. 'Wait and I'll slow it down.'

'Do it!' I shouted. 'Do it now!'

Ultimate Man lifted his hand off the glass as if to say something. I thought he was waving at me.

'Now!'

Something else buzzed, and the entire restaurant came to a complete and instantaneous stop, which threw me and everything in the place right up in the air. I screamed as the sudden inertia tossed me like a rag doll across the thickly patterned carpet.

When I looked up, Ultimate Man had vanished from beyond the glass.

Chapter Forty-two

I stood, my mouth open, my heart pounding.

'RU ... ' I started to scream, but even in my horrible panic wasn't daft enough to say his name out loud.

'Ultimate Man.'

It's then I realised that before, in fact, I wasn't truly frightened. Obviously I must have thought I was; must have felt scared or strange.

But this – this was utter empty terror. There was no air in my lungs, no breath in my throat. The cry I was making tailed off; I was a completely empty vessel and my brain felt like the lightning that had moved on outside was carrying on here, was flashing across my mind with terrible thoughts: that he was dead; that I'd killed him, or caused him to be killed; or that I was all alone and now about to be abducted, killed – I didn't even know the awful things that were about to happen to me and there was nothing, absolutely nothing I could do about it and nobody could reach me, even as the sirens grew louder outside. They didn't know. They couldn't get here.

If Ultimate Man couldn't get here, nobody could get here.

I'm sure Nelson had tried his best, but there was no help left for me.

I realised, as if from a distance, that my teeth were chattering. Frederick Cecil ran up.

'Shit!' he was saying. 'Shit, shit shit. I thought he had suckers on.'

'He did,' I said weakly. 'He ... he took his hand off ... '

'Oh for *God's* sake,' said Frederick Cecil. 'You are the worst sidekick ever. What was he doing? Blowing you kisses?'

He stared out.

'Christ.'

I couldn't even hear him. He took me by the shoulder and I smelled again that sharp aftershave and felt, through my numbed skin, once more the oddity: that someone would wake up, determine to do terrible things to people that day and still take the time to put aftershave on, to smell pleasant for the people. What was this?

'Move,' he said. 'Move now.'

My knees gave way. He didn't have to lift me up or force me at gunpoint. Slowly, as if in a dream, he took my shoulder from behind and gently steered me, stumbling across the highly coloured carpet filled with shreds of broken crockery which tinkled and trailed beneath my feet as I dragged myself along; glass everywhere; crockery; ominous creaking noises still coming from the kitchen – whatever Frederick Cecil had done to the structure of the revolving tower, it obviously hadn't taken it very well.

There was a noise outside, a pounding. It took my white-out head a moment or two to realise that the emergency services had arrived and couldn't get through the locked lifts. They pounded and pounded. Frederick Cecil raised an eyebrow. Then there was a huge, racketing sound as I collapsed to the floor, hands on my ears. They had shot out the lift door. The noise was unbelievable, and the entire area filled with smoke as the large bullets they had shot through it carried on and shattered throughout the glass of the restaurant window. Immediately, the creaking got louder and the wind rushed in. The restaurant was really starting to wobble now; the carpet was tilting under my feet.

'Oh come on,' said Frederick Cecil. 'Seriously, I should have just Tindered you and told you to meet me up there.'

'I wouldn't have come,' I managed to spit.

'You might have,' said Frederick Cecil, dragging me to the stairwell.

The doors of the lift were being pulled apart as we continued to move. Inside was a SWAT team. Thank God, Nelson had got to the right people. They were dressed in black riot gear, with masks over their faces.

'Mm,' said Frederick Cecil. 'Bit toasty for today, isn't it?'

'Drop her!' shouted one, as the others came out brandishing their weapons. There was a moment's silence accompanied only by the creaking and wobbling of the two-storey restaurant structure.

'Thanks for coming by,' said Frederick Cecil. And quick as a rat, he took a grenade from his pocket and threw it far away, down into the floor; the noise was amazing. It was huge and tore a hole straight in the bottom of the structure. Immediately the entire edifice lurched even harder to the side. Two of the SWAT team fell over. The others steadied themselves against doorframes as Frederick Cecil pulled me up the alarmingly tilting staircase.

Through a fog, I dimly heard bullets follow us up, but they couldn't shoot straight, as the restaurant started to tilt more definitely, and I heard all the forks and crockery and glassware crash down to one side as if they had fallen off a table. The helicopter on the roof was already in the air and ready to go, and Frederick Cecil easily grabbed and pulled me out of the collapsing room and onto the unfurled rope ladder which came from it, climbing it with one hand and holding me with the other.

I should have refused; I should have fought him there, in the wind and the rain, terrified, on the roof of a collapsing building, hanging halfway out of a helicopter.

But I couldn't: even if I had had the will left, the second I turned around I felt the structure – the entire restaurant – vanish, quite simply fall away from beneath my feet, and my feet were on the ladder, and then I was being pulled into the helicopter, watching the glass and the metal drop away from beneath me, and I couldn't believe my eyes, as it tumbled down onto the viewing platform far below in the most extraordinary crumple of metal and glass; then a huge shockwave followed, which pushed the helicopter up and sideways and I lurched back, just as a vast plume of smoke started to rise up from the collapsed restaurant, and even as I saw injured and shocked SWAT team members pull their way out, I couldn't, anywhere, see a single flash of purple; no, no one.

Chapter Forty-three

I knew I should have logged where we were headed, but apart from establishing that it was south, somehow, someway, I couldn't figure it out as we flew away from the island of Centerton, the plume of smoke visible far behind us way after we'd left the buildings behind, and I sat on the floor of the helicopter, even though the pilot had indicated I should take a seat, and curled my hands around my knees and rocked and sobbed and sobbed and sobbed.

I thought once again of Rufus looking out over the beautiful darkened gardens in the deep moonlight, telling me how lonely he was, being the loneliest man in the world, and great choking sobs came up through me, although nobody could hear me over the noise of the chopper and, to be frank, who was there left who could possibly care if they did hear me? After what I'd done; what I'd risked; what the hell I thought I was trying to prove.

After a couple of hours, I was all cried out, and I noticed we were coming down to land. I looked below. Incredibly, although it felt like this afternoon had lasted for ever, it wasn't even that late; we were coming down to a glorious sunny late afternoon, several degrees warmer than Centerton, and it had been plenty warm there.

The helicopter set us down on what felt soft; white sand flew up. I couldn't get up off the floor for exhaustion after crying; Frederick Cecil basically had to kick me out – then it took off again immediately. I lay down on what I gradually realised was warm sand, but I still had no tears left. I felt completely emptied out, and suddenly utterly knackered.

'Are you planning on staying there?' drawled Frederick Cecil eventually. 'Only if you are, I'll get some factor 40 – that freckly skin of yours can't take it.'

I looked up at him, face full of misery.

'What are you going to do with me?' I hiccupped.

He sneered down at me. 'Obviously, take you for my bride and reveal your true beauty underneath ... Marta!'

He shouted, and – squinting in the sun – I gradually realised he didn't mean me. I looked up. Walking down the sand was a ridiculous vision, so mad I thought for a moment that perhaps I was unconscious, that I had not realised in fact was happening to me, that I was dreaming.

A motherly-looking woman with her hair drawn back and an apron on came down onto the sand.

'Marta,' said Frederick Cecil, opening his arms to her. 'This is Holly. She had rather too much to drink at the reception ... I think she took something else too. Anyway, I said I'd bring her back here to sleep it off. Can you help us out?'

Marta moved towards me and smiled politely.

'You okay, huh, missus?'

I blinked at her.

'Well, my friend got thrown off a building by your boyfriend. So not really.'

She laughed in a tinkling fashion and said, 'Oh my, she is in a bad way.'

She put her arm around me.

'Hey, why don't you come take a shower ... or a dip?'

I blinked. This couldn't really be happening. As if in a daze, I let her lead me up the beach, my brain unable to understand what was happening. Frederick Cecil had gone somewhere else.

'But,' I said. 'We have to escape! We have to get away ...'

'Sssh,' said the lady. 'Ssh. Don't worry.'

Just up the beach, through a soft dune, was a house.

There were steps up towards it: a New England, gabled pale blue dream of a house, with a veranda wrapped all the way around it, and wooden steps. There was a tower on the side, also in pale blue, with a widow's walk and a weather vane. The windows were huge, the deck sandy. In different circumstances, it would have been the most beautiful house I'd ever seen.

Beside the swing seat on the front deck was a table laid out with fresh lemonade.

'No!' I said, turning round to Marta. I stared around behind me. But when I looked back, there was nothing except a perfect white beach, fringed with palm trees, and a huge, fathomless blue sea ahead. 'NO!' I screamed.

'Sssh,' said the woman. 'Here, drink a bit of this lemonade. You look thirsty.'

And like a child I did, and after that, I didn't remember a thing.

Chapter Forty-four

All I could hear were waves. Gentle, soothing, splashing waves. It was so comforting. So relaxing. It was like a lovely spa treatment where they played those wave tracks with dolphins singing on them ... except, I realised gradually, that wasn't a tinny backing track. Those were ... those were real waves.

My head hurt. I groaned loudly. What the fuck? *What the fuck?* I decided I would just stay here, wherever the hell I was, listening to the wave noises until everything else went away.

This lasted about four seconds before I then realised that the wave noises made me absolutely desperate for the bathroom. I groaned again and, slowly and painfully, opened my eyes.

The plain white room was full of the soft pink light of a Caribbean dawn. It was stunningly lovely. I was lying on a spot-less white bed, covered in pillows, with a patchwork quilt thrown over the sleigh bottom. Overhead, a fan was turning lazily, but the open windows let in a beautiful breeze, gently stirring the white gauze curtains. Oh God. What the ... ? I knew something bad had happened. Something really bad. But my fuzzy brain wouldn't take it in quite yet.

I stumbled over to a door, guessing it was a bathroom. It was. There was a roll top bath, pale aqua marine tongue and groove, and a little lighthouse out of the window. I went to the loo, then, to my surprise, threw up. I took a long, long shower, first cold, then hot, and after a while, with my back against the tiles, I sank down onto my heels and let the heavy water cascade over me, and tried to figure things out.

Rufus. Oh my God. Rufus.

He had come to save me again. And he had died in the attempt.

I covered my eyes with my hands. And now Frederick Cecil had taken me anyway. Why? None of it made sense, except I was completely alone in the world and in terrible danger.

There was a white fluffy dressing-gown hanging on the back of the door. I blinked. It didn't compute, not at all.

The main door, of course, was locked.

I sat down on the bed, which was bigger than the entire bedroom in my apartment, and buried my face in my hands. What was going on? Where was everyone? What was happening? And I realised that all I could think of was Rufus.

I didn't know where Nelson was, but I assumed he was fine, along with those horrible rat finks in the restaurant, who'd taken their dime and run.

But they'd know I was missing, wouldn't they? Gertie and my mum would be going nuts. Nelson would have told everyone. I looked around for a television, but there didn't appear to be one. Would they have reported me?

Something else caught at my heart. Oh my God. Oh my God. They'd think I was dead. They'd think I'd perished in the rubble of the Revolving Restaurant.

I had no bag, no phone. Nothing. All I had to do was prepare for the end.

Eventually my wrenching sobs began to quiet, and I remembered something I'd heard about prisoners: in cells, the innocent ones would pace all night, terrified and panicking after being arrested; the guilty ones would sleep because there was nothing they could do about anything now. The game was up and that was that. And I felt a little like that.

I stepped towards the French windows. To my total and utter astonishment, they were open. I was in a wing of the house, and I stepped forwards carefully into the soft heat of the new day.

It was so stunning outside I wondered briefly if I'd died already: the sky was a paradise blue, the sun warm and gentle on my skin. I glanced around.

On one side, far away, I saw now, was a fence, presumably guarded. But there was nothing except a few feet of sand between me and the ocean. As a way of escaping they had presumably thought it impossible, but I stepped forwards anyway, closing my eyes as the sun flooded my face.

There wasn't a sound around, nothing but the waves calmly rolling on for ever and the occasional bird. I took another step forward, a little worried in case I was going to be shot by a sniper, but there wouldn't have been much point bringing me all this way then, would there?

I continued to walk on. Nothing, except the caw of a bird in the palm trees behind the house. I walked on – my feet bare, my eyes shut – right to the water's edge. I took one step into the water, then another. It was warm as a bath; soft and salty on my skin. Suddenly bold, caring about nothing, driven half mad, I shrugged off my white dressing-gown, hurled it on the sand and dived into the sea.

Chapter Forty-five

I don't know how long I floated there, completely untethered, slightly mad, utterly free. I stared up at the blue, wondering what on earth was going on in my life, what on earth was going to happen, what would happen if I just kept on floating out to sea. Would a friendly coastguard pick me up? Would I drift elsewhere, or catch a passing cruise liner? They must come by here; this was patently paradise. I lay on my back and hummed to myself, forbidding my thoughts to focus on anything, anything at all that wasn't straight ahead of me, feeling slightly separate from myself and everything I knew.

Suddenly a roar cut through the blue, obliterating the gentle noise of paddling toes and soft crashing waves on the ever more distant shore.

'What the hell are you doing?' came a voice, and something – a lifejacket and a pair of shorts – were hurled at me.

'Why do you have to be so bloody unpredictable all the time? Where the hell did you think you were going?'

I looked up from my dreamy stupor, surprised. Frederick Cecil was on a sharp black boat. I realised he'd taken off his mask. This made me jump. His eyes were a very bright green. His kiss-curl was back, sticking up from his head.

'Get in,' he said.

'Don't want to.'

He sighed, and one of his henchmen dragged me in, none too gently, until I was lying on the boat. There was another white dressing-gown there and I covered myself with it and stared up at the sky, ignoring him.

'You are no end of bother,' Frederick Cecil said crossly. 'Why can't you just sit down and look frightened?'

'You left the doors open,' I said sulkily. 'What did you expect me to do?'

'Go for a swim where it doesn't look like you're drowning!' said Frederick Cecil. 'We're not animals.'

I remembered the convulsions of the SWAT team as the great building had shifted on its axis.

'Yes, you are,' I said, quietly.

'There was also a perfectly good swimsuit in your size.'

The boat dropped us off back at the shore, and Frederick Cecil took hold of my elbow.

'Eat breakfast,' he said. Sure enough outside my room was a tray with a coffee pot, orange juice and what, if I wasn't dreaming – and I was totally unsure at this point – was fresh croissants.

'What the hell are you doing?' I said. 'What are you doing to me? Why?'

Frederick Cecil blinked.

'Well, it's a mystery to me too,' he said. 'But Ultimate Man has an interest in you – for whatever reason – seriously, I can't see it myself. Anyway. I wanted to bring him but, as you saw, there was something of a SNAFU.'

I blinked.

219

'You killed him! You monster!'

I launched myself at him, trying to claw at him.

'What?' he said, effortlessly batting me backwards. 'Stop it!'

'But,' I said, still clawing the air. 'But he's dead! I saw him! He fell off a ninety-storey building!'

Suddenly something in my heart caught light. Was it at all possible that . . . ? It couldn't be, could it? Could it possibly be that he was still alive somewhere? That he had . . .

I remembered the look on his face as he had fallen . . . and fallen.

Frederick Cecil looked at me. 'Seriously? You thought he was dead? I thought you knew him!'

My heart was thudding at a million miles an hour.

'Oh no, you can't kill that tricking freak that easily,' he said. 'It's like trying to squash a rubber bloody ball. No. I want to talk to him.'

My knees nearly gave way, and I sat down at the little table with breakfast on it.

'He's still alive,' I said. 'Oh my God. You think he's still alive.'

Frederick Cecil rolled his eyes. 'Like cockroaches after the apocalypse. As we will soon see, hopefully. Anyway. Now psychically call him and lure him here please. Maybe eat a croissant first, give you the strength.'

I looked at the food. Inside I just felt a gushing enormous overwhelming sense of relief. And, annoyingly, suddenly I was absolutely starving.

But I wasn't eating in front of this monster.

'What's your plan?' I said.

Maybe just a little bit, with some butter. To celebrate Rufus being alive.

'Oh yes, why don't I just tell you everything?' said Frederick Cecil prissily. 'Eat!'

I took a sip of the orange juice. It was heavenly. The coffee was still hot too. I decided to butter a croissant, but to do it in quite an angry way so he would know I was still very cross and upset.

'So, just send him a signal,' said Frederick Cecil.

'What?' I said, realising too late that I had just spat crumbs everywhere. It was a good croissant though.

Frederick Cecil smiled. 'Oh, maybe you don't know. He is slightly psychic. He can pick up on thoughts. I hope you didn't have any very specific ones while he was close by! How naughty of him not to tell you. Anyway. Think about him now – and I can tell you are; your tongue is hanging out – and he'll be here in a jiffy. Nice.'

This time I slowed right down and took my time, enjoyed every flake of the croissant, licked the crumbs from my fingers, even as I noticed his fastidious face recoiling a little bit. Yes, you find *that* disgusting, I thought to myself. But finally. I had some leverage.

'Well,' I said. 'Here's the thing.'

I took another sip of my coffee.

'He put a psychic barrier on me when I asked him to,' I said. 'He won't have the faintest idea where I am. So you should probably take me home.'

Chapter Forty-six

So, that was a big mistake. Big. Huge.

Chapter Forty-seven

I was led through the beautiful house – and it was so beautiful – brusquely, through exquisite rooms with stunning artworks and rich rugs and polished tables. I saw no signs of the girlfriend. I guessed she'd been lifted off. I wondered if she'd ever been more than a prop. I wondered if everything I was looking at was a prop, designed to hide from satellites, from prying eyes; to make it look like nothing more than a billionaire's fantasy island.

Behind the huge kitchen, which was done in tasteful shades of grey, was a locked door. Not just a locked door: one which, while painted to look like wood, I realised as I glanced closer, was in fact solid steel. Lots of it. We looked at it for a second. Just for a second. I didn't want to go beyond that door.

'Perhaps you could call him?' said Frederick Cecil.

I wanted nothing more, nothing more in the entire world, than to call someone who could save me, who could rescue me from all this. But to lead him into a trap ...

'No.' I wasn't going to give him the phone number I'd memorised. Not after Rufus had trusted me with it.

'Why don't you call him, then we'll go eat lunch? My man

223

caught some crayfish this morning, and I have a very acceptable Chablis chilling. We can just hang out, you know. I have a new first edition Eliot I could show you, very rare.'

He kept looking at me. I sighed. Oh, how much easier it would be to just give in. But how could I? How could I betray someone who would fall off the top of the highest building for me?

It was just as I had thought or imagined – or in fact, slightly worse. Underneath the exquisite Cape Cod beach house was a war room. Silent men in black patrolled beeping machinery; there was a radar, maps, satellite linkings and surveillance everywhere, plus several ominous machines called long strings of numbers, and I didn't even know what those were.

'What's all this?'

Frederick Cecil sighed.

'Now,' he said. 'You've seen how beautiful my little island paradise is, no?'

'Yes, yes, you've watched a lot of Nora Ephron films,' I said. 'What's this about?'

He took me further inside and pointed to another door.

'What's that?'

'I'm just saying.'

'Saying what?'

'There is a door within a door.'

'What's behind it?' I said, my heart beating strongly.

'Persuasion,' said Frederick Cecil.

I gasped.

He went on. 'I think … I mean, I really wish. I want you to contact Ultimate Man. I want you to tell me everything you know about him. I think you know him. I think you know his real name and where he lives.'

224

'I thought you were in charge of the internet,' I said, trying not to look at that door, although every nerve and every sinew in me was straining to back away, to get away.

'And I thought you liked hiding behind dark doors,' he said. I glanced at him quickly.

There was a long pause.

Chapter Forty-eight

I'm not proud. I'm not. I couldn't. I couldn't deal with torture. I'm sorry. I was so, so scared. So horrified. So frightened. So desperate to see Ultimate Man again, just to prove to me that he was. And I needed him; I needed him so save me.

Frederick Cecil didn't say a word. He stood there, with his fine hair and his bad skin cleaning his nails with his knife. Occasionally he would hold it up and let it glint. The men working around us didn't look at us; there was no interest from them in me at all. I wondered where Marta was; how much she knew. She must know, surely?

I quivered and I acquiesced and I cried in terror as Frederick Cecil knocked the knife against the metal of the door and scraped it down.

Yes, I was prepared to sacrifice another's skin to save my own.

I told him the telephone number to save my own skin.

I hope you would have done differently. I hope you can understand why I could not.

Chapter Forty-nine

Frederick Cecil jotted it down and nodded. Then, anyway, he turned open the steel door, and I closed my eyes in horrified anticipation. Now, the real imprisonment would begin. I trembled as I waited to see the torture chamber; closed my eyes.

When I opened them again, I realised I was staring into a cupboard. Or, more precisely, it was an armoury: a locked collection of hunting rifles and munitions. A storage cupboard. Frederick Cecil made sure I saw it – in my horrified puddle of a state – then pulled the door closed and sealed once more.

'Safer that way,' he murmured, smiling. He looked at my horrified face.

'Don't worry,' he said. 'Everyone cracks straightaway. There's clothes in the wardrobe in your room. Get changed. We're taking a walk.'

He pushed me towards my room.

I opened the wardrobe. Inside was a selection of dresses and shirts, all in my size. This was absurd. I had never been luxuriated to death before. They were all expensive and beautifully cut, in shades of white and aquamarine. I chose a floaty white dress, something I would never have worn in the city; it was light cotton with a broderie anglaise top and a layered skirt, and it fluttered down over my head like a dream. My hair had dried in the sun and looked streaky with sand; I'd even caught a little colour on my face. For someone in the most dangerous situation of her life, I found myself musing in the mirror, I actually didn't look too bad. I immediately felt awful for even considering this.

The knock came at the door, and I went to it obediently. He looked me up and down.

'That's better,' he said. 'You looked half-dead when you came in yesterday.'

I blinked.

'I was,' I said.

Frederick Cecil opened the back doors of the kitchen and sunlight flooded in. It was utterly, ridiculously beautiful out there.

'Walk with me,' he said.

Chapter Fifty

The sand was warm beneath my feet, and the soft breath of the air was gentle on my skin. I closed my eyes.

We strolled quietly along the beach and into a verdant forest of shady palm trees. Birds and crickets cooed lazily.

'Holly,' said Frederick Cecil eventually. 'You have to make him stop this.'

'*You* have to stop!' I said. 'Why are you doing this? Why? *Why?*'

He blinked, and looked a little hurt.

'I thought ... I thought it would be obvious,' he said.

'No, it isn't,' I said. 'Apart from you being evil!'

He looked around.

'Really? You think this is so much worse than Centerton?'

'No, this is beautiful,' I said. 'Lots of rich people get rich by being evil. You must have had to rob a lot of people.'

He laughed.

'Not at all,' he said. 'No.'

'How did you make your money?'

'Tech,' he said. His voice changed. Sounded downbeat for

once. More serious. 'I worked at . . . Well. Everywhere you've ever heard of, I worked on most of it.'

'So why did you turn to evil?' I asked, genuinely curious. 'Why did you turn off the internet?'

'I'm *not* evil,' he said, turning round. For once his voice sounded anguished, impassioned, which it normally wasn't.

'I'm not! Look! Look at the world the internet has built! Look at it.'

'What? What do you mean?'

He started ticking things off on his fingers.

'Faster trading and worldwide panics mean permanent instability in the stock markets, which mean traders who get rich from instability get stinking rich whichever way and everyone else is scrabbling about in the gutter. How much did you make last year?'

'You don't want to know.'

'That's right. Because all human capital – music, creativity, writing, anything beautiful or useful – has been completely degraded and destroyed by the internet, because apparently everything is free now, and human creativity is worthless.'

He ticked off another finger.

'Meanwhile, you've got a huge boiling mass of pustules; of people externalising every inner slight they've ever suffered, and causing a massive explosion of hate and shame and ridicule and doxing over whatever moving target they like. Is that making the world a better place?'

I thought back to all the horrible comments when my knickers had shown up online. I'd pretended to laugh it off, but some of them had hurt terribly.

'What about a generation of children who can't engage with their peers; who can't deal with life without a screen in front of them; who are obese and unhappy and anxious and caged by themselves and their devices in a prison of their own making? Is *that* making the world a better place?

'Oh, and now your government can spy on everything you do and everywhere you go, as can every big corporation you use, as can Facebook and everybody else, and they can sell that information to the highest bidder, and you have happily thrown them complete insight and complete control into the very heart of you: your searches; your deepest desires; your innermost fantasies and wishes and personality.

'You have thrown it open to the world in return for funny cat pictures, and you hope and keep your fingers crossed that no one will use that against you.

'And your Ultimate Man of course, the little tame Judge Dredd, protecting the strong, attacking the weak.'

He blinked, his curious green eyes full of melancholy.

'Evil is when good men do nothing, remember? And now the internet can instantly disseminate the worst, the most evil political and religious philosophies, and it becomes valid, because enough people will watch it and be scared of it and conform to it and even leave their homes and ruin lives by going to fight for it. Isn't that bad enough for you?

'And even beneath that. You can keep going down and down and down. Even under that is the other stuff. The silk road. The dark web. This astonishing discovery that the deepest, most corruptible, most appalling part of human existence is now a shared experience.

'No matter how awful things are, they are now out there where they can be laughed about and discussed and shared and shared and shared, and it can happen over and over and over again, and it can happen to children, and it happens to children every day, just so the great maw internet can have it.'

231

His voice had gone very quiet now. There was an extremely long pause. Then he said the next bit so quietly I could barely hear it.

'And once upon a time, one of those children was me.'

Chapter Fifty-one

We didn't say anything for a long time. His head was bowed, his entire face staring fiercely at the ground. He was crying.

'What happened to you?' I asked him quietly.

'I was raised in an orphanage. Or rather, should I say, a "facility".' His tone was soft.

'I can't talk about it. Please. You can certainly search for me if you need to know more.'

I would have thought it went against all my natural instincts, but suddenly his rough skin was against my shoulder, the tears wetting me as he sobbed. I did not put my arms around him, but I didn't hurl him away either. Instead I stood there, and I thought about him; about Rufus; about Nelson.

All those motherless boys.

'Sssh,' I said.

'It's all right,' he choked, straightening up. 'I've had a lot of therapy. I mean, a lot. All of it, I think.'

'Who with, Doctor Octopus?' I said, but he didn't hear me.

'Seriously, ask your therapist for a refund,' I added. Then, more gently, I patted him on the arm.

'All this talent, all these brains and money you have,' I whispered. 'Why couldn't you take all that skill and cash and do something heroic?'

'But that's *exactly* what I'm doing,' he said. 'Can't you see that?'

Chapter Fifty-two

'You can't uninvent the internet,' I said, when he'd finally stopped crying and we were still standing there, in that paradisiacal glade. 'You can't turn the clock back.'

'It's a massive tap of fetid poison pouring into our homes and our eyes and our children. We invented sewers. We cleaned up the water supply. We have to clean up the internet. Which means, in tech terms, turning it off and turning it back on again.

'We built it wrong. It's wrong. It's putrid and sexist and filthy and it has become a repository of our darkest desires, refracted in an echo chamber of wasted lives and misery and futility and poured out rage.'

'You tried to destroy the city because of *internet comments*?'

I was trying to cheer him up, I realised, which I hadn't exactly expected.

'I'm not trying to destroy the city. I'm trying to save it.'

'Why do you keep killing all those people?'

'I don't kill anyone!'

'What about that SWAT team?'

'They had fair warning, and they all pulled their parachutes, believe me.'

'What about all those fights with Ultimate Man?'

He looked at me.

'Who got hurt in those fights? I didn't throw a punch.'

'What about your men?'

'Yes. Ultimate Man beat them up. Without provocation, may I add?'

'Don't you care about them?'

'Are you kidding? After getting into a fight with Ultimate Man, they all write their own tickets. They're amateur boxers, most of them. Giving them a leg up. Everyone wants to work for me.'

There was a long pause.

'The only person who's committed any violence,' said Frederick Cecil, 'is your boyfriend.'

'You kidnapped me!'

'Yes, I did. So Ultimate Man can come and find you and we can finally have a conversation without him wanting to kill me.'

He leaned forward, his green eyes boring into mine.

'I'm sorry: you must be finding everything terribly awful and difficult. Here.'

He took out a flask he'd been carrying.

'Mango juice. Freshly squeezed this morning. From our own mango grove.'

'What about all those people you mugged?'

'Oh yes, all those innocent venture capitalists and corporate lawyers and barflies and professional wives who trample on everything and everyone to get a millisecond's advantage in the financial markets,' he said. 'Via the internet.

'Actually, believe it or not, I tried asking nicely. But everyone is like a dog with a bone when it comes to their devices. Don't touch. Don't go near it.

'We've become a species of snarling, grabbing self-centred

hedonists, whose entire existence is entirely focused on and exuding from themselves. We are building seven billion worlds for ourselves in which we are the suns and everything else rotates around us and must serve our every desire, and to hell with the consequences and the fact that this can bring nothing but individual existential misery on a gigantic scale.

'To hell with the human detritus that gets in the way of the naked or the ultraviolent or the hysterically religious echo chamber you want beamed back at yourself from your pocket. To hell with all the screams of the innocent. You can't hear them with your headphones in.'

Chapter Fifty-three

'You know,' I said, as we headed back slowly to the house through the surf, 'I think Ultimate Man works alone.'

'So do I,' said Frederick Cecil. 'And I think it's time to come together. So we can all make things better.'

The sun was setting incredibly quickly, a deep pink over the horizon. Frederick Cecil had asked me to join him for dinner and I had, feeling a little like *Beauty and the Beast*: completely unsure as to the nature of this strange animal.

Fresh fish, just pulled out of the turquoise water and wrapped in coconut leaves then baked over an open fire in front of us, was being served up on the veranda in front of the well-stocked library, along with freshly baked bread and a freezing cold Chablis.

'How long were you planning on keeping me here?' I said. I was, I realised, starving. I tried not to tear at the bread. It was one of the best meals I'd ever eaten.

'We're waiting for him, that's all.'

'I need to call my mum.'

'Of course,' said Frederick Cecil.

'She'll think I was up that tower.'

He shook his head.

'I'd never scare anyone like that,' he said. 'I told the restaurant manager to say you'd got out.'

'Well, she'll still be panicking,' I said. Well, I hoped she would. She'd probably take that as enough; assume I'd gone off with my friends.

Frederick Cecil smiled.

'I didn't think there'd be that much ransom for you. It's not like Centerton is short of twenty-somethings who want to work in the media and eat too much ramen.'

'Excuse me,' I said. Then I smiled. 'Okay, fair point. No ransom.'

He smiled back.

'I promise I'll give you back completely unharmed – well, you have a tiny bit of sunburn on the top of your nose.'

I instinctively felt for it.

'No, it's okay,' he said. 'It brings out your freckles.'

'Ugh,' I said.

'I like them,' he said. 'I think they're cute.'

I blinked and didn't say anything. Creep.

'What are you planning?'

'What I've already done. But better. More safeguards. All the trains will head straight back to depots to replace the old signalling. I've already fail-safed the hospitals, although I didn't do as well as I should have done on the traffic lights. Yes, that was a problem. A design flaw. I can fix that.'

'A town without internet?'

'Centerton becomes a haven of cafés and bookshops and conversation and universities and talk. No cars on the roads at weekends. Street food and people spending time with their families and each other.'

I looked at him.

'You're mad,' I said. 'That could never work.'

'On the contrary. I think it's the only system that ever has.'

He ate another forkful of fish.

'Do you want to have children one day?'

The setting and that soft voice of his completely shook me up for a moment; for the tiniest split-second, I thought he was asking if I wanted to have children with him. I looked at his fine profile, his skin still a little bad as he stared out over the ocean into the setting sun, bare feet on the white sand, the warm breeze ruffling his kiss-curl.

I shook my head.

'Um,' I said, pushing my fork around my plate. 'Maybe one day. Yeah. Sure.'

'Have you noticed how quiet children are these days? On every flight, in every coffee shop, in every buggy, in every home. They are plugged in as surely as in *The Matrix*. Plugged into another world altogether, where they are forever the sole lord and master. Where they never share or climb a tree or interact or ask questions or do anything except endlessly tap tap tap. And those, let me tell you, those ones will be the lucky ones. Is that how you want them to grow up?'

'No, well, I wouldn't do it like that,' I said.

'Everyone thinks that,' said Frederick Cecil sadly. 'We have to change. I'm taking a stand.'

'But you're the baddie,' I whispered.

He refilled my glass.

'Yeah, I know. I'm so sorry about all of this inconvenience,' he said. 'I really am.'

I looked at him.

'The first time I saw you ... in that bar. You were very sure of yourself. Very controlled. Now you seem very nervous. What's changed?'

240

'Because I did it,' said Frederick Cecil. 'I did it. I made it work. What I'd been working towards for so long. I suddenly realised I could make it happen and it did happen. And I . . . I was scared. Stealing a few phones – that's small fry stuff. Put on a swagger of confidence and you can get away with just about anything. That wasn't me: I'm just a tech guy. But now, changing the world. That's the real deal.'

'There were fights, you know,' I said. 'On the street. People were fighting on the street because there wasn't any Wi-Fi. There were fires. Accidents. Burning. It all started to fall apart.'

'I know,' said Frederick Cecil. 'That's how awful it's got. How awful the world has become. None of them were fighting over the fact that there's an epidemic of homelessness in the city. That TB is back despite the fact that we successfully eradicated it fifty years ago. That children have to rely on food parcels in the richest country on earth. Those are the kinds of things I want to make people angry. Those are the kinds of things I want people to notice. Instead of doping themselves, drugging themselves with pictures of the Kardashians, or horrible pornography, or snuff videos, or video games, or worse.

'The government is fine with the war on drugs. We're pretty much behind the war on tobacco, and we're gearing up for the war on sugar. Why aren't we waging war on this?'

I paused and stared out to sea.

'You didn't really think there'd be a ransom demand for you?' said Frederick Cecil. 'You went on and on about Ultimate Man, but you scarcely thought about one for yourself. Why is that?'

'Oh, I'm not worth a ransom,' I said.

Frederick Cecil blinked.

'Of course you are,' he replied. 'Everyone is.'

Chapter Fifty-four

The sky was such a perfect purple fading down into night. Little fires had been lit in candle-holders all the way up the drive, which kept the bugs away and scented the air with a delicate citrusy smell which contrasted beautifully with the heavy sweetness of the pink and purple bougainvillaea.

Huge stars began to pop out overhead, and I felt slightly woozy from a second glass of the exquisite wine. Frederick Cecil went into the library to choose a book for himself. He asked me if I wanted one and I realised I'd almost forgotten what reading a book – doing nothing else, not surfing the net, not DMing anyone, not playing *Candy Crush* – was like, so I let him choose one for me, and he was just coming back, carrying something called *I Capture the Castle*, when I caught sight of what I thought was a tiny star, except it was moving rather rapidly. I stood up to get a better look, but Frederick Cecil was already charging into the house.

'Lockdown!' he was shouting. 'It's lockdown!'

Immediately, steel shutters began to roll over the entire house. The dot in the sky grew bigger and I realised it was a small jet, travelling incredibly quickly.

As it grew closer, I realised another thing: it was purple.

Frederick Cecil picked up the old-fashioned telephone which was next to him.

'Confirmed? Is it Ultimate Man?' he barked, receiving an answer in the affirmative. He banged down the phone.

'Don't shoot him down!' I said.

He looked at me.

'Seriously, are you thick? Have you not listened to a single thing I've said?'

'Yes,' I said. 'But I didn't know whether to believe you.'

He looked at me.

'Was it difficult?' he asked, taking me by surprise. 'Memorising a phone number?'

'Yes,' I said. 'Yes, it was.'

He shook his head.

'We are losing so much. So much.'

The noise of the jet as it approached got louder and louder, drowning out our conversation. I thought it was going to go right past us, but instead I saw it had two odd landing devices on it, like blown-up feet, and it came in to land – absolutely spectacularly – on the water just in front of us, setting up huge plumes behind it as it did so.

'Wow,' I said. A posse of henchmen had materialised. I glanced back at them nervously.

'I thought you weren't going to hurt me.'

'They're to protect this place.'

Frederick Cecil took me by my upper arm. I recognised the touch immediately. It felt new and familiar all at once.

'Don't try anything, please,' he said. 'This is our best chance for everyone to get out of this peacefully and properly.'

'It isn't,' I said. 'He won't work with you. He won't let you win.'

'Good always triumphs,' said Frederick Cecil in that low voice.

'That's what he thinks,' I said.

Ultimate Man waded through the dark water towards us. The moon had risen: it was almost full, and incredibly bright, making it almost as clear as day. Behind us, the path braziers crackled gloriously in the cooling evening.

Frederick Cecil was standing stock still with me beside him, my long dress flowing in the wind.

'Good evening,' he said calmly.

Ultimate Man's costume, whatever it was made of, wasn't even slightly wet as he emerged from the waves. His eyes were hidden beneath the mask, but I could tell he was looking at me very intently.

'Are you all right?' he said, striding up to the sand towards me.

'Stand back, please,' said Frederick Cecil, as the henchman shifted menacingly behind us. 'You're still susceptible to bullets right? Maybe not one, but sixty rounds in you would just about do the job, yes?'

There it was again. That cold, dead lizard voice was back. It sent shivers through me in a way the rest of the day hadn't at all.

Ultimate Man ignored him.

'Tell me you're all right, Holly.'

I hoped I didn't have salad between my teeth.

'I'm fine,' I said. 'Thanks for asking. I'm fine. Can I go home?'

I could feel Frederick Cecil stiffen a little just beside me and realised I'd hurt his feelings.

'Yes. Yes, you can,' said Ultimate Man. 'First, I have to teach this little runt a proper lesson. To get out of Centerton. To leave our city alone. Once and for all.'

'A drink first?' said Frederick Cecil. 'Come, sit down. Have dinner. Let's meet properly. Finally. Let me welcome you to my home.'

And he walked towards him, holding out his hand.

Then Ultimate Man did something I wasn't expecting at all.

Chapter Fifty-five

The beautiful citronella braziers which lit the way up the steps to the villa were just to the right. Ultimate Man moved, faster and deadlier than a snake, to that side very quickly, and booted the first one over, hurling something – propellant? – over the top of it.

'MOVE, HOLLY!' I heard a distant voice. 'MOVE!'

Immediately, the flames leapt up, and the next fire caught, and the next one, quicker than you could imagine, and in a matter of seconds, great clouds of choking smoke were everywhere and the very last two had caught, right on the front door of the beautiful old timber-framed house. I whirled round in shock. It went up like matchsticks.

'Nooo,' said Frederick Cecil, watching as first the door then the timber frames of the window caught fire. 'Not my library. Nooo! Is everyone out?'

Frederick charged back into the house, whereupon he started ushering out staff – including the cooks, and Marta – all of whom came out and stood, tear-filled and ashen on the sand as the house burned behind us. I was watching it too, slightly horrified, when Ultimate Man came up and grabbed me.

'Get in the jet,' he growled. 'What did you do?'

'I was creating a distraction!' I said.

'He. Is. Your. Kidnapper,' shouted Ultimate Man. 'It normally takes more than twenty-four hours for Stockholm Syndrome to kick in. Can you get in the goddamned jet?'

'But! He just wants to talk to you.'

There was a bank of machine guns trained on us, I realised. One of the men looked round, as if awaiting a signal. I watched the entrance of the house with bated breath. No more staff emerged. But there was still no sign of Frederick Cecil.

'In the jet!'

'I need to see if he's all right!'

'I'm never rescuing you again.'

'Good. Next time you'd probably burn down a rainforest!'

There was a long pause. The henchmen were still looking at each other, unsure of what to do.

'*Seriously,*' said Ultimate Man. Then he picked me up again and threw me over his shoulder.

'Put me down!' I screeched. 'Put me down! Go rescue him! Frederick Cecil is in a burning house.'

And I started hitting him on the back with my fists.

'RESCUE HIM! Frederick Cecil!'

Just at that instant, a blackened face, his blonde hair dirty, his kiss-curl all over the place, appeared finally in the doorway of the house, which was such an inferno that we had to back away because of the heat.

'Hang on,' Frederick Cecil was shouting. 'We need ... we need to talk! Please!'

In his hands, he was holding a large bowl of tropical fish. And a second later, the bowl had cracked and started off a volley, and suddenly we were in the middle of a gun fight.

247

Chapter Fifty-six

It was chaos. In the heat of the fire, I didn't realise at first that nobody was actually shooting.

The heat must have reached the gun cellar and started setting off all those rifles. At any rate, suddenly we were surrounded by gunfire.

The henchmen all dived to the ground as one, as did we. Only Frederick Cecil stood there, looking down at his dying fish, horrified. Then he started to scoop them up and went to put them back into the sea. As he ran, a stray bullet caught him in the leg and he dropped like a stone.

Completely unthinking of her own safety, Marta the housekeeper ran forwards to look after him.

'Oh, Mr Cecil,' she called out. And that was the last thing I saw, because Ultimate Man pushed me down to the ground, and pulled me along like a sack of potatoes, into the water, and shoved me up into the plane which, to my total astonishment, lifted up off the waves like a jump jet, as indeed it was.

Furious, sopping and horrified, I looked beneath me at the flaming remnants of paradise, the bullets still exploding in the air, the house still burning, the woman tending to Frederick Cecil on the beach.

'Bloody amateur,' grunted Ultimate Man briefly, concentrating very thoroughly on getting the plane up through the clouds. In the air, it was cramped and very, very noisy. I stared down as we moved further and further away, gathering speed and then we were through the clouds and powering through the sky at tremendous speed, Rufus's jaw steely, reflected against the glass of the jet's window.

He passed me a blanket to wrap around myself, but neither of us said anything. My teeth were chattering. He didn't seem to notice the cold.

'You didn't need to burn down his house!' I said eventually.

Ultimate Man ignored me for what felt like several months.

Then he said, 'He tried to destroy the entire city.'

'You didn't speak to him about it! He was just trying to get people to chill out a bit.'

'Was he?' said Ultimate Man grimly.

'He thinks the internet is evil.'

'Tell that to the people whose lives have changed immeasurably for the better because of it. Notably speaking, everyone ever.'

'No, he says it's a ... '

I didn't have the words I realised, to be as persuasive as Frederick Cecil had been. I could barely remember what he'd said, just that I'd been very convinced at the time.

'He says what?'

'He says it's a filth delivery system.'

'That's what they used to think about novels,' said Ultimate Man. I looked at him.

'It's not the same.'

'It's the medium, not the message.'

I frowned.

'You probably think guns don't kill people; people do,' I said.

'Actually, I don't think that. I never use guns. Perhaps you'll notice that I wasn't the one with a munitions bin in their basement.'

I sniffed.

'Don't you think that's odd? To have a massive underground arsenal?'

'But he's peaceful!' I said. 'He didn't want to harm anyone.'

'Then he should stop destroying city landmarks. And kidnapping my friends.'

Ultimate Man banked to the left.

'And watching the company he keeps. I recognised every single one of those henchmen he had with him. I've put most of them away, several times. They've done things, Holly ... things I wouldn't even want to talk about with you.'

I fell silent. With what seemed amazing rapidity, the lights of the Eastern seaboard approached.

'I'm sure he was charming, Holly,' he said eventually. 'I'm sure he had his reasons. They all have their reasons.'

'They were good reasons,' I said mutinously.

'Holly, he broke the emergency services network.'

I didn't say anything.

'All my instruments indicated there was a lot of technical equipment in that house. I mean, *a lot*. Not just weapons. Computers, power generators, nothing good.'

He looked at me.

'A normal house wouldn't have gone up like that. Do you realise? Do you realise the danger you were in?'

Quietly, I nodded. I stared out of the window. Everything below was passing in a blur.

250

'How fast are we moving?' I said, a little breathless.

'Too fast for anyone to see us,' said Ultimate Man, and I looked at him, focused intently on the controls.

'You can,' he said, and suddenly he sounded more like Rufus again. 'You can say thank you any time you like, you know.'

And I realised, truly, what he'd done for me. And how I had betrayed him.

'Oh my God,' I said, bursting into tears. 'I'm sorry. I'm so, so sorry. I mean, thank you. Thank you! Thank you! Were you all right when you fell down?'

'The falling down was easy,' said Rufus, almost smiling. 'It was the crawling back up that was hard. That tower is big.'

'Ninety storeys.' I nodded. 'Oh my God, how is everyone? I mean, am I famous? Is everyone worried about me? Am I in all the papers and everything? Missing believed dead?'

'No,' said Ultimate Man. 'Gertie just thought your date had gone really well.'

'Oh God,' I said, my head dropping into my hands. 'And you still came to get me.'

He looked at me.

'Of course. I always would.'

Chapter Fifty-seven

We landed in his grounds of his house. Across the water, the lights of the city sparkled, with one glaring difference: Centerton Tower was no longer lit. Repairs had already begun but it looked like a tooth missing in a mouth.

I wondered briefly, traitorously, whether Frederick Cecil was okay.

'He'll be fine,' said Ultimate Man. 'Hopefully with his base destroyed, and half his men in hospital, and you back safely, he'll finally see that as a good reason to give up. He's got nothing left. He can't even vaguely beat me. Us,' he added patronisingly.

'I thought you weren't reading my mind any more.'

He rolled his eyes as he peeled off his mask.

'I blocked my psychic abilities, Holly, not my basic brain.'

'He had ... he had a really terrible childhood,' I muttered.

'Well, that I know a little bit about,' said Rufus.

Standing there – the air was cooler here, although still not cold – I looked at him: that ridiculously handsome square face; his hair, slightly ruffled from being under the costume, although you'd have to know him quite well to notice; his slightly reticent stance, as if he were ashamed of his height and physical presence when he wasn't covered up. My hair was all frizzed, falling over my face. He turned round and gently tucked it behind my ear.

And I stretched up as far as I could and kissed him, full on the mouth.

Chapter Fifty-eight

It wasn't planned; it was completely spontaneous and I felt terrible instantly. He staggered back across the grass. It was the first time I'd ever seen him look surprised about anything.

'Sorry,' I said straightaway, feeling wrong. 'Sorry sorry sorry. I shouldn't have done that.'

His hand went to his mouth, and he looked at me.

'Sorry,' I said again. 'I am so sorry.'

He shook his head. He looked at his fingers as if trying to work out what had just happened.

'I shouldn't have ...'

'No,' he said. His costume was torn from the explosions, and his tone suddenly sounded quiet and defeated, even though he had just saved me, and goodness knows what else.

'No. You should have. I ... I liked it.'

This last bit was almost too quiet to hear. I moved back a little towards him. He was staring at the ground, but he didn't move away. My heart was beating rapidly. I had ruined our friendship, of that much I was sure.

'Do you ...?' I tried to keep my tone normal, but my voice

sounded husky. I wanted to feel those cold, marble lips one more time. The rippling of his muscles under my hands. The strength of him. I was done pretending to be friends. I couldn't play nice.

'Do you want to do it again?'

He wouldn't look at me and I couldn't figure out why. Then I realised that my dress was ripped across the top, exposing my bra, and he was averting his eyes. I rolled mine.

'Hey,' I said. 'It's okay.'

He looked at me.

'I ... I can't,' he said, quietly.

'What, it's a code?' I said. 'Are you like a monk or a priest or something?'

He grimaced.

'No. Well. Yes. A bit. I mean, I have to focus.'

I drew level with him; or rather, level with his chest. It occurred to me to look into buying a small stepladder.

'Never?'

He blinked and didn't reply, which I took as agreement.

'Would you like to?'

He didn't answer that either. I didn't cover up the rip in my dress. Instead we stood, looking out and down at the lights across the water.

Trying to read his thoughts seemed as impossible as his trying to read mine, which were all over the place. Could he? Physically, I meant. I mean, he looked like a man. But he wasn't quite a man. He was more than a man. A scientific accident had changed him; changed the very structure of his DNA.

And now: what if he was full of molten metal, or transformed into – I don't know – a giant bee or something afterwards, or impregnated me with an alien baby or something? Did he even have a thingy? After all, he looked pretty smooth in that suit. I sighed, and chewed my lip distractedly.

He was still staring at the darkening sky, his jaw tight. Then he turned abruptly and headed into the house. He didn't tell me to follow him. He didn't tell me not to.

I hesitated at the door.

'My . . . my dress is wet,' I said. He nodded.

'You can take a shower,' he said. There was a pause. I stared into his blue eyes. I wanted him more than I had ever wanted anything in my life.

'And after?' I couldn't help saying, pathetically.

He stood out of the doorway, to let me pass.

'Holly. I don't think so,' he said. 'I don't.'

'That's fine,' I said. I half smiled. 'Actually, my dress isn't that wet,' I said, feeling foolish and suddenly desperate to get out of there. 'Do you think . . . do you mind if someone could drive me home?'

'Oh! Yes. Yes. Of course.'

I walked through the house, padding across the soft carpet, as I heard him pick up a phone and ask his chauffeur to bring the car round. I felt rejected and awful and completely and utterly stupid.

Stupidly, even though I realised it was different with Rufus – that he was different, too different, that it wasn't anyone's fault – he reminded me of some men Gertie and I had dated in Centerton: the ones who were all over you until you gave in to them and let them get close, whereupon they ran a mile. They were fuckwits, every one, and Gertie and I had sworn blind not to get caught up in it again.

This was obviously a completely different situation. But as I walked, head bowed, somehow, it felt exactly the same.

*

I was nearly out of the house when I heard the voice, and at first I couldn't tell if it was in the hallway or directly in my head. His voice went through me, right into the heart of me.

'Holly,' it said, deep and low. 'Holly. Please. Stay.'

And fatefully, I paused, and turned round and then I saw him; oh, just the outline of him in the dark corridor against the light coming in from outside, his arms dangling by his sides, his head leaning on the side of the doorframe as if he had succumbed, as if he were exhausted, as if he simply couldn't fight it any more.

Chapter Fifty-nine

And then we did it, which obviously I can't talk about.

Chapter Sixty

Oh, I'm just messing with you.

Chapter Sixty-one

Okay, so I am going to tell you everything in the interests of full disclosure, but I am not saying that it goes for all supers, okay? So if you do find yourself in a compromising situation with someone who's just saved an entire city, and it's just one big mass of writhing tentacles down there, don't blame me, okay?

Also don't blame me for obvious scaling issues. I don't care how charming Ant Man is, or how intriguing Dr Manhattan. You so knew what you were getting into.

Anyway. I ran the entire length of the corridor, straight into his outstretched arms, and he picked me up and spun me around, then put me down, and then, as soon as he had stood down the chauffeur, I followed him into the beautiful bedroom. Rufus instantly looked more nervous than I did. He stood on the other side of the huge bed.

The huge, untouched bed. I turned to him.

'You seriously have never done this before?'

'Um? I've been really busy.'

I looked at him.

'I mean ... but you do ... you do want to? You have the urge?'

He nodded.

'I ... I think so. I just ... '

He looked at me.

'I just don't know what the consequences might be. Do you realise that? The risks? With what I am.'

I nodded. Because I also had no idea. Because all rational thought had in any case been completely overtaken by want, by need.

He looked down at himself. 'Do you want me to keep the suit on?'

I burst out laughing.

'You don't mean that.'

'I get a lot of mail from people saying they would like to do it with me with the suit on. I mean, a lot. Ninety or ninety-five per cent, easy.'

He looked a little hurt.

I moved towards him. I wanted to take that suit off. I didn't know how, but I was going to. I couldn't look at anything else purple, not right now.

'That's what I mean ... I mean, you can't have been short of offers.'

He looked down. His thick eyelashes cast shadows on his high cheekbones. God, this man was beautiful.

'I know. But I couldn't. With my job. It kind of feels morally wrong ... I mean, there were just so many people who wanted to and, well, I didn't really know what to do with that.'

'Why not?' I said, thinking back to the blonde.

'Well, in one life, all they saw was the suit. And in the other, all they were thinking of was the money ... or my eligibility or my house or ... And there was just absolutely no way of marrying the two.'

He looked at me ruefully.

'Until *somebody* caught me halfway between both.'

I wasn't finished though.

'Why not? Because you could see inside their minds?'

'I don't mean to. I'm not prying. I just can. This city is full of people with ... ambitions.'

I nodded.

'How do you know I'm not thinking those things?'

He smiled.

'Because the last things I caught from you were that I am slightly irritating and you think I look weirdly overgroomed.'

I shrugged. I couldn't really argue with that. I took hold of his hands and looked into his eyes.

'Biologically speaking. Nothing weird is going to happen, is it? You're not going to "vamp out"?'

'I don't know what that means.'

I took a deep breath. My heart was thudding painfully in my chest.

'Are you going to hurt me?'

He looked straight into my eyes.

'If I was ever going to harm you, I'd stop.'

'What if you can't stop?'

'Controlling myself is what I do.'

I shook my head.

'Then I don't think you know what this is like.'

He was standing as still as a statue, even now. There was nothing natural about him. I barely knew what he was. I wondered if he had ever felt it amid all that training, all that work.

Truly. Not to have done it before now. Did he really feel desire through his veins? Or was he dabbling in being human, like eating a pretzel?

He looked so strained. It also put me in the awkward position

262

of being the aggressor, if you like, for the first time ever. I was much more a kind of 'mutual drunken fumble' girl generally. I preferred a faint messiness which shrouded the embarrassment and clumsiness.

But here I was, in a room, stone-cold sober, with a virgin, who I wasn't one hundred per cent sure wouldn't actually kill me or impregnate me with an alien baby or something. Well. This was an odd state of affairs.

I looked out through the windows at the city. He turned his head to look out too. My heart lurched. Even though I was right here, he just seemed alone, so alone. I reached up and turned his head around so he was looking back at me. I leaned up to him. I could feel his heart beat too. It was a lot slower than mine.

'Are you sure?' I said.

He nodded. I reached up and kissed him. Then again. His lips were cool, unyielding, and I pressed myself against his long body, as he began slowly to reciprocate. His body felt so firm against mine, like granite. I began, gradually and steadily, to touch his chest; I ran my hands across his broad shoulders and realised as I did so how long I had wanted to do exactly that.

'Do you want me to take the suit off?' he said, breaking off. I nodded vehemently. He disappeared to the bathroom and reappeared a microsecond later, completely starkers.

Oh Lord. I couldn't help it: I dissolved in laughter.

'What?' he said, looking offended. I felt awful. There can be nothing worse than disrobing for the first time to peals of hysteria. Thank God Rufus didn't have the easily torn ego of other men.

'What is it?'

'Nothing,' I said, trying to stifle my giggles. 'I never get tired of seeing you doing that.'

I calmed myself down.

'Um. Shall we lie on the bed? Don't run over there too fast; I'll laugh again.'

'I take it speed isn't a useful quality under these circumstances.'

'Are you making a joke?' I said, giggling still.

He didn't reply, but instead strode over towards me. He was glorious, utterly perfect. He looked like Leonardo da Vinci's Vitruvian man, except with republican hair – and to my complete and utter surprise, lifted me into his arms like I was thistledown. I grinned up at him. Then the oddest thing happened: suddenly I wasn't wearing any clothes either.

'WHAT?' I said, my hands jumping up compulsively.

'Sorry,' he said. 'Sorry sorry sorry – was that wrong? Was that bad?'

I looked down, then back up at him. He was holding me, completely naked, in his arms. My hair cascaded down over his arms; he'd unpinned that too. My clothes were folded up in the corner of the room. I threw back my head and laughed, and this time he laughed too.

'You know, no,' I said. 'It saves a lot of awkward wriggling. Although I will say, sometimes awkward wriggling can also be nice.'

Gently, he laid me down on the huge bed. The mattress was springy and firm; just as I had thought, it had never been used. The expensive white sheets were brand-new, clean and fresh. The lights from the city twinkled through the uncurtained windows, the garden still and mysterious under the moonlight. Nobody could see us here. He lay down beside me, his head propped on his arm, looking down at me. I smiled and kissed him again, and this time, he put more of himself into it; I felt closer to him, stronger, and my body started to yearn to be closer to him, to move instinctively towards him, to draw what heat it could from him.

'Oh,' I said; my breath was coming shorter now. His skin was cool but so firm to the touch, every muscle so carefully and beautifully delineated under the white light of the moon.

'Do you ...?' I said, as we paused. 'I mean, you understand the mechanics, right?'

He nodded.

'I know all that stuff,' he said.

'Yeah, the theory,' I said. 'This is the practical.'

There was another pause then, carefully, slowly, he started to caress me with his giant hands. My eyes began to close but I forced them open, not wanting to miss a moment; wanting to see him; desperately hoping to break that unbreakable exterior, to find a crack in him.

I could not find it yet, even as he carefully, thoroughly, thrillingly caressed my breasts, my thighs with those huge cool hands, and I found myself writhing beneath him. My breathing tightened in my throat; I started to twist my hips to reach up closer towards him. My body started to beat with something beyond my control, to follow its own rhythms as my thought patterns twisted, became confused; my brain started to kaleidoscope, to fold in on itself.

'Is this right?' he said calmly, far more calmly than I was now. I reached up for him, but he carried on maddeningly, exploring my body with his fingers and hands; fascinated, it seemed. I felt – I was being – examined; I watched how his eyes darted rapidly from his hands to my face, reading precisely, exactly what I liked, what got a reaction and responding instantly to it.

He was a quick study.

It was the absolute opposite to what I'd expected: I thought I would be guiding him, showing the naïve virgin what to do. Instead, in almost no time at all, I was breathless, close to begging, desperately trying to pull him closer to me, my entire body squirming to his touch, desperately wanting more, as if this was all brand-new to me.

'Is this right?' he asked again.

'Shut up,' I said fiercely. 'Shut up and just do it. Do it.'

I wanted him to lose control so badly; I needed him so furiously. I was mad with myself in that I clearly couldn't have him in the same way as he very clearly could have me, but my frustration, my desperate need, didn't care about that right at that moment. Instead, I simply reached for him, tried to pull him on top of me, although I might as well have tried to pull a lump of solid rock: I absolutely could not budge him.

'Please,' I said.

He blinked and stilled his hands.

'Of course,' he said, polite as always, and right then I could have screamed at him – and I think perhaps I did.

He moved on top of me, carefully not to squash me, and his marble body was still cool, and I felt him finally – oh, and it was steel – as I had thought; as I had known it would be – cool, not warm, still, but now I could feel something pulsing in him, something pulsing there, and I looked up at him and there was no smiling, not now, and he saw the strain on my face.

'Am I hurting you?'

He stopped immediately.

'No,' I said in a breathless panic. 'Don't stop.'

'But I can't hurt you.'

'Some types of pain are all right,' I said, clenching the sheet with white knuckles.

'I can't believe that.'

'Believe it,' I said, almost howling in frustration. 'You have to. I promise. It won't hurt for long.'

'But—'

266

'Do it!' I yelled, then I yelled out again, and again he tried to stop and again I wouldn't let him, and my eyes flew open and I was staring into his, and at last – at last I saw him and he saw me; at last we connected, not as other, through gender or superpowers or anything else; finally I saw the flow between us of connection, the way two souls become fluid, joining together, pushing together, and I couldn't help it, I yelled again; and now he started making noise, he who was so contained, so controlled, whose heartrate did not change when he ran down the side of a building, when he covered bombs with his own body; now he was letting out great tortured cries, his eyes imploring me to tell him what was happening, what was happening to him, but he did not – could not – stop and we moved tumultuously together, and I grabbed his sculpted face with one hand, sweat dripping from both of us and growled at him:

'Say it. Tell me what we're doing.'

And he shook his head, breathing hard.

'I don't … I don't swear.'

'You have to understand. That things you think are bad aren't. It's just a descriptive word. It's okay. It's what we're doing. Tell me what you're doing. What you want to do.'

'I have to do it?'

'You have to. Tell me.'

He groaned from deep within himself, sped up and said it.

'I'm fucking you.'

'And is it bad or is it good?'

'It's … it's both.'

'Tell me again.'

'I'm fucking you.'

I came then so violently and unexpectedly out of the blue that he could do nothing else but try and hold onto me, looking terrified and muttering, 'What was that?' but I couldn't answer him; I was barely conscious, and he tried to soothe me but as he did so, suddenly he was compulsively and hugely and completely overwhelmed, and for the first time I was scared as he reared up, roaring like a lion, taking me with him, and jammed us both up against the headboard so hard the boom echoed in the room and, just for a microsecond, the electricity fused so that through the uncurtained windows the entire city – the entire city – went dark; and I did lose consciousness, and when I came to, the plaster on the walls had cracked apart, and we were staring at each, horrified, as powder drifted and settled prettily around us.

He didn't swear. But I knew he wanted to. I did compulsively. It felt like the only way I could get my breath back; get myself back. Rufus had jumped up, got off the bed and, without compunction, punched the wall. The crack got markedly worse. But thank God, just as the sirens started wailing in the dark, there was a stutter, and gradually the electricity came back on across the water, the lights popping on one by one over the bridge.

'Are you okay?' he said, his voice sounding strangled in his throat.

'Yes ... no ... yes,' I said, completely unsure. My legs had turned to jelly; nothing seemed to move.

He turned to me.

'Are you okay or not?'

His face was a furious mask. I felt the back of my head. There was a huge bump there and I winced tentatively. He looked as if he wanted to curse again.

'I knew it.'

'What are you doing?' I said, rolling over, despite my seemingly atrophied legs. It was so uncharacteristic of him. His face was a mask as he stood back and examined the damage to the wall.

'What?'

I felt scared again.

'What is it?'

'You have to go,' he said.

I shook my head.

'No, thanks. No. I'm not buying that. None of this BS. You don't treat me like this. You're meant to be a hero, remember?'

He turned to me.

'I ... I could have killed you.'

I realised suddenly I was bleeding. I felt up: I had a cut on the back of my head which hurt like hell. I touched it dubiously and blew plaster dust off my fingers.

'Well, you didn't.'

He shook his head.

'You don't understand. I lost ... I completely lost control.'

He sat down on the edge of the bed. He looked completely bereft.

'Yes. That's what it is,' I said gently.

'I didn't ... I didn't realise.'

'Well, you can't learn everything in books.'

He hung his head and sighed.

'All I wanted ... All I wanted to do was to try ... to have one shot at being normal. One. Come here.'

I thought he was going to hold me, and I sure as hell needed it right then. But instead, he pressed his hands against the back of my head, where the cut was, and gently manipulating his fingers, sealed it. It was the oddest sensation. It was also not much more personal than getting a pap smear.

'... with someone normal.'

'Thanks for that.'

'I lost myself.'

He shook his head in disbelief.

'I've never . . . '

'Never?'

He shook his head.

'I can't. I can't do that. I don't know what I'll do.'

'Well,' I said. 'From now on, we'll just do it on bouncy castles.'

He shook his head then pulled me to him.

'Are you all right?'

I looked at him straight.

'I don't know.'

'I didn't know that's what other men do.'

I shook my head.

'That's not what other men do.'

He frowned and put his head in his hands.

'Stop it,' I said. 'Please. This is the bit when you come over and sit down next to me and hold me and it's lovely.'

He shook his head.

'Holly,' he said. 'I can't. Because I'll want to do it again. And next time . . . who knows what will happen? I might blow out half the building,' he said, casting his eyes away.

'Rufus,' I said. 'It's just sex. It's sex. It's not power.'

'It is.'

'It's not. It's lots of things. It can be funny, and tender and sweet, and brutal and everything. It's not just one thing. Let me show you.'

I reached my hands out to him, but he pulled them away.

'It's too powerful,' he began unhappily.

'You knew this might happen,' I said.

'I feared it, yes.'

'That's why you never ... '

He nodded, and I felt strange. I placed my fingers on his arm. And he flinched.

I stood up at that.

'Well,' I said. 'I'm not easily embarrassed, but someone being terrified of being with me can certainly do it.'

'It's nothing to do with you.'

I turned round to him.

'Oh great. Thanks.'

He sighed.

'You don't get it.'

'Oh, I do,' I said. 'Everything's a power struggle with you. Everything is black and white, good or bad. Anything bigger than you, or you can't understand it, you fight it. You destroy it. You wouldn't even talk to Frederick Cecil. You can't even entertain a different point of view.'

I blinked.

'You think sex is a kind of power, a kind of thing that you can take or lose, and if you can't control it, you aren't interested.'

I looked at him sitting there, so beautiful in his nakedness; so beautiful and so unconcerned as to whether he was naked or not (I wasn't one hundred per cent sure he even knew nudity was a actually state); that he had made me feel so beautiful too. I looked at him, my heart drooping because I knew he didn't understand, not at all.

'Well, if that makes you feel any better, actually I've changed my mind. Maybe I have met a lot of men exactly like you.'

'Holly,' he said.

'It's okay,' I said. 'I'm done.'

'I did ... I did say I only wanted a friend.'

Chapter Sixty-two

John the chauffeur drove me back in silence, thank goodness. I was absolutely and completely weary to my very bones. The last forty-eight hours had spun me around and I felt like I'd been through a laundry cycle. I wanted to go home so very badly. That was all. And to sleep, for a very, very long time. It was three o'clock in the morning. I would take the next day off. I didn't even care what Liz thought. What Liz thought was extremely low down on the list of things that made me sad these days. I stared out of the window at the twinkling bridge, and let the tears steal quietly down my face.

I crept into the apartment, determined not to wake Gertie and DuTroy, but there was to be no chance of that; all the lights were on. I really, really was not in the mood for them asking about what I'd been up to – as far as they knew, I'd spent the weekend at Nelson's or Ultimate Man's after I'd escaped from the Centerton Tower accident. I knew they were calling it an accident; there was a newspaper in the back of the car. Hit by lightning, accidental fault found which made it susceptible, fortunately nothing but minor injuries among restaurant staff. I hoped that horrible manager had lost a nose or an ear or something unpleasant and disfiguring.

But I really wanted just to stumble into bed without the third degree. Unfortunately Gertie flung herself on me in a whirlwind of incoherence the second I stumbled in.

'HOLLLL!'

'What?' I said. 'What is it? Is everything all right? Was it the power cut?'

'Ooh, yes, I know, everyone panicked and thought it was like the Wi-Fi again. Seriously, that mayor is getting voted out at the next election. You'd better make sure you hang on to your job.'

Another thing to add to my long list of ridiculous things to worry about later. I really wanted a bath. We didn't have one of course. I thought with some envy of the amazing sunken tub Rufus had in his bathroom. No. Screw it. Don't think about him. One day you'll be able to laugh about it, I kept telling myself, like a mantra. One day it would be a funny story. About the girl who slept with Ultimate Man. One day it would be funny. When I stopped feeling like this.

'HOLL!'

I realised belatedly that Gertie was waving something in my face, but I was too bleary and tired to take it in.

'What?' I said. 'What is it?'

Then I focused and understood. DuTroy was standing at the back of the room, looking shy and genuinely sweet and embarrassed.

'We're engaged!' she shouted. 'There was a power cut and DuTroy got all romantic!'

As these things go, I didn't do too badly. I'm no actress, but I think she was too giddy to notice. She told me all about it: the walk down the pier, DuTroy telling her that after the last few days of things happening, he wanted them to move somewhere safer. To go and build a life: their life. Together. Somewhere quiet; to build something lovely for them. A life, not, as Gertie put it, scrabbling by in this shithole.

'Because it's all right for you now,' she said brightly. 'Isn't it? You and Ultimate Man hanging out! It's great.'

'Can we double date?' said DuTroy. 'I mean, so you and Gertie can hang out, okay, not just because I want to meet him. Can I meet him though? We'll invite him to the wedding. I mean, he probably wouldn't want to be my best man, but obviously if he'd like to . . . '

I waved my hands. I was going to explain, but they both looked so in love and so overflowing with happiness and overjoyed with everything that I couldn't bear to rain on their parade, to spoil their amazing day and happy night; both their faces were so bright.

I felt about a thousand years old; someone who had seen so much, suddenly. I felt like a survivor coming back from a war zone, where people got blown up in munitions fires; where you got rescued by a seaplane in the middle of the night. Where everything went terribly, terribly wrong. For me, for Rufus, for poor old twisted misguided Frederick bloody Cecil. It was all awful.

'I am so, so happy for you guys,' I said. 'So thrilled.'

And I drank far more than my share of their celebration champagne. Because I wanted it to make me fall asleep. And it did.

Chapter Sixty-three

I took a day off to deal with my hangover and my utterly filthy mood. I cried a bit.

I cried all day.

Did he call?

Did he fuck.

Tuesday I cried all morning, then I went and replaced my phone, which they upgraded because I couldn't stop crying even though it wasn't actually their fault, although it did make me think of all the other times: they had so many people crying in their shops they actually needed to have a policy about it and maybe they should just improve their network, and that made me think perhaps I was feeling a little better, so I headed into work.

I'd expected Nelson to be keen and puppyish and pleased to see me. Or possibly really, really sorry that he'd left me there, deserted me on the top of a tower with the bad guy.

But he wasn't either of those two things. Instead he was snotty and a bit distant, not at all the sweet gentle guy I knew he really was.

'Hey,' I said, trying to get him to talk to me. I couldn't bear the silent treatment.

'I'm glad you're all right after the lightning strike,' he said stiffly. I looked at him.

'But the girl,' I said. 'The girl on the tower. You remember? It wasn't a lightning strike.'

'I didn't see any girl,' he said. 'You just said you did, remember? They said it was probably you just imagining things with the lights and the cloud and you sent me out. There wasn't anyone up there who wasn't accounted for.'

I frowned. Someone had got to Nelson.

'Okay,' I said, and swung back to my computer. I looked at him. He obviously wasn't finished.

'So.' He cleared his throat. 'Did you have a nice weekend at Ultimate Man's house?'

I looked at him. So that was what this was all about. He was jealous! Oh goodness, of all things.

I remembered our lovely lunch – our lovely, simple, straightforward funny *human* lunch of two people doing two completely normal things – and I wanted to cry again. Why couldn't I be an innocent in this? Why could Frederick bloody Cecil and Rufus bloody Carter just have nothing to do with me at all and couldn't we just forget all about it and why couldn't I just have met the nice, schlumpy mensch at work and have had a few lunches and a few dates and got on really well and ended up – why couldn't we end up like Gertie and DuTroy? Why did everyone else get it except for me?

I paused.

'Not really,' I said quietly. He looked at me, and I was cross because there was a momentary expression of satisfaction which crossed his face before it returned to neutral again, which was mean from Nelson; it was a mean thing to think and it was me who'd made him feel mean like this, who'd made him think these things.

276

'Sorry to hear it,' said Nelson, but he wasn't the least bit sorry, not really, and that was my fault.

And after that, we were totally plunged into work. The mayor was taking an absolute battering in the polls after the Wi-Fi outage, followed closely by the power cut, even if the latter had only lasted ten minutes or so. Neither of these things were her fault, but she was up for re-election in November so we were all systems go. I churned out endless press releases about good news, about gardens being planted and charming stories about dog walkers and small acts of city kindness, and fed them to the hacks at the *Globe*, who rolled their eyes (but often used them, I noticed, given they were incredibly short-staffed, and we produced a lot of this stuff).

I would think, while going into the office or talking to them on the phone, I have a story for you. A big one. You know that fancy boy that keeps turning up in your gossip pages? The business leader, the philanthropist who sponsors every charity event going? You know what else he gets up to? It's not particularly charitable. And you can speculate about him and various society blondes as much as you like. I know what's going on.

If I did, of course. In my darkest moments through those months, as Gertie and DuTroy sat poring over gift catalogues and wedding napkin booklets and table plans; as I lay in bed, sleepless, I would think, Maybe I got played? Maybe I was right the first time I went out there? Maybe the chauffeur spent his life taking girls out there, who all got the 'let's just be friends' spiel, the 'hey I don't know, let's try this penis, see if it works' spiel, all of us falling for it. Falling for it every fricking time.

And I thought again of the loneliness in his eyes and remembered the dust settling around us, and I thought, No. No. He's lonely all right. He's by himself all right.

But I wasn't the one who could help him out of that. I wasn't enough. And that hurt.

I had worried a lot at first if Frederick Cecil would come back. Whatever he'd said on the island, he was – I saw clearly once out of his web – a loose cannon. An unpredictable madman. But surely he'd been neutralised now, his base destroyed. Every time he'd come up against Ultimate Man he'd lost, and lost very badly. Surely now he'd retreat, go somewhere else. Centerton was clearly protected. A tiny bit of me wondered if I might not have managed to persuade him, just slightly, to stay exactly where he was.

Except that even as no one had heard from Frederick Cecil, no one had heard from Ultimate Man either. Sightings, which were usually nightly, had dropped down and down. People were staying at home more, worried about going out without a neighbourhood vigilante to protect them. This wasn't great for the mayor's business either. Where is he? she kept asking. All the usual routes and pleas to him hadn't worked at all.

Centerton had been vanquished of an evil villain, it seemed, and the Revolving Restaurant had been repaired. I thought there was no way they'd get anyone back up that thing, but apparently it had reminded a lot of local residents that it still existed, and its reopening was one of its rare popular success days, and then it was booked out for months. I disliked seeing the smug face of the manager, who was still there, grinning madly in front of all his staff, minus, I noticed, that serving girl, the one who'd helped me. I wondered what had happened to her.

So it was a quiet autumn. I didn't mind. I took to hanging out more often at Vinnie's, as Gertie's bride tendencies got ever more pronounced. It was quiet there. Plus I managed to persuade him to let me use his bath. I called my mum so much she got worried, which is annoying when mums do that. It's like you hardly need Ultimate Man to have psychic abilities when there are mums in the world.

I watched the leaves turn glowing orange and brown in Meridian Park and tried a mindfulness yoga class, at which I sucked most mightily, particularly when I saw all the incredibly slim and toned women in the class run straight out of it, dashing to their phones in case they'd missed a teeny tiny bit of nothing which referred to them during the sixty minutes.

I couldn't help but notice that though; as if Frederick Cecil had opened my eyes somehow. That if an alien came to earth, he would think we carried our hearts in our pockets. Or our babies. Or something unbelievably precious to us, more important than our children, who stumbled while we were fixated; more important that our legs, as we tripped downstairs, eyes distracted; more important than our lives, even, as people checked their social media while trying to drive cars.

And I became attuned to the low-level misery, the bad reviews, the rape threats, the comment sections of newspapers; the great broiling cesspit which spilled out into the world constantly from the net. It didn't find its way into my press releases, which stayed lovely and positive and desperately, almost aggressively upbeat, about Centerton, even as the muggings escalated and the streets got dirtier (I hadn't realised until he vanished that Ultimate Man also spent a vast amount of time telling people off for littering. This made me feel slightly softer towards him than I was inclined to). The press releases were sweet. But everything else – the beheadings on Facebook; the bodies on beaches; the women doxed and attacked – everything else that caught my attention seemed to be making things just that little bit worse. And there was a tiny bit of me, as I got into my lonely bed at night, listening to the shouts of the streets outside and the noise and the music, which slightly wished I was in a white bed, on an island, curled up with a book and the sound of the waves.

Chapter Sixty-four

I suppose there are more lonely situations than setting off to try and persuade your introverted brother to come with you as your plus-one to your best friend's wedding, but I couldn't think of any that morning.

There was a touch of frost in the mornings now, the beauty of the sky and the leaves tempered by the knowledge that we were about to plunge into an icy world of darkness for months on end. I had recently had another dream about being back on Frederick Cecil's island. I could smell the frangipani on the trees. Then I saw the tree catch fire, and everything caught fire, and everything was burning, and Gertie had to come in and sit on my bed until I calmed down.

I had called Vinnie several times – and called Mum, who had sniffed and said it was cruel to force him out like that and I had said wasn't it cruel not to and she said no it wasn't. Nevertheless, I didn't hold out much hope when I set out after work on a rainy afternoon.

Nelson caught the lift just ahead of me. His broad shoulders looked defeated; his jacket was a little crumpled. He had barely spoken to me for a month. He had seemed saggier, more defeated; had turned up, worked quietly and then moved on every day. Liz had made a couple of remarks about lovers' spats, but neither of us had risen to the debate. It felt absurd: the man I had wanted to make friends with wouldn't because I wouldn't date him; the man I had tried to date ... I wasn't thinking about at all. Not at all.

As Nelson wearily pushed open the door of City Hall, on impulse borne out of sleepless nights and sadness, I caught him up.

'Hey,' I said. I knew he lived off in the suburbs, so I knew where he'd catch the subway, and it was near Vinnie's place. 'Can I walk with you? I'm going that way.'

There was a pause.

'Sure,' he said.

At first, it was awkward, walking along, him with his usual slightly ponderous shuffle; he was even slower than usual. Then we both got splashed – drenched, in fact – by a passing cab, so all-encompassingly – I was soaked from head to foot more or less, and sent out a stream of proper Centerton swear-words in the cab's wake, and took his number – that we turned to look at one another and simply couldn't help laughing.

'Maybe I look better wet,' said Nelson, wiping the drops from his glasses. 'Like Ursula Andress.'

I grinned, trying to wring out my sodden coat.

'I think you're more of a Halle Berry type,' I said, and he smiled back at me. We squelched on and decided to go and get a cup of coffee, then we steamed up the tiny artisanal coffee shop and a man with a beard looked very unhappy with us for dripping all over his impeccably sourced stools, so that was also problematic, and I realised I was giggling for the first time in months, and

I had completely forgotten what easy company Nelson was, how interested he was in me – not in saving the world, or destroying it, or his own tortured masculinity, rescuing me like a sack of puppies from a river. He asked me questions about myself and how I was and how I was feeling, and it was like a cold drink of water on a hot day, a balm.

We left the coffee shop and I slowed down to his more even pace – much to the annoyance of bustling Centerton residents trying to pass us – and we meandered along the pretty streets of the south village, and I found myself sad when I ended up outside my brother's door, realising even as I did so that Nelson was miles out of his way and had obviously enjoyed walking and talking with me as much as I had.

'So this is me,' I said reluctantly. Nelson, ever the bumbler, slightly tripped over his own feet as he stopped, and I stood on Vinnie's expensive art deco steps. Even a step up from him, I was nowhere near his height.

'Okay,' he said. I buzzed Vinnie.

'Um,' said Nelson.

The door clicked open – Vinnie had seen it was me and had let me in straightaway, which was definitely a good sign, plus I was going to need a bath – but I lingered. Nelson had gone bright pink.

'It was nice to catch up,' he said, staring at his shoes.

'Normal,' I told myself, internalising a stern voice which I wasn't sure who it belonged to. Definitely not my mum, who was far more bohemian and interesting than I would ever be, and didn't really care who I dated as long as Vinnie was all right. 'Normal. Nice. Human. Suitable. Someone you can really get on with. Someone who understands you.'

More than that. Someone who would make an effort to

understand me. Something none of the other males who'd crossed my path had shown the slightest effort to accomplish.

'I ... I really enjoyed it too.'

I smoothed my wet hair down with my hands.

'I am so, so sorry about what happened before ...' I said. 'I was in terrible shock, and I didn't know what I was doing and it all got ... Well, it got more complicated than I can explain. But it was really. I mean. Is there any chance we could ...?'

A light rain started to fall, and we both smiled as we got even wetter, but it simply didn't matter. Then Nelson's face lit up and he retrieved an umbrella from his satchel and I burst out laughing and said, 'Now? *Now* you let me know you have one of those?'

And he said, 'I know. It's a very special umbrella: you have to be completely soaking wet before I'll let you use it.'

And he held it up over my head on the stoop and I found myself smiling up at him, into the glasses streaming with water. I didn't notice the dark shape looming through the frosted glass of Vinnie's apartment door.

'Sis! What are you doing?'

Vinnie looked immaculate as always, in the same white shirt he habitually wore, but angry at having to come downstairs. I realised then that the door must have buzzed open several times but I hadn't been paying attention, had completely missed it in fact, which must have upset Vinnie's sequence of events.

'Oh hi,' I said, feeling slightly warm around the face but still, somehow, happier than I had been in months. Vinnie straightened up, taking in the fact that I wasn't alone. The two men looked at one another.

I fumbled and felt embarrassed and a little silly about everything and it was ridiculous – it was hardly like Vinnie was going to care about who I dated or whether I did; he didn't really have the ability to care about anything I did at all. Sometimes I wasn't entirely sure that I actually existed for him the second I left the room. Mind you, in my state of mind these days, I felt like that about most men I knew.

'Um,' I said, then I smiled. 'Vinnie, this is Nelson.'

They looked at each other for a long time.

'No, it isn't,' said Vinnie.

I looked at him.

'What do you mean?'

Nelson looked shocked suddenly, and started backing away. He was, I noticed, wiping his face quite carefully with a handkerchief; as the rain came down harder, he pulled the umbrella further and further down over his face.

'His name isn't Nelson,' Vinnie said, in that monotone of his. 'His name is Frederick Cecil.'

Chapter Sixty-five

I froze. So did Nelson.

'No,' I said, shaking my head, almost laughing. 'No. No.'

I was frantically trying to think about when I'd come over. That day we were watching the picture appear, and he plugged in his old dial-up connection ... No. I must have mentioned his name. I must have. Mustn't I? Or had I just called him the baddie?

And Vinnie's visual recognition was awful. Of course. It was simple confusion. He must have got mixed up. Didn't get out enough. Didn't see enough people. People weren't really his thing after all. That must be what it was.

'No,' I said, trying to clear my throat. 'No, Vinnie. That was me talking about someone else. Someone else altogether. This is Nelson Barmveyer.'

There was a very long pause.

'No,' said Vinnie again, in that voice of his which had little time for ambiguity. 'I was at school with you. This is Frederick Cecil.'

My brain was racing fast. Could it be coincidence? Maybe that was Nelson's other name. It couldn't be. It couldn't be. Everything about them – Nelson was taller. Fatter. His voice. His skin was smooth, not rough; his hair was flat, without the ...

Nelson stood there in the rain, looking at both of us as if completely unsure what was going on. Maybe he was: someone had just walked up to him and accused him of being someone else altogether.

Or maybe.

I looked at his thick hair. The rain was getting in, running down the back of the umbrella. I looked. And I saw it. Unmistakeably. That damn kiss-curl popping up under a welter of thick dark Brylcreem dye-looking stuff, which even now was starting to run just a little.

'No,' I said. 'This is impossible.'

I ran towards him, even as he backed away. But I only had to do one thing. I put my wet hand up to his wet face. And when I pulled it away, my palm was lightly tinged with make-up.

Then he turned and ran – with a slight limp, in a most un-Nelson like fashion – off into the crowd.

Chapter Sixty-six

Vinnie didn't even think to make me a drink to deal with shock, so I managed it myself with an unopened bottle of whisky I found in one of his pristine cupboards.

'It's not,' I tried to explain again. 'It's not Frederick Cecil. Frederick Cecil is the bad guy. The guy who kidnapped me. Which I didn't tell you about because it would freak Mum out and also because you wouldn't really care, which would make me feel bad.'

Vinnie blinked.

'I would care,' he said. 'Why would you think I wouldn't care?'

'I don't know,' I said.

'Is this why you keep having bad boyfriends? Because you think nobody cares about you? Because you think Mum only cares about me and I don't care about anyone? Is that why you have to keep doing stupid things which you think are brave but are actually only rash and stupid? Because you think Mum and I won't notice you?'

I was started by how acute his analysis sounded.

'Actually yes,' I said. 'And . . . '

'Oh,' he said. 'Well, don't think that. It's not true.'

I looked at him, eyes goggling.

'That's not Frederick Cecil,' I said. 'I've been close to them both. It's not. Nobody can disguise themselves like that.'

'It was a terrible disguise,' said Vinnie. 'I recognised him immediately.'

'But he was fatter.'

'Fat suit.'

'And Frederick Cecil has really bad skin.'

'Make-up.'

'And Nelson is taller.'

'Shoes.'

'And Nelson ... smells different.'

Vinnie rolled his eyes at me.

'Frederick Cecil was in grad school with me.'

Vinnie had been the most brilliant student in his year. He'd lasted about five minutes in grad school before he'd been recruited by a firm.

'He was as good as me. I don't know how I didn't see it. The Wi-Fi. He's about the only other person on earth who could do it. I can't believe I didn't figure it out.'

'I can't believe I didn't figure it out,' I echoed weakly. 'But I googled ... '

'You can google me too,' said Vinnie. 'Won't find me.'

He hadn't left me in the Revolving Restaurant. He'd taken me there. I hadn't been kidnapped. I'd gone willingly. All that stuff about having no family and moving to the city ...

'Did Frederick Cecil have a family?' I barked at Vinnie suddenly. I felt such an idiot. Why hadn't I asked my brother more, found out if he knew any tech geniuses I could investigate?

Vinnie screwed up his face. 'There was something about that ... I never listen to family stuff.'

'Right,' I said.

'But I think . . . I think he was brought up in care.'

I put my head in my hands.

'This is twisted as fuck.'

A job the day after the heist. Sitting next to me. Asking me all those questions about myself. It wasn't about me. Of course not. It was just a way to reach Ultimate Man; to get closer to this person who for whatever reason had taken an interest in me. He had been working under all our noses this entire time. No wonder he'd used the mayor's office: it was handy. It was all reconnaissance.

'Oh fuck,' I said. 'Oh fuck oh fuck oh fuck oh fuck.'

And the even more chilling thought: Ultimate Man burning down his base hadn't stopped him. Hadn't stopped him at all.

Chapter Sixty-seven

There was nothing to do but wait. I knew I should call Ultimate Man. I steeled myself, dug the landline up, dialled laboriously the only number I had ever learned by heart that wasn't my mum's.

It rang out. I tried again. Still nothing. I hated the idea that he was sitting, looking at the phone, rolling his eyes because here she was, his crazy stalker lady, ringing him day and night. Gah, it was annoying.

The Wi-Fi was still on. But there was something else. It didn't matter how good your ad blocker was, or your pop-up blocker or whatever: every time you turned it on, there was a large white square in front of your screen. Only for a second, then it would disappear. People thought it was a glitch. It made you feel strange when you saw it though.

I did not think it was a glitch.

Vinnie slowed it way down frame by frame and called me, which was a miracle as he never called anyone. I went round and watched it over his shoulder. Sure enough, these white pop-ups weren't actually all white at all: there were tiny flashes, tiny uncomfortable flashes, just a millisecond long, too quick for the human eye to see or the brain to register, but they were there nonetheless – scenes of slaughter and destruction, meat markets and slavery. Terrorist recruitment images. Homeless and derelict people. Death camps. And slogans too: Wake up! Wake up! Look around! Live in the world! Live in it! Live in it!

'Jesus,' I said.

'What does he want?'

'He still wants to take down the internet. Permanently.'

Vinnie whistled through his teeth.

'That's ambitious.'

'Is it possible?'

'Well, anything's *possible*.'

'Will he just keep on at it? Until the entire internet is just a white square?'

'I'd say so. That's what I'd do. If I wanted to take over the internet. But why would you want to do that?'

Weirdly I found I didn't want to say. Frederick Cecil's pain was his own, and too vivid to share.

'Because he's a crazy bad man,' I said.

Vinnie nodded. 'Well,' he said. 'I'd back up your photographs.'

'Come with me to Gertie's wedding.'

'I don't actually give a shit about your photographs.'

'That wasn't a bargaining chip,' I said. 'I just want you to come to Gertie's wedding with me.'

'No.'

'Pleeeeease. Come on. It might be the last social event before the apocalypse.'

'Deterioriating Wi-Fi is not the apocalypse.'

'It is,' I said, thinking back to the young boy's tantrum. The fights in the street. The breakdown of everything. 'It is. It's the beginning of the end. The end of civilisation. Like when they decommissioned Concorde.'

'Nobody cared when they decommissioned Concorde. The world kept turning.'

'No,' I said, shaking my head. 'No, it didn't. It admitted that sometimes we go backwards. That sometimes progress doesn't succeed. And this is going to be just like that. Except worse. I don't think we could wrench our personalities back into the real world. I think it'll be too much for us. I think the internet keeps us calm by showing us how frightening things are out in the world where you don't mindlessly eat and consume and watch stuff and fiddle. If we're no longer anaesthetised . . . who knows what might happen?'

'Are you drinking Kool-Aid?' said Vinnie.

'No,' I said. 'But I'm very, very frightened. I know what this man is capable of. Ultimate Man's vanished. There's no one to save us. We're all going to die. So. Please come with me to Gertie's wedding.'

Chapter Sixty-eight

Gertie and I were sitting in the park the night before. It was a sunny evening with a distinct chill this late in the year. Tomorrow was going to be absolutely perfect. We were sharing a half-bottle of champagne and telling ourselves very firmly that this was going to be absolutely it and Gertie had to be going to bed at 7 p.m. to give herself that new bride glow, as if her and DuTroy hadn't been living together for a year.

'Nothing's going to change, you know,' said Gertie, as we watched some oversized seagulls eat discarded chips out of a fast-food container, which seemed as good a metaphor for my life as any.

'Of course it will, Gert,' I said. 'Everything will change. You'll move somewhere nice in the suburbs and I'll just carry on getting older and more bitter, and then I'll get a cat and everyone will pretend they really like my cat but instead they'll feel sorry for me and I'll give the cat a really stupid name like Mr Snuggleupicus and people will want to weep when they hear it and I'll buy clothes for the cat and give it a birthday and have a party and make everyone come.'

'I will always come to your cat birthday party,' said Gertie gravely.

'Oh God,' I said.

'DuTroy is disappointed,' she said. 'He really hoped you might get Ultimate Man to come to the wedding.'

'Seriously?'

Gertie nodded.

'Seriously. Honestly, he was beside himself.'

She took a long pull of the fizz. Fortunately, I had actually secretly bought two half-bottles as I know us quite well.

'I wonder sometimes ... I do wonder if he's settling for me.'

'DuTroy?' I said. 'Are you nuts? He's crazy about you.'

'I mean, look how awestruck he gets around Ultimate Man. I must be second best to that kind of life.'

'Believe me,' I said, popping the other cork and taking a drink. The bubbles went up my nose. 'That kind of life totally sucks. Totally.'

Gertie looked at me.

'Are you sorry it didn't work out?'

I thought back to that one night.

'Yes. Of course,' I said. 'But it's BS. The entire thing. It's all about the guy and about him nobly saving the world. How the hell would I fit into that? Back for supper, darling ... Oh no, I see. Out endangering yourself again. That's fine; I'll just wash your fricking cape, shall I? Oh sorry, I can't, I've been kidnapped again because that's what happens to hero's girl-friends. I'll just swing here upside down while you go to another function ... '

I took a deep breath.

'No,' I said. 'It can't work.'

'Something will,' said Gertie ferociously and slightly tipsily, putting her hand on my arm. 'You're good and brave, and attractive when you make an effort.'

'Uh, thanks, I think,' I said.

'It'll work out for you. Don't aim too high.'

'All right, Mum.'

'And . . . I hope DuTroy isn't aiming too low.'

'You are *mad*. Completely demented.'

'I'm allowed a little wobble the night before, right?'

'You're the most loved-up girl in the universe. He's the most loved-up boy. It's going to be fine. It's going to be better than fine. It's going to be super.'

Chapter Sixty-nine

The next morning did indeed dawn as the most perfect autumn day you could imagine. Beautiful. The leaves were golden-red and brown in the trees; there was a crispness in the air. If you didn't look at the litter and the graffiti and the dog mess on the pavements, or listen to the sirens or look up at the police helicopters, it was heavenly.

Gertie and DuTroy had (unexpectedly) gone for a hipster vibe (although thankfully DuTroy had avoided the beard).

Gertie was wearing a vintage frock from the twenties, with a flat cream front, and a long skirt which came up just above her ankles. On her head was a veil with a band around it, which could have looked fancy dress on someone who wasn't as beautiful and glowing and lovely as she. Her skin shone; she glowed with happiness. DuTroy was in a pale cream suit and loafers. They looked like something from an old movie, as if they moved in sepia through the drifting brown leaves on the pavement.

The normal array of grumpy derelicts and panhandling drunks left us alone as we all casually walked down to the ancient church. Vinnie looked uncomfortably stiff in his white shirt, but I insisted on holding his arm anyway. I was wearing a pretty floral dress. Even though I had about a million floral dresses in my wardrobe already, I'd decided I needed a new one and this had tiny sprigs of daisies on a green background and chimed very nicely with my informal bridesmaid role, in which I had point-blank refused to organise the hen party (although I had sung loud karaoke and ended up having a very long confusing conversation with a stranger in the bathroom about why my love life was such a disaster. I can't remember what she said, but it was probably along the lines of because I sang loud karaoke at hen parties, then spilled my guts in the toilets).

There was a motley collection of friends and family – Gertie's mum and about nine thousand of her aunties had flown in from Antigua and were definitely not dressed for a hipster wedding, which I reckoned actually made it more hip – plus the old gang from college, and I realised how much I'd been neglecting my friends. I sighed, looking at everyone, so many people paired off already, and remembered that stupid advice they always give you in magazines: get on with making yourself happy and everything else will fall into place. Whereas I'd spent half the year caught up in mad events beyond my control, and thinking endlessly about one guy (two guys, my traitorous heart whispered, but I ignored it. Sometimes, two), fixating on my love life. Which was almost certainly why I didn't have one. I sighed, then pasted my smile back on for the cameras.

'Hey, what's been happening?' said Simone, who was engaged to an uptown banker and made a lot of fuss about how her ring was too big to go through airport security every time they were on their way to yet another glamorous expensive holiday destination.

I tried to figure out how to answer that question. I couldn't.

'Oh, the usual,' I said.

298

She tilted her head and battered her false eyelashes winningly.

'It will happen to you one day!' she trilled. 'Totally! Although you should get a move on!'

'Okay,' I said unconvincingly, and suddenly desperately wanted to shout, 'By the way, oh yes, I nearly forgot: I totally boned Ultimate Man in his gigantic mansion and it was more awesome than any sex you've ever had ever.'

Then I remembered my brother was there, and wisely decided against it. Someone passed me a bottle of champagne. I drank quite a lot of it.

'I would like,' DuTroy was saying, holding Gertie's hands in his. She was gazing into his eyes – they were pretty much level when she wore heels. Her face was absolutely rapturous with excitement and love. I smiled, feeling a little teary. She deserved this.

'I would like to make you laugh every day. To hold you every day. To wish you good night. To be happy when you are happy and to comfort you when you are sad. I will always, always be on your side. I will always, always be on your team. I will.'

'You may kiss the . . . '

'OW!'

'ARGH!'

There was a loud crashing noise as suddenly, all around, people were jumping back. I felt a glowing in my pocket. My phone was red hot, untouchable. That was the noise from everyone else: they were dropping their phones on the ground.

'What's happening, man?' shouted someone. There was general disquiet. On the screens of all the phones, the white square was appearing, spreading. Everyone had their phones now placed on the ground or on the back of the chair in front of them, glowing hot, the square growing until the entire screen was white. The party fell silent, apart from two of Gertie's noisier aunties, who didn't have them.

'Don't stop the wedding!' said Gertie, but the celebrant was already crouched down, comforting a child who'd been using their iPad.

I slipped away to the side towards Vinnie, holding my hot phone with my cardigan.

'What's he done?' I said to Vinnie, who simply shrugged his shoulders. 'He'll have reversed the voltage to make them burn up. Pretty tricky stuff. He's just taken control of all the phones in the city.'

He said this in a completely emotionless way.

'Not just the phones,' I said. Two other children had been gaming in the corner, and now both of them were crying. 'Oh my God.'

I placed mine down. 'Can you reverse it?'

'I'd need my own computer to have a shot at a workaround, and let's just assume for the minute he's got at those too.'

Suddenly every single phone in the place – and in the street outside; in the entire city – went off, with a hideous cacophony of bells and calls and whistles and, in one case, the 'Macarena'.

'Somebody wants our attention,' said Vinnie.

'He's got it,' I said.

I stared at my phone on the nearby table. Everyone else's was pure white. But I noticed that on mine, there was a tiny flicker. There was something. It was the cursor. The little, green flashing cursor.

Using my cardigan, I grabbed the phone towards me. It was utterly scorching. I hid myself away from everyone else. The cursor flashed, then very slowly the letters appeared.

```
>H-E-L-P M-E
```

Chapter Seventy

'What are you doing?' said Vinnie, as I pointed it in his direction. 'What is that?'

'I think it's Ultimate Man!' I said. 'That's his secret way of contacting me.'

'Through time travel?' he said, examining the ancient green script. Vinnie doesn't know how to be sarcastic so I have to assume he meant it.

I pulled the cardigan over my fingers and tried to type on it. I was rubbish.

```
>WERERABBIT U?
```

'How often do you type "wererabbit"?' asked Vinnie.
'Shut up.'

```
>WERE YOU?
```

'That's the wrong usage of "were".'
'SHUT UP!'

I stared at the cursor, willing it to life. It flashed once ... twice ...

>H E L.

And then, nothing.

I grabbed Vinnie.

'You can find out,' I said. 'Find out where that was from. Can't you?'

He screwed up his face.

'Frederick Cecil was ... I mean, he was the most brilliant programmer I ever met. He made the rest of us look like level one of *Donkey Kong*.'

He picked up the phone. 'Ow! Hot!'

'Vinnie, sometimes it is actually okay to pay attention to what other humans do.'

He didn't listen and took out a handkerchief to cover his fingers. He could still feel the heat through it though, as he winced and jabbed at the phone, somehow uncovering a screen behind the white, and after that, lines and lines of computer code I hadn't known were there, or were accessible. Of course, they probably weren't.

'This is good,' he said. 'This is very, very good.'

'He's a horrifying monster!' I said. 'Hurry up.'

I was touched that my brother, normally so intractable in so many ways, so difficult and complicated, was doing this for me. It was not easy for him to put himself in other people's shoes. Even though it hurt him, clearly, to type, to find out what was happening, he kept at it, occasionally sucking his fingers like a wounded bear. His blink rate intensified.

'There,' he said, pointing out a line which of course meant absolutely nothing to me.

'What's that?'

'That's the rough position of where the signal's coming from. It triangulates from three points, so it's coming from one of those. I can get into the sat nav ... '

'Where is it?'

Then he told me.

Chapter Seventy-one

'Where the *hell* are you running off to?'

Gertie was in tears as the room was deteriorating into chaos all around her. It was her wedding day, and all anyone was talking about was their phones and the outage and was this the Wi-Fi thing all over again and what was going to happen to the world. Everyone had stopped taking pictures, obviously, and filming things, and she couldn't share her day any more with her grandpa, who was too old to come but had been watching it on Skype. And now her maid of honour – me – who was due to give a speech in five minutes' time, was charging outside with one of the other guests in tow.

When the signal had been pinpointed as coming from inside this block, I had immediately jumped, panicking. The worst thing was, we didn't know exactly where. Vinnie stood in the middle of the room, scanning the guests. Could Frederick Cecil already be here in disguise? It seemed unlikely but I could no longer put anything past him.

'You can't leave.'

'We're not leaving,' I said gruffly. 'He's here.'

'Is it Ultimate Man?' said DuTroy, standing by his almost-wife's side. 'Is he fixing it? Does he need you? Because he could totally come by here afterwards for the reception if he'd like to.'

I didn't think that telling him that I actually had to go and rescue him would do much in the way of easing the obvious tensions.

'Don't worry,' I said, which was crap because this was very much a time when everyone should be very, very worried.

DuTroy shook his head.

'Of course I'm going to worry,' he said. 'Do you think he's nearby?'

I nodded.

'I think he's here. Or very close.'

He turned round to the room and held up his arms.

'Don't worry everyone,' he said to the scared-looking aunties. 'Everything's going to be totally fine. I just need you all to head to the bar two blocks down, and Gertie's going to lead you there, keep you out of trouble. It'll be fine.'

He bowed his head slightly.

'You're coming with me!' screamed Gertie, her face a picture of panic.

'I will,' said DuTroy. 'I'll lock up and be right down. I promise.'

Gertie stared at him.

'Don't,' she said. 'Don't you think this is your moment. Don't you think you're going to be like Ultimate Man.'

DuTroy bowed his head in a humble way and turned his brown-eyed gaze fully onto Gertie's face.

'I have to,' he said, touching her lightly on the face. 'It's my destiny to protect you.'

All the aunties tutted and sighed. I glanced in panic at my watch. Gertie looked like she was going to melt.

'Then come with me.'

'Two minutes,' he said. 'Just so I'm sure everyone is out. But go. GO NOW.'

'You're my hero,' she said as they started to shepherd everyone out together.

Vinnie held up my phone and tugged my sleeve urgently. He'd pulled up plans of the ancient church, and pointed one out.

'Catacombs,' he said.

'What?'

'There are catacombs underneath the church. Where they used to bury their dead.'

'Here? In Centerton?'

'Yup. Most of them were cleared when they built the subway. Most of them. But according to this map, not all of them. Unless he's up in the bell tower.'

I looked up and down. Which was most likely? We had no time to choose. Up or down?

Chapter Seventy-two

'Down,' said Vinnie.

I looked at him.

'Why?'

'Connections. Cables. Subways. Everything you need. Down. Go.'

'Thank you.'

Gertie had led everyone else out. DuTroy stood at the entrance, looking tough but solemn, his jaw jutting. I almost smiled to see him.

'The faintest *hint* of trouble,' I hissed at him. 'You call me, okay? You call me.'

I had absolutely no idea what I'd be able to do. But it might be better than nothing.

DuTroy nodded quickly, and I turned around and went.

The door to the old sacristy was locked, and we had to persuade the verger to open it for us. We told her that we could fix her online bridge group, and she seemed mollified enough. I had no idea who Frederick Cecil would have down there. Plus I needed stealth. I had looked at Vinnie, but he had looked back at me and shaken his head.

I completely understood. I had already taken him so far out of his comfort zone, dragging him out to this wedding; pushing his boundaries. This would be a step too far. And he had already helped so much. I nodded briefly. He didn't wish me luck. He didn't think in that way. Which was probably for the best.

The great old wooden door clanged hard behind me; the tunnel was dark, lit only by small bulbs here and there, dotted along the earthen tunnel. The earthen tunnel that was filled with bones.

I shivered and told myself not to be such a wuss. Ultimate Man had scaled Centerton Tower to come and rescue me. Although of course he had magic powers. Whereas all I had was an overdraft, a good WPM and a selection of slightly daring berets.

I couldn't hear anything but a slight rushing wind in the air, and I could feel it too: a draught on my face. Where was it coming from?

The path I was on continued to descend; we must be out of the church grounds now. It was freezing; I pulled my cardigan around me, my heart sounding treacherously loud, wondering what I would meet at the bottom. I was using my hot phone as a torch now, its glowing white light showing me the way. I turned it towards the wall of the catacombs and immediately jumped back as a skull grinned at me. I squeaked but managed not to scream; I wanted to lean against the wall, which of course I couldn't do. It was utterly horrible, however much I told myself that they were dead and gone, that there was nothing they could do to me.

In contrast to what lay ahead.

The lamps had run out the further and deeper I got. I was entirely reliant on my phone now. But the wind kept blowing stronger and stronger.

Suddenly I heard a terrifying noise: a rumble which turned into a roar. I dropped my phone in shock, then found myself dropping to the floor, covering my head and my ears, closing myself off to the deadly noise, wishing myself anywhere but there.

Chapter Seventy-three

The terrifying noise faded away. I glanced upwards, but could see nothing around me; it was just me, in the dark, with hundreds of ancient skeletons. I panted, trying to fend off a massive panic attack.

Somewhere ahead, as I blinked, the darkness around me like a blanket, there was the tiniest pinpoint of light. I could see it. The tiniest trace of something.

I flashed back suddenly to hiding in the cupboard at the office. In a funny way, it made me feel stronger. If I'd felt scared then, it was a million times worse now. And I was much stronger. Much.

Slowly, gradually, I straightened up, put my arms out in front of me – shuddering whenever they brushed a bony protuberance from the wall – and started, quietly, to move.

I don't know how long that dark, horrible tunnel went on for. It felt like for ever, like an age. The noise didn't come back and I could hear my own panicky breathing in the terrible silence, and the horribly growing fear that this was not the way, that I had made the wrong choice and that even now, Frederick Cecil was destroying Ultimate Man on top of the bell tower and taking his helicopter to freedom.

But he wouldn't destroy him, would he? He just wanted to talk to him, didn't he?

Then I thought of how he had lied to me as Nelson, how untrustworthy he was and how I had absolutely no idea what he was capable of. He was burning the hands of children.

The dot of light grew larger and larger and I realised it was opening into some kind of a cavern. Just as I moved more sure-footedly towards it, I heard a rumbling noise again; a great wind blew into my face, and I recognised it, and couldn't believe I hadn't recognised it before: it was a subway train, rollicking past. We must be just above the tunnels. It was horrifyingly loud, and the lights now flashed across the entrance. What was it? An access spot?

And what was I going to find in there? I kept moving forwards.

Chapter Seventy-four

I crept up to the entrance and peered in, my eyes blinking in the light.

It was a large underground cave. The walls were studded with bones, including skeletal fingers still wearing rings; locks of hair, once lustrous and beautiful, were now dried out hanks.

At one end, there was a hole which obviously led down to the train tracks beneath. Must be how they got in.

Ultimate Man was trussed up, upside down, in one corner of the room, hanging from the ceiling in heavy metal bonds. He was obviously coming round from some massive dose of drugs as he looked very woozy, and I wondered how Frederick Cecil had got close enough to administer them ...

He didn't see me. Once again, I cursed getting rid of the psychic abilities.

On the other side was Frederick Cecil. He was holding something in his hands about the size of a ping-pong ball, which glowed.

'Just join me,' he said. 'Join me. Join my campaign for good.

For re-education. Stop trying to thwart what I'm doing here, it's all I ask. It's for the good.'

Ultimate Man, muffled, shook his head.

'You're wrong, Frederick Cecil. You're wrong. People won't give it up. It's lifted people out of poverty. It's promoted freedom of expression all over the world. It's allowed us to share injustice and messages and brought humanity closer than it's ever been.'

'It's promoted the worst, the most filth-addled reprobate whims of that humanity,' spat Frederick Cecil. 'It has made the very worst of humanity.'

'And the best,' said Ultimate Man. 'It has disseminated more than you could ever imagine.'

'Very well,' said Frederick Cecil, sighing. 'I have tried and tried with you.'

'And I will still stop you.'

'I didn't want to do this. I really didn't. All prophets begin with the best of intentions. But I'm going to have to kill you. If I can't get round you and I can't get past you, I'll just have to get through you.'

And he pulled out the knife. That shining knife. And every single doubt I'd ever had fell away. But I almost, *almost* screamed the wrong name.

'R . . . ULTIMATE MAN!' I screamed and hurled myself into the chamber. The strange metallic ropes were like hard wire, but I had the element of surprise on my side.

Unfortunately, I completely muffed it by running full pelt into Ultimate Man, banging my head on his elbow, and set him swinging like a pendulum.

'Holly!' they both shouted at the same time.

'How did you text me?' I shot at Ultimate Man.

'I can do tongue stuff . . . GET OUT!'

Frederick Cecil looked horrified, perhaps by the mention of tongue stuff, and lowered the knife slightly.

'What ... what are you doing here?'

'Friends are there for one another.'

I walked up to him, face white.

'You said ... you said ... Are you going to hurt him?'

He looked at me, his face twisted in embarrassment and shame.

'I gave him every chance. This can work, Holly. But we all have to be on the same side.'

Behind me, the metal chains were still creaking and twisting.

'You said you abhorred violence.'

He put his hand out.

'We can still make it right, Holly. We can still have a better world. Without this crazed, violent vigilante. This killer.'

'OH! All you motherless boys!' I shouted. 'You're all nuts. NO. Stop it. Give me that knife.'

The tables had turned completely. I found I was no longer afraid of Frederick Cecil.

'Give it to me!'

He looked me straight in the eye. They were so green. How could I never have noticed that Nelson had that direct stare too? Brown eyes, not green. But I had simply thought he was a naïf, an innocent farm boy.

Was there ever even such a thing?

His face twisted into a snarl.

'You asked for it,' he said. And he twitched his hand with the knife and brought it up to my chest, and was about to jam it straight into my ribs. I pushed him back, and then I saw he really was angry.

'No one lays another hand on me,' he screamed. 'No one! No more!'

And I felt the point of the knife on my vintage dress, and I saw, as if in a dream, it cut through the layers of chiffon to the pale freckled skin beneath.

Chapter Seventy-five

You know how when you're a kid there's always another kid at a swing set who says he knows someone who once swung all the way over the top, all the way over. And you can try and try, but it never happens?

The creaking grew louder and ever louder, and I found I simply watched, paralysed, as the knife entered my body; as everything I had feared in my darkest nightmares, since that very first night in the bar, started to happen.

Next, there was a huge crashing noise as the chains turned over from the hook they were held from, and *bang!*, suddenly, in a great rattle, Ultimate Man – no longer doped up – was in between Frederick Cecil and me, his body huge. He was panting hard, his chains wrapped around his neck, his arms above his head still tied together, but his body was there, and he pushed, quickly, knocking Frederick Cecil completely off his feet.

And then the knife was in the air, glinting and tumbling as it flew – the knife Frederick Cecil had always carried, had always meant to use. The way he had got into my head suddenly horrified me completely: I took a step back as Frederick Cecil and Ultimate

Man both desperately reached for it, and WHOOSH, there was a train again, on the tracks below, roaring like a dragon and blowing the knife up on its updraft.

They both stopped whereupon it rebounded, pinging, sparks flying, against Ultimate Man's chains, then shot straight down. And by the time I'd turned my head, Frederick Cecil was nowhere to be seen, but now there was a very tiny white shape, just like a ping-pong ball, flying through the air.

Chapter Seventy-six

My eyes darted around in panic. Where was he? Behind me was a great noise: Ultimate Man was still trying to wrestle himself out of his strange metal electric bonds. But Frederick Cecil . . .

Then I heard it. Heard a groan. I rushed over. Down the hole, gripping on with all his might, was Frederick Cecil, the knife stuck in his shoulder. Beneath him, I could see a great drop to the tracks.

'Holly,' choked Ultimate Man's voice behind me. 'Holly, move. I need to get down the hole. Get rid of the bomb.'

'Wait,' I said. 'Frederick Cecil, can you pull yourself up?'

'I . . . I don't know . . . ' came the voice below.

'Get out of the way.'

I turned round to confront Rufus. But he was holding the tiny glowing spherical device. And it was ticking.

'I need to get that down there!' he shouted, desperately trying to contain the glowing ball. 'GET OUT OF THE WAY!'

I looked down the hole. Frederick Cecil's terrified face was staring back at me.

'Get him up!'

'There's no time!'

I reached my hand down.

'Climb up! Move! Now!'

But the knife was twisting in his shoulder, and he couldn't move.

'GET HIM!'

The bomb was ticking louder than ever. I threw myself onto the ground to get my arm further down the hole.

'Take my hand!'

Frederick Cecil slowly shook his head.

'No,' he said. 'I'll pull you down.'

'But you'll die!'

He looked up at me. And his voice was very quiet and calm once more, just like the first time I'd ever heard it.

'I think. Maybe that's all I've really wanted since I was eight years old.'

I shook my head.

'No! No, that's no good! You owe me!'

He blinked.

'You set me up! You pretended you liked me. You followed me around so you could get to him! You cheated me!'

He blinked again, his large eyes startled.

'No,' he said. 'No. I didn't. I actually liked you. Did that never even occur to you?'

I looked at him, my arm desperately dangling down to reach him. But it could not.

'MOVE, HOLLY!' It was Rufus yelling. But it was too late.

One desperate stretch by me and I touched, only just, the edge of Frederick Cecil's cold fingers.

There was that familiar rush of air of an oncoming train; then I saw through the hole the flash of sparks on the tracks and the rumble sped up and became a roar and I thought I heard a scream, but it may just have been the sound of the train on the tracks, though I did hear a great crack and a wet squelching noise – and then the train passed and it was gone and there was nobody in the hole and I couldn't hear a thing.

And then Rufus was hurling himself at the back wall of the crypt, curled up in a ball, and I knew nothing except a huge great roar of exploding dust, and then I knew nothing at all.

Chapter Seventy-seven

'MOVE! MOVE! WAKE UP!'

Where was I? It was freezing cold, and I was lying somewhere hard. Had I fallen out of bed?

'MOVE!'

I blinked and blinked again. With effort, I took in my surroundings. I was sprawled on the subway line on top of Ultimate Man, whose arms were still chained. Our legs were twisted together. There was soil all around us. Ultimate Man, I realised, was lying in an incredibly awkward contorted position.

'Can you move?' I said, thinking surely he could lift me off; my arm was hideously painful suddenly, and felt like it must be broken; everything came flooding back.

'You have to move first!'

'No, you do it.' My ankle was also in agony.

'I can't,' he said. 'I'm lying on the live rail. If I move, you'll get it.'

And I realised that he was jerking; pulsing up against me.

And I realised something else: there was another rumble. Why couldn't they stop the trains? Why didn't anyone know about us? Why not?

And then I got it. Of course. Frederick Cecil's new fail-safes. The trains were heading to the safety of the depot. There was no safety for us.

'I'm getting up!'

I struggled and twisted in pain. The noise got closer and closer. The lights were approaching in a roar.

'MOVE!'

My ankle was twisted and trapped, and I finally managed to pull it up. But there wasn't time: the two lights of the oncoming train had us in its gaze, like the eyes of a vast hunting animal, and the sides of the tunnel were incredibly steep; there was no way I could climb out in this state.

I paused for just a millisecond. Then, with a tremendous heave, Ultimate Man lifted his legs and threw me, with the most almighty kick, up and over and onto the platform, then rebounded and dropped back onto the rails. I collapsed in a broken bleeding heap in horror, as the train rolled right over the top of him. And even then I remembered to do nothing more than whisper:

'Rufus.'

Chapter Seventy-eight

I lay there in the darkness. I don't know how long for. Bruised and broken, on a filthy platform, waiting for the end of everything. I didn't feel I could turn my head. Couldn't bear to take in what would be there. What would be left.

There was, I heard gradually, a horrible groan. Was it coming from me? If not, from whom then? From Frederick Cecil? No. Nobody could have survived that. No human.

He was almost unrecognisable: his face was a mess of blood and dirt; his purple suit completely torn and hanging off him in shreds. He hauled himself up, like a broken toy, then collapsed onto the platform.

'Oh my God,' I said, starting to cry, even though I still couldn't move. 'Oh my God. Rufus.'

His head hung so heavily. His expression was so, so grave.

'Oh my God, you're all right.'

He looked at me, utterly blasted. He was so very far from all right. He coughed.

'You chose him,' he said. 'When it came down to it, you chose him. Over me, when I was holding the bomb. You chose him over me.'

I looked at him, blinking, feeling in too much pain to do anything more; too much pain to even be able to identify where it was coming from.

'Rufus,' I said softly. 'Rufus. Look at you. You just survived a train running over you. He was just a man. He was just a *man*. A dying man.'

'I'm a man,' said Rufus hoarsely.

I shook my head.

'You're not. You're so much more than a man. You're different. You're not a human. And you can't behave like a man. We are all just ants to you. Insects to be saved or destroyed. A mass of humanity you stand outside of. You can't behave like a man.'

His face was pained.

'I tried.'

'I know,' I said. 'But you can't do it. You couldn't do it. You couldn't respond to me as a man; you couldn't respond to me as a human.

'I'm sorry. I'm sorry that at the end I was with the human. He needed me. You never could. You can rescue me, of course. You always do; you always did. But it's not the same thing.'

There was a long pause as we looked at one another in our absolute depths. He didn't say anything and I thought he started to turn away as we heard the ambulance sirens. Our entire time together, I thought, I will remember because of the sirens. Wherever we went. They were our tune.

And now my heart was breaking. I'd thought I couldn't weep one more tear over this. I was wrong. I had told myself sternly. Not one more tear. Enough now.

But they kept on falling.

When he next spoke, his voice was quiet and low.

'Two thousand, three hundred and eighty-five,' he said.

'What?' I said.

'Two thousand, three hundred and eighty-five. You have two thousand, three hundred and eighty-five freckles.'

'You counted them?'

'I can see them. Every one. You have seventeen different types of colour in your hair. Raw sienna and tumbleweed and antique brass and desert sand and peach.'

I didn't move.

'But you dumped me,' I said.

'I couldn't be with you.'

'You barely tried.'

'We fused the city. I could have killed you.'

'Some people would have called that a good time.'

Two medics and a policeman ran into the subway and started hurling questions at me and shining lights into broken bits of me.

'We killed someone,' I said. 'We killed Frederick Cecil.'

'We didn't,' said Ultimate Man. 'Frederick Cecil was hell-bent on his own destruction from the moment he started stealing handbags. And probably a long, long time before that.'

And I knew that this was true. But that it didn't change a thing.

'I only ... I only ever wanted a night out,' I choked.

He nodded, still covered in dust, then – as more and more people began to approach – he was in an instant of course, as always – gone.

325

Chapter Seventy-nine

'So thanks for saving the city, Holly,' I said grumpily, sitting up in bed. Gertie was there, being cross with me. 'I mean, come on.'

Because it had turned out that the bomb, the tiny one which had detonated completely surrounded by Ultimate Man, who had absorbed the entire blast, would have permanently knocked out every comms device in the city. It had been designed to be set off down the cable which lay alongside the subway tracks and permeate outwards, connecting every internet-connected device which had already been activated with a virus of Frederick Cecil's demonic invention. It would have knocked Centerton back to the dark ages. And I had saved it, because it hadn't gone down the hole.

I had a broken wrist and a twisted ankle and a few cuts and bruises after they'd cleaned me up. Not much in the scheme of things. Not much at all. Gertie was still furious I'd ruined her wedding, although DuTroy had been recommended for a medal from the mayor's office for quickly ushering everyone to safety and, despite Gertie's admonitions, staying in post. He was the happiest I'd ever known him.

Liz was moved to another position in the office for hiring a Nelson Barmeyer who didn't actually exist and had no credentials she'd bothered to check beyond the basics.

I got Liz's job; Bettina didn't want it. I hired a new girl for the office. I didn't want anything more to do with men, nothing at all.

Frederick Cecil left no family and no friends. Almost no trace at all, except a few classmates and teachers who remembered him as the most brilliant mind they'd ever worked with.

There was no funeral.

It was a beautiful chilly day in Centerton: snow on the ground, but sun and pink clouds in the sky. The Christmas decorations were lighting up the town, there were skaters in the parks and fires in the lobbies. The world might be a dank, corrupt place but it had its beautiful spots too.

DuTroy and Gertie were looking at me severely.

'What?'

'Don't have a cow,' said DuTroy who, even though he hadn't had to stop any baddies outside the church, did slightly strut around like there'd been hundreds of them. And fair play: he'd stood there, a faithful sentinel, until we'd finally remembered about him in hospital.

'I'm just saying that in advance,' he went on.

It was their newly planned wedding day. We were all wearing the same clothes, except with fake fur over the top.

'What?'

'We asked him,' said DuTroy. 'Because he saved you. Okay? And because we're kind of . . . I mean, like I did a cool thing too now. And he said yes, all right? He's an ordained minister.'

I felt a mounting sense of dread.

327

'Seriously? Great. I'll invite all your exes, shall I?'

'Don't be daft,' said Gertie. 'Come on. One thing. It's special.'

I was pulled down to the wedding venue with bad grace. They were holding it in the new park: an anonymous billionaire donor had bought a huge plot of land downtown in one of the worst neighbourhoods and turned it into the most exquisite park. There were babbling streams and baby ducks and pergolas and a bandstand and chessboards and swings and a boating lake. It was utterly stunning.

The one stipulation about the park was that there was no Wi-Fi in it and phones were banned.

Friendly volunteers staffed the four wrought-iron gates and carefully filed your phone away for the duration of your time there. Which meant it was always full of people reading, and children playing, and there was no blaring from people playing music; but instead sometimes the sweet sound of an acoustic guitar, the clicking of draughts and knitting needles and people talking, chatting, hanging out or turning the pages of a book. It was beautiful.

'St Cee's Park,' said Gertie. 'Isn't it glorious?'

I was annoyed because it was and it made me miss him. It had raised property values too, and cut crime in the area. And weirdly, I loved it for another reason too: I felt at home there and I didn't know why. For the first time, it seemed, since I'd arrived in this great, strange city in the great, mad country of America.

Gertie and DuTroy stood under the heated bandstand. Ultimate Man was wearing the suit as the celebrant, of course. He couldn't give himself away now, could he? Couldn't fit in or be bloody normal. Had to have all the attention on himself. Hectorio was taking the photos. He tried to get all up in Ultimate Man's grill and make him take off his mask. It didn't work of course, but it was clearly annoying, which pleased me.

328

'You are my hero,' said Gertie as they did the vows again, staring at DuTroy (they were about the same height when Gertie had her heels on). 'You are my hero, my protector for ever.'

DuTroy beamed.

'I do,' he said.

Rufus didn't look at me once. I didn't look at him either. He didn't stay for the reception.

'By the power vested in me by the state of Centerton,' he intoned, his cape billowing behind him, 'I now pronounce you man and wife.'

And everyone clapped and cheered as Gertie and DuTroy kissed long and hard on the bandstand, and the boats going past on the cold, muddy river honked, and we threw confetti in the air and watched it dance on the wind, a promise of the new spring that would come around again.

Chapter Eighty

I'm not sure who was more surprised, Vinnie or me. No, it would have been me. Vinnie didn't do surprise particularly well.

Anyway, when I'd got out of hospital with my broken arm, my mum had breezed into town and insisted that I move in with my brother, seeing as Gertie and DuTroy were of course off to the suburbs, which they were, being married and all that, and I had nowhere to live. And Vinnie had been absolutely adamant about it, then sheepishly said that actually a new apartment had come up in his building next door to him and he'd bought it so that he never had to worry about talking to his neighbours and Mum had yelled at him until he'd agreed to let me stay there for a pepper-corn rent, so that was something. It really was quite something, actually: I loved it. And I wouldn't say that I was always popping into Vinnie's for us to share cosy suppers, but it felt like since he'd helped me out so much, there was something more between us which hadn't been there before. So that was good. I didn't make him come with me to Gertie and DuTroy's second wedding though.

And the new promotion helped of course, and I liked heading

out of the city over the bridge – a little wistfully, sometimes – to Gertie and DuTroy's new place in the burbs, with a nursery space Gertie kept looking at meaningfully. And I loved that, because I liked seeing DuTroy so anchored and happy. It took my mind off having to worry about the lonely, lonely boys I had known. And how lonely it made me too.

Chapter Eighty-one

It wasn't an email – that was the peskiest thing about it. It was a letter. A really beautiful, handwritten letter. Oh, he was infuriating. I hadn't received a proper letter since my grandfather died. Birthday cards, yes, occasionally; lots of dribbly invitations to product launches which local businesspeople thought the mayor might like.

But this was something different altogether: a stiff envelope with my name and address written in beautiful, old-fashioned handwriting by fountain pen; then, when I opened it, a short note. I was standing in my pyjamas, still getting used to the emptiness of my new apartment – none of DuTroy's gigantic boat shoes to stumble over in the hallways; no scented candles burning (Gertie was obsessed; I thought we were all going to die in a conflagration); no heroin addicts in the stairwell. Just me.

Strictly between us, I had been looking at cats in pet shop windows.

Anyway, I looked at the words on the page, rubbing my eyes, going through to make coffee. It was a chilly day in February.

They were very simple.

I was thinking of making dinner if you'd like some. Car at 7.

That was it. Of course, no identifying names or marks; nothing on it at all. The handwriting was beautiful. Some superpowers really were worth having, I thought. I too would like beautiful handwriting. If I could choose.

I hummed and hawed all day. I wanted to talk to someone about it, but I couldn't bear to get into the fact that there was now nobody left on earth who had ever met me who trusted me to go on any kind of an outing at all.

Oh, all the reasons. I knew all the reasons. When I thought back to that night – that one, extraordinary night. I couldn't put myself through it again. Couldn't torture myself again.

So don't go, my better voice urged. Don't go. Don't stir yourself up again. He's made of steel, right?

He is cold and hard as iron. And when it mattered the most, you betrayed him. When it came down to making a choice, he could not choose me. And I did not choose him.

So why dinner? A settling of scores? A rueful entente?

I stood in the window, looking down at the car for a long time. It was a long, sleek, black thing again. At least it wasn't purple. I blinked. Stood up. Sat down. Put on a dress. Took it off.

At 8.30 p.m. it hadn't moved. I sighed. It wasn't really fair to keep John sitting out there. That felt like the flimsiest excuse of all time.

I would go, tell him why I couldn't see him any more, why we couldn't be casual friends. Why it was all right; I knew he was terribly good, he didn't have to 'forgive me' again, nor I him. These things had happened, they had marked us and that was all there was.

'Good evening.'

John opened the door for me and I smiled and thanked him as we glided through the city, which was quiet tonight, unusually so. As if everyone was finally turning in; everyone was calm and sleepy at last, happy to take a night off from doing the crazy noisy work of cities everywhere, whether we like it or not; the electricity of all the people interacting, bouncing off each other as electrons; sparks alighting connections and changes and advances and new ways of doing things. Some good, some bad, all moving us forward, just as the car moved sleekly under the bridge and onto that funny, secret little workman's slip road, and the tarmac under the wheels turned, as the great gate opened, into gravel, and little fires – proper, gas-fired lights – flamed up in lamp posts all the way up the driveway as we moved towards the great house.

John let me out and vanished, and I stood there, my heart in my throat, outside the great door. Swallowing – which did nothing to relieve the lump – I picked up the great brass knocker.

He was there, door open.

'I hate it when you do that,' I said. 'Honestly, move at normal speed. Pretend you're in slow motion or something.'

'Oh,' he said. 'Okay.'

We looked at each other. He was dressed casually again, wearing light cotton trousers, a pale chambray shirt and those heavy black-rimmed glasses. He looked like he'd spent a lot of time and effort trying to choose something which looked like he hadn't spent any time deciding at all.

In contrast, I had completely panicked at the last moment and gone totally over the top. I was wearing a slim-fitting black dress which I'd worn for a function, then felt was far too sophisticated for me to wear. It wasn't me at all: it was quite a heavy material, sleeveless, which zipped all the way up the back and forced me to stand up straight and, when moving, to wiggle.

'Wow,' he said. Then he smiled, just a tiny bit, those white teeth just visible beneath those chiselled lips.

'Are you going diving?'

I looked at him.

'Hang on,' I said. 'Was that actually a "joke"?'

'Um,' he said. 'Dunno. I thought I'd start with "quips" and see how we got on from there.'

I couldn't work out what it was about him. Then I realised. He was properly nervous. I'd seen him a little down before, a little unsure. But never nervous.

'So,' I said. 'You wanted to see me.'

'Um. Yeah.'

'Your park is ... ' I paused. 'It's beautiful.'

'Thanks.'

'St Cee's. What does that mean?'

He shrugged.

'I thought you might like a "C" for Cecil.'

I didn't know what I thought about that at all.

'Would he have liked it? You knew him better than I did.'

'I didn't know him at all. I doubt anyone ever did.'

'How's Vinnie?'

'Exactly the same. Except ... '

And I told him about the apartment. He smiled. 'That's great!'

'Sure!' I said. 'Obviously I miss the rats and hearing every tiny thing Gertie and DuTroy are up to and the homeless man who used to play the drums outside the window. But apart from that, it's tremendous.'

Rufus rubbed the back of his neck.

'I thought you might be hungry.'

He ushered me inside and followed me down the dimly lit hall-way. I could smell something delicious coming from the kitchen.

My heels rapped on the polished parquet, making a stupidly loud noise. I felt his eyes on me as I moved forward.

'You look lovely,' he said suddenly. I whirled round.

'Don't,' I said, suddenly and mortifyingly realising that I was on the brink of tears and my throat was closing over. 'Don't ... don't be nice to me. Please.'

'But ... '

'Don't.' I stopped. I shouldn't have come. I knew it. I was an idiot. I could tell myself till I was blue in the face that I wouldn't fall for him again, and here I was and I couldn't bear it. I absolutely couldn't sit here, and eat with him and joke with him and tease him and get into that car and go home, knowing for ever that it was like looking at a specimen under glass: we could never be together; I could never kiss him or touch him or hold him; he wouldn't allow it; he absolutely didn't want to; we were a security risk.

And, at the end of the day, when it came down to it, it wasn't just about him thinking he was too different. It was me too. I had chosen someone else.

'Sorry,' I said. 'This is a bad idea. We can't be friends.'

I turned. The tears were almost blinding me now – regret. Being shown everything I could have won. Loss – all the stupid pointless wasted loss.

'Can you ask John to come back round?'

Rufus took a deep breath.

'Can I just show you something? Something I've been working on?'

'Is it another terrifying threat to the city and our peace of mind?' I said. 'Because I don't think I can go through that again.'

He shook his head.

'No. No, it isn't anything like that. Please?'

There was a catch in his voice. He sounded nervous.

'It'll only take a minute.'

I looked at him. Oh God, why did he have to be so fricking beautiful?

'All right.'

I followed him downstairs into the basement, feeling nervous. I hadn't been down here before. Mind you, given the size of the house, there was a lot of it I hadn't been to before, I knew that. I quashed immediately the fact that the words I had so wanted to hear – come to the bedroom, right now, and let the world go to hell – hadn't been forthcoming. Of course they hadn't. Of course they never would.

There was a large rec room downstairs, with a red billiard table, a huge TV, a bar in the corner which looked spotless and ridiculous and unused.

'Yeah,' said Rufus when he saw me looking at it. 'I designed this when I was a lot younger. Thought it would be cool.'

'Mmm,' I said. 'Elvis would have liked it.'

He blinked behind his glasses and pointed to a door I hadn't noticed at the far end. 'Through that door.'

It looked like the tunnel. It looked like the tunnel in the catacombs. I realised suddenly I was frightened.

I started backing out hastily, my heel turning over in my rush; I wasn't used to moving in high shoes at all, couldn't work them.

'Ow!' I screamed, as my stupid weakened ankle turned over again. 'Ow, ow, ow, GODDAMIT!' and then I completely dissolved.

The speed of him. The way things were done – so fast; without hesitation. He had scooped me up once more; I was in his arms; his hand was on my ankle, setting it, manipulating it, which made

337

me scream out loud for a second and then instantly it felt better; it was fine, and I was gasping in his arms as he went to set me down.

'You okay?'

And I wanted to scream, No, no, of course I'm not okay, you bastard, you made me fall in love with your ridiculous irradiated self and you never even gave a damn, how could you? How could you? But I was winded, from the ankle and the feel of being in those arms again, and the closeness to which I'd nearly hurled his glasses onto the floor, and I was unutterably miserable and sank to the ground in tears.

'Hey. Hey. It's all right. It's all right. You'll be all right; it's not broken.'

I looked up at him through my red eyes.

'I'll just go home.'

'Don't be silly; you're hurt.'

'It's fine now,' I mumbled.

'Let me just show you though. Can I? Let me show you; then you can go.'

There was a pause when I thought, Maybe he'll just hold me. Maybe he'll hold me for ever.

So of course he set me down.

Hardly limping at all, I followed him across the vast room, miserable and confused. It was a huge, heavy door, more like a safe than a room. I heard a hiss of steam volts. What the hell was in there?

Inside was pitch-dark and, curious despite myself, I leaned in. There appeared to be a short tunnel.

'Just tell me what it is,' I said.

'I can't,' said Rufus. 'I need to show you.'

'Is it, like, an oven for hungry children?'

He looked at me.

'Seriously? You still don't trust me.'

I couldn't tell him the truth: that I trusted him with my life. But I couldn't trust him with my heart.

Then thank God he put the lights on, and I followed him into the strangest thing I'd ever seen.

Chapter Eighty-two

The closest I could get to describing it would be a submarine submersible: one of those balls which go all the way down to the bottom of the sea. It had steel walls, God knows how thick. There was light coming in from somewhere, but I couldn't tell if it was moonlight or anything else. On the ground was a built-in sofa and mattress. It looked like a strange shag pad of James Bond's from 1965. It was completely stable, but I realised that around us, the wall was actually spinning incredibly quickly, as if we were inside a gyroscope; he had started it up as soon as we had stepped through the door, so it was as if there was no door there at all. It made a low humming noise.

I squinted around me. It was large and airy, and through the glass in the ceiling, I thought I could see the stars, but I wasn't sure. If he'd said we were in space, I'd have believed him.

'What the hell is this?'

Rufus looked at me.

'Um,' he said. He actually went pink. I didn't know he could even do that. 'I built it. I ... I built it. For ... um ... us.'

'What do you mean?'

He looked even more embarrassed now.

'Well, I kind of hoped we would have dinner first . . . chat about it. This isn't quite how I thought it would go . . . '

'I don't understand. What is it?'

He swallowed.

'Well . . . also maybe some wine . . . '

'Get on with it.'

I sat down on the sofa to rest my ankle. It was incredibly soft and comfortable. The walls had calmed down to a dull shimmer I barely noticed, although the room felt like it was bobbing about, just a little.

'Well, it's kind of . . . it's a capsule.'

'Does it fly?'

'No . . . no, it wouldn't. It's lead-lined. Not just lead. It completely neutralises my . . . well, my powers, if you like.'

There was a long pause while I looked around it, my heart starting to pound against my chest.

'Oh my God!' I said quietly. 'Oh my God. It's kryptonite.'

'It does . . . Yeah. It works kind of like kryptonite. Except on me.'

I looked at him.

'So it makes you . . . what? More like a normal man?'

He nodded.

'Yes. Um. Yes, it does.'

He moved forwards a little.

'Holly, at first . . . that day when you saw me. Saw me transform, and then recognise me. I thought it was a disaster, that my cover was blown. Then I thought maybe we could be friends. Maybe for once in my life I could have a friend.'

'But I betrayed you,' I said. 'I turned your telephone number over to Frederick Cecil.'

341

'You never did,' he said. 'Not for a second.'

'I did.'

'You didn't. You gave him my number, who cares? I was always going to beat him. But you never, once, told anyone my name.

'And here ... I only have one name.'

My heart was starting to pound incredibly fast.

'Is that what the glasses are for? I thought they were fashion.'

'Oh. No, it turns out in real life I have a mild astigmatism.'

I laughed and stood up again. It didn't seem real.

'Can I ruffle your hair?'

'It seems so.'

He looked at me.

'You said ... you said ... you needed a man. A person.'

I looked back at him.

'Here. Here I'm a person. Whether I'm the type of person for you ... well, of course that's up to you.'

There was a very long pause then.

I looked around. My voice, when it came, was very quiet.

'Is this ... is this a space for us? Could this be a space for us? To do normal things together?'

He blushed bright red again.

'Um,' he said. 'Well.'

'Like watch boxsets and do our taxes?' I said, smiling a bit. He grinned back.

'Those are two things, yes.'

'So if we were doing normal things ... if we were just hanging out. Watching boxsets ... '

'Watching boxsets ... '

'Yes. Watching boxsets. Do you think you would, for example, be able to watch boxsets without nearly killing anyone or fusing the city?'

342

He nodded gravely.

'Yes. This is a space in which I believe someone could watch boxsets without doing any of those things.'

I looked at him.

'What's it made of? No. Don't tell me. Don't. Never ever tell me what else is in the walls, protecting you,' I said in a rush. 'In case I ever ... in case I have to protect you. I will always try, I promise. But I can't. Not always. I'm not like you. You have to know that.'

He nodded. 'I do know that.'

He looked straight at me.

'But I will always protect you,' he said.

'That doesn't seem fair,' I said.

'Um, might you make it up to me?' he said, nervously, half-smiling.

I stood up and moved closer to him; felt that cool body, towering over me. Different. But the same. A shiver of delight and excitement went through me.

'Well,' I said. 'You may want to get out of those clothes.'

There was a moment's pause. Then he glanced down, looking confused. I burst out laughing.

'No way!' I said. His brow furrowed.

'Hmm,' he said.

'You can't get undressed!' I said. 'You really don't work in here!'

'That's odd,' he said. His fingers went up to his buttons. Then they came down again. I burst out laughing.

'You're not serious.'

'What?' he said.

'Undo your buttons,' I said.

'Ah,' he said. 'This seems more complicated at normal speed.' Then he looked at me, and I looked at him. And we both laughed.

'Come here,' I said. 'I'll show you. Later when we get to the advanced stage, I'll do shoelaces.'

He laughed again, and sat down.

'Ow,' he said. 'That bumped.'

'I will,' I promised faithfully, 'be very, very gentle.'

And very slowly – for once – very, very slowly and carefully and intently, we moved towards one another.

And when we emerged, much, much later, starving hungry, both of us only the tiniest bit bruised, but unutterably happy, both of us in absolute awe that not only had we not fused the city but that there was a single brick of it still standing, we stood, holding hands, looking out over the lights. Rufus was completely naked – he didn't really seem to see the point of clothes after all, and I saw a lot of point in just looking at him – we stared at the pod in silence for a long time, then carefully, sweetly, he took me up to that huge bed in that beautiful bedroom, the untouched sheets, the unfussed pillows, the warmth of the room, and sat, stroking my hair, until I dozed off.

'One night,' I murmured, just before I fell into a deep sleep. 'One night, will you sleep there with me? Can we stay in there?'

He looked down at me with utmost tenderness in his eyes, the deep kindness of a man who wanted – who needed – to help everyone. Everyone in general and, somehow, at last, me in particular. He stroked my hair.

'Yes,' he said. 'And you know I always keep my promises.'

'I do know that.'

My eyes were heavy.

'Tonight?' I whispered, my thoughts jangling together confusingly, already beginning to circle that plughole of sleep.

His eyes left my face for a moment, ranged out across the

344

balcony, down the beautiful garden and straight across the water. In the distance, I could hear a siren.

'No, my love,' he whispered gently, running his strong hand down my face once more. 'No, my love. Not tonight.'

And as filled with sleep as I was, I half watched him through nearly shut eyelids: his strong, huge body, as it moved gracefully across the room. He turned the handle on the French windows, sped through as sprightly and swiftly as a dancing shadow, stood outlined by the light from the moon for a moment on top of the old stone balcony until I could see only the huge, dark silhouette of him and noticed, just at the last, that he was wearing the suit once more, and I must have fallen asleep then – did I? – because the next thing I noticed, he had vanished into the night and all that was left in the great garden was an owl, hooting mournfully in the empty dark.

Chapter Eighty-three

But I didn't tell him about my other letter. Also beautifully written. Not a letter in fact: a postcard, with nothing on it but my name, and a picture of grass rushes blowing on a white sandy beach far, far away.

Acknowledgements

Thanks to Tim Holman and his amazing team at Orbit. Anna Jackson, Gemma Conley-Smith, Joanna Kramer, Jenni Hill and everyone there, particularly the sales team.

Thanks also to my wider LB family, including Maddie West, David Shelley, Emma Williams, who makes an extremely difficult job look easy – thank you especially for the website, which was beyond generous (www.jennycolgan.com, which updates on everything I do across the board). Felice Howden, obviously too; Manpreet Grewal, Stephie Melrose and the team at BBC books too, particularly Justin Richards, Kate Fox and of course Albert dePetrillo. I am so lucky. Special thanks to my agent Jo Unwin, and Isabel Adomakoh Young.

About the author

Jenny Colgan is the author of numerous bestselling novels, including *Christmas at the Cupcake Café* and *Little Beach Street Bakery*. *Meet Me at the Cupcake Café* won the 2012 Melissa Nathan Award for Comedy Romance and was a *Sunday Times* top ten bestseller, as was *Welcome to Rosie Hopkins' Sweetshop of Dreams*, which won the RNA Romantic Novel of the Year Award 2013. Under the Jenny T. Colgan pen name, she has also written the *Doctor Who* tie-in novel *Dark Horizons* and *Doctor Who* short stories 'Into the Nowhere', 'Long Way Down' and 'All the Empty Towers'. Jenny is married with three children and lives in London and France. For more about Jenny, visit her website and her Facebook page, or follow her on Twitter: @jennycolgan.

Find out more about Jenny T. Colgan and other Orbit authors by registering for the free monthly newsletter at www.orbitbooks.net.

Interview

If you could have any superpower, which one would you choose?
We have given this a *lot* of thought and discussion in our family, and have come to the conclusion that teleportation is the one to have. It lets you fly (as long as you teleport away before you hit the ground), gets you out of trouble immediately, works as invisibility if you need to steal something and saves a lot of airport time and cash.

What was the inspiration behind *Spandex and the City* and how did the idea develop?
Well, I suppose because I watch a lot of superhero movies and I always feel for the girlfriend. Like, who the heck would want to do that? They're never there, they're always late, they're always in trouble and you're always getting captured. Except of course they're meant to be very attractive because they're the hero. So. I wanted to write about that.

Who's the sexiest superhero?
Michael Keaton's Batman. I know, I was surprised too.
Honourable mentions to Chris Reeve's Superman, Charles
Xavier, and Mark Ruffalo's Hulk.

Who's your favourite supervillain?
Bane. He's terrifying, sexy and kind of hilarious all at the same
time.

**What was the most challenging thing about writing this
novel?**
Avoiding copyright infringement.

**You've written several *Doctor Who* novels and two books
for Orbit now: how have you found the transition to
writing sci-fi?**
I'm a very lucky writer – even luckier than just being a writer,
I mean – to get to play in lots of different sand-boxes, and I
enjoy it all really. But I don't see it as a transition at all; I enjoy
writing all sorts of stories, some with aliens and some without,
but it's not a particularly different experience to me. I would say
writing *Doctor Who* is more different to sci-fi/rom-coms, because
you're writing about someone else's creations so there are a lot
more rules. Fun rules though.

**Was it more fun playing with a world of superheroes and
supervillains in *Spandex and the City* or a world of aliens
and conspiracy theories in *Resistance Is Futile*?**
Well, I loved writing superheroes because when you strip it
down, they can be so funny. I wrote *Spandex and the City* before
Deadpool came out (and mine is nothing like as foul-mouthed!)

but I think we share an attitude of being affectionately teasing about that world.

Can you tell us a little about your writing routine?
Well, I can but it's very boring! I walk the dog, go to the gym to watch *Frasier*, order a sandwich and type for two hours in a coffee shop.

What's next on your reading list?
The new Tana French; *Commonwealth* by Ann Patchett; *The Tourist* by Robert Dickinson; Jon Ronson on Donald Trump; and *Sweetbitter* by Stephanie Danler.

Look out for

RESISTANCE
is
FUTILE

also by

Jenny T. Colgan

Discover an irregular love story ...

Connie's smart. She's funny. But when it
comes to love, she's only human.

As a brilliant mathematician with bright red hair –
Connie's used to being considered a little unusual.
But when she's recruited for a top-secret code-breaking
project, nothing can prepare her for working with
someone quite as peculiar as Luke.

From the *Sunday Times* bestselling author Jenny Colgan
comes a charmingly quirky tale of love, friendship ...
and the possible obliteration of mankind.

www.orbitbooks.net